Betrayal in the Cotswolds

By Rebecca Tope

THE COTSWOLD MYSTERIES

A Cotswold Killing · A Cotswold Ordeal
Death in the Cotswolds · A Cotswold Mystery
Blood in the Cotswolds · Slaughter in the Cotswolds
Fear in the Cotswolds · A Grave in the Cotswolds
Deception in the Cotswolds · Malice in the Cotswolds
Shadows in the Cotswolds · Trouble in the Cotswolds
Revenge in the Cotswolds · Guilt in the Cotswolds
Peril in the Cotswolds · Crisis in the Cotswolds
Secrets in the Cotswolds · A Cotswold Christmas Mystery
Echoes in the Cotswolds · Betrayal in the Cotswolds
A Cotswold Casebook

THE LAKE DISTRICT MYSTERIES

The Windermere Witness · The Ambleside Alibi
The Coniston Case · The Troutbeck Testimony
The Hawkshead Hostage · The Bowness Bequest
The Staveley Suspect · The Grasmere Grudge
The Patterdale Plot · The Ullswater Undertaking
The Threlkeld Theory · The Askham Accusation

THE WEST COUNTRY MYSTERIES

A Dirty Death · Dark Undertakings
Death of a Friend · Grave Concerns
A Death to Record · The Sting of Death
A Market for Murder

Betrayal in the Cotswolds

REBECCA TOPE

Allison & Busby Limited
11 Wardour Mews
London W1F 8AN
allisonandbusby.com

First published in Great Britain by Allison & Busby in 2022.
This paperback edition published by Allison & Busby in 2023.

A CIP catalogue record for this book is available from
the British Library

10 9 8 7 6 5 4 3 2 1

ISBN 978-0-7490-2869-5

Typeset in 11/16 pt Sabon LT Pro by
Allison & Busby Ltd.

The paper used for this Allison & Busby publication
has been produced from trees that have been legally sourced
from well-managed and credibly certified forests.

FSC
www.fsc.org
MIX
Paper | Supporting
responsible forestry
FSC® C171272

Printed and bound by CPI Group (UK) Ltd, Croydon, CR0 4YY

For Roger and Nikki

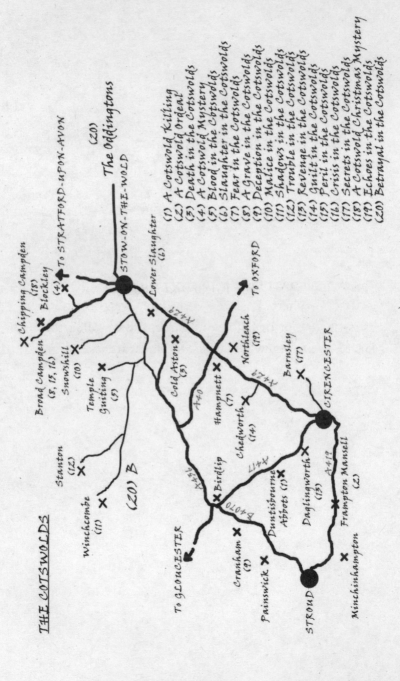

THE COTSWOLDS

Chipping Campden (18)
Blockley
TO STRATFORD-UPON-AVON
The Oddingtons (20)
Broad Campden (8, 15, 16)
Snowshill (10)
STOW-ON-THE-WOLD
Stanton (12)
Temple Guiting (5)
Lower Slaughter (6)
Winchcombe (11)
(20) B
A424
Cold Aston (3)
Hampnett (7)
Northleach (19)
TO OXFORD
Birdlip
A436
Chedworth (14)
A40
Barnsley (17)
A417
CIRENCESTER
A429
TO GLOUCESTER
Cranham (9)
B4070
Duntisbourne Abbots (1)
Daglingworth (13)
Frampton Mansell (2)
A419
Painswick
STROUD
Minchinhampton

(1) A Cotswold Killing
(2) A Cotswold Ordeal
(3) Death in the Cotswolds
(4) A Cotswold Mystery
(5) Blood in the Cotswolds
(6) Slaughter in the Cotswolds
(7) Fear in the Cotswolds
(8) A Grave in the Cotswolds
(9) Deception in the Cotswolds
(10) Malice in the Cotswolds
(11) Shadows in the Cotswolds
(12) Trouble in the Cotswolds
(13) Revenge in the Cotswolds
(14) Guilt in the Cotswolds
(15) Peril in the Cotswolds
(16) Crisis in the Cotswolds
(17) Secrets in the Cotswolds
(18) A Cotswold Christmas Mystery
(19) Echoes in the Cotswolds
(20) Betrayal in the Cotswolds

Author's Note

Upper and Lower Oddington are real villages, very much as described here. Positano is entirely invented, however, as is the layout of fields and gardens. The village street has also got somewhat wider in this incarnation.

Prologue

It was late April. The children had gone back to school and life was relatively quiet. Thea Slocombe had been approached for a new house-sitting commission in six weeks' time and she was presenting herself in Lower Oddington for inspection and instruction.

The village was readily located, a short way east of Stow-on-the-Wold and parking was easy. *The same only different,* Thea said to herself as she parked her car outside Umberto Kingly's handsome stone house with its perfect symmetry and colourful garden. He let her in and introductions were made. She waited in vain for him to say 'Call me Bert'. On closer inspection, it was perfectly obvious that this was never going to happen. Which was in no way a problem, since 'Umberto' was a splendid name by any standards. She liked the 'Kingly' too, because he was, rather. Very straight back and an authoritative look in his eye. But quite a lot less rich than a king, to judge by the state of his clothes and property. He might be a man of substance in the physical sense, but there was a shabbiness about him that could not be mere eccentricity. The house oddly suited him –

surrounded by second homes belonging to stockbrokers and barristers, only an initial careless glance could make it fit the Cotswold stereotype. A gutter was hanging at a precarious angle, paint was peeling from the window frames and the incongruous locked gate that opened onto the pavement was rusting in places.

Umberto was affable, with a large oval head and a matching paunch. His thick wavy hair was dark grey, having obviously mutated from black. He had an air of impatience with the world. Thea earned his approval by returning his gaze without flinching and replying to his remarks with very few words. He succinctly explained the nature of her commission and she replied with equal briskness. She was to remain in place for five days, taking care of three dogs, and a roomful of old cameras and binoculars.

Thea's first impressions of Upper and Lower Oddington were nowhere near as favourable as others had been in other places. This was nothing more than a street lined with old houses, the occasional new ones standing out vividly – custard-yellow amidst the mustard and caramel of their neighbours. She spotted an Old Post Office and Old Malthouse, evidence of lost businesses. There was no sign of a shop and The Fox Inn looked as if it was very slowly being renovated or refurbished or something. If she wanted a pub, she would have to go to the Horse and Groom in the other Oddington.

Umberto's house boasted the name of 'Positano', which struck Thea as highly unsuitable, even if it confirmed an

Italian dimension to the man. It had an iron gate and a keypad, as did about half the properties she had passed. The gravelled area outside the gate was adorned with a prominent 'No Parking' sign, and a smaller one asking people to prevent their dogs from fouling it or its strip of grass. The sign was particularly sinister, with a pair of eyes watching closely for canine misdemeanours.

'So welcoming,' Thea muttered to her dog. Hepzibah had been given permission to share in the house-sitting and had come on this preliminary reconnaissance to be approved by Umberto.

As he showed her round the house, he explained the business – which she had already understood was more of a passion that generated no more than a very modest income. An upstairs room had become home to numerous examples of his stock-in-trade. Cameras of every shape and size lined the walls. 'I buy them at auctions mostly,' he explained. 'And get them cleaned up and working. Then I take them back to where they were made – which is Germany for the most part. I'm especially passionate about Voigtländers.' He clearly wanted to say more about this, but thought better of it. 'I'm sorry. You don't want to hear all that now. I keep this room locked, as you'll understand. And I'd be glad if you wouldn't mention it to anybody. They might be rather specialist, but a burglary would be most unwelcome, all the same.'

'Of course,' murmured Thea, thinking about her grandfather who had shown her how to work his precious Leica when she was about eight.

'So I'm going off for a week in June on a selling trip. It's the first one since I got the dogs. Since . . .' he hesitated. 'Since we had some family trouble last year,' he finished. Thea's curiosity was instantly aroused, but she bit back the questions. Umberto reverted to his plans for the trip. 'You meet such wonderful people,' he sighed. 'Absolute experts, most of them. It's a privilege to know them.'

'Must be sad to see the old equipment gradually disappearing,' she said. 'Can you even get film for them any more?'

He laughed and told her that there were specialist companies still valiantly producing thirty-five-millimetre film, as well as older formats. 'Not for much longer, I suppose,' he sighed. 'I hate progress, don't you?'

Thea had no answer to that, and realised that he didn't really expect one. He was happy in his bygone world, which apparently was even now quite lavishly populated with fellow Luddites.

'So come and meet the girls,' said Umberto, as if everything else had been a rather insignificant preamble. 'I'm sure they'll like you.'

Thea had already realised that the dogs were even more dauntingly precious than the cameras – pedigree salukis, with infeasibly long legs and shining brown coats. 'They just need company,' their owner told Thea. 'And somebody to stand guard over them. Don't *ever* take them out. They've got all the space they need here.' And he showed her his field, strongly fenced and scattered with doggy toys and a kind of miniature set of jumps and hurdles worthy of a gymkhana. Patches of untended long grass added variety, and Thea was excused from having to clean up their excrement. 'They mostly go at the far end, so just watch where you tread down there,' said Umberto.

He recited their names, which she jotted down on the notepad she carried. 'They're beautiful,' she sighed, in all sincerity.

'They are,' he agreed. 'The loves of my life.' And he offered her more than twice her usual fee for keeping his darlings happy. 'But do remember that they're vulnerable to being stolen,' he added with a very poor attempt at carelessness.

'I'll remember,' she assured him, and then changed the subject. 'How long have you lived here?'

'Oh – that's a complicated thing to explain. My mother has lived here most of her adult life and had us all here as children. When my father died, she insisted she couldn't be here on her own, so the four of us organised a sort of rota to stay with her. None of us has properly managed to leave home, you see,' he said with a sigh. 'I moved in permanently at the beginning of last year, just to save money. I never dreamt that Mama would go and die on me. It came as quite a shock.'

'It must have done. Was your mother fond of the dogs?'

'I didn't have the dogs then. They're not even a year old. I only got them six or seven months ago. It's all very recent, you know.' Thea remembered the remark about family trouble. 'We're still settling down, actually. I wake up some mornings thinking my mother's still in the next bedroom to mine.'

'She died unexpectedly, did she?'

'Yes, she did. It was horrible.' He was suddenly unreasonably snappish, his face turning pink. 'It was last summer. Must be nine or ten months ago, now.'

'Oh dear,' said Thea feebly.

He took a breath and forced a weak smile. 'Sorry. It's still quite raw. She just dropped dead, halfway through a sentence. Never a day's illness in her life, everything to live for, no will or anything. Threw everything into a spin for a while. We're a very close family, you see.'

Thea wasn't sure she did see, but she smiled understandingly. Umberto went on, 'The house came to me more or less by default. But it's still the focal point for the others as well. The grandchildren all love it. Not that any of them are mine.' He grimaced, and changed the subject. 'So you think you can manage my lovely girls, then?'

'They'll be fine with me,' she assured him. 'And it's not for very long, is it?'

Chapter One

Now it was mid-June and she was back in Lower Oddington with Hepzie and a bag of clothes and books, for the whole week, while Umberto Kingly went to Germany to sell old cameras.

She got out of the car and pushed a button on the keypad; then waited twenty seconds for a voice to crackle out at her, and then click the mechanism to let her in. While she waited, she examined her immediate surroundings, the same phrase as before echoing in her head. *The same only different.*

It applied very aptly to Lower Oddington; it was indeed 'the same only different'. Every Cotswold village was different from every other, and a single glance could effortlessly distinguish Chedworth from Snowshill or Daglingworth from Cranham. Then there was lovely Naunton, and overrated Broadway, and tiny Hampnett and tourist-ridden Bibury. The list grew longer with every passing month, as the Slocombes made new discoveries. None of them had even registered the existence of the Oddingtons until a few months ago, which was not unusual. When twelve-year-old Stephanie had mentioned Hillesley the whole family had stared at her blankly. When nine-year-old Timmy checked it on a map, they all decided it was too far south to properly count as Cotswolds. 'But don't tell anybody we said that,' cautioned Drew, their father. 'It might hurt someone's feelings.'

People's feelings were sacrosanct, as nobody could deny, and Drew found himself the main enforcer of sensitive behaviour. His work as an undertaker gave him special powers in that respect.

Umberto was looking much smarter than before and the house was tidier. He quickly took her out to see the dogs, and repeated his earlier instructions. 'I've written it all down for you,' he said. 'The main thing is exercise, really. You need to throw things for them, and run around with them, two or three times a day. If it's fine, you might want to sit out here with them.' He indicated a swinging hammock, big enough for a person and three – even four – somnolent dogs. 'They should be fine with your spaniel, once they get to know her,' the man added for good measure.

The dogs looked bigger than Thea remembered, which she observed aloud. 'They've filled out a bit,' Umberto agreed. 'And they're even more playful than ever. I love them as if they were my children.' His eyes were moist with Latin sentiment. Thea could only suppose he had not heard about her past record with other people's dogs – which was a shameful one. There had been deaths and damage, desertion and disasters. But for some reason he had wanted her specifically, and the set-up here in Oddington looked to be almost completely foolproof. The spaniel would, as Umberto predicted, cause no difficulties. Hepzie was skilled at winning over affection, whether human or canine – even salukis, which were essentially hunters, and might be tempted to view her as prey. 'You will have to keep a very close eye on them, and keep the front gate locked,' he emphasised. 'Don't forget about the cameras upstairs. There aren't so many now, but there's still about ten grand's worth.'

'They'll be fine,' said Thea.

'I'm waiting for one of the girls to come on heat,' he went on. 'I won't breed from any of them this year, of course – but early next year it'll be time for the first one.' He rolled his eyes. 'I'll need my sister's help with that. But if it goes to plan, I should be able to boost the coffers quite nicely, even with one litter a year.'

Thea swallowed back the cautionary tales she could tell him about the perils of relying on animals to *boost the coffers,* as he charmingly said. 'Let's hope it works,' she said.

'Even if they paid for my council tax, that would be a huge help,' he said with a smile that suggested such modest aspiration was absurd. With a decent amount of good fortune, he obviously expected the pups to cover quite a number of essential bills.

Thea forced a confident smile, and willingly redefined her role as dog warden, rather than house-sitter. Umberto apparently cared rather less for his inanimate property.

The interior of his home did not suggest much in the way of domestic pride in any case. A good proportion of the ground floor was available to the dogs, with a large comfortable area at the back of the house furnished with saggy chairs and warm sheepskin rugs. It opened directly out onto the back garden and field, and had a small scullery with a sink and doggy feeding bowls. Throughout the house, the furniture was nothing special, apart from the old-fashioned mahogany desk in the study. 'I work from here, obviously. I used to have to go to auctions all over the country, but now I can do most of it online. I still like to go to the viewings, though.'

'Who minds the dogs?'

'Usually my sister Imogen. Sometimes my nephew lends a hand, and there's a local chap who'll give them a game outside. We muddle through. Once in a while I take them with me, if it's somewhere nice. We went to a funny little place in Herefordshire last month.'

'I thought they never left these premises?'

'Hardly ever,' he nodded, apparently unconcerned at his own inconsistency.

They both knew that now he was leaving there could be no turning back from the arrangement. Any hint of anxiety or second thoughts must be quashed. The plan was for Umberto to transport an impressive number of antique cameras in a slightly battered Bedford van, across France and into Germany. His dark eyes were focused on schedules and paperwork, the dogs a box already ticked.

Thea made no attempt to hide her surprise when she realised how he would be travelling. Umberto laughed. 'You think I'm dodging the export tax?' he said. 'Well, I'm certainly going to try. There's a risk I'll be searched and required to explain myself, but it's a risk worth taking. You would never believe the bureaucracy involved if I try to send it all by plane. It's not so much the tax I want to avoid as the paperwork. Not that there's any real escape. Just getting myself and the van across is bad enough. The truth is, I really love driving and this is a perfect excuse.'

'I see,' she said, wondering at his frankness. How many people knew what he was doing – and wasn't there a fear that one of them would report him?

He caught her expression and laughed. 'Please don't worry about it. Now – be sure not to get bored, won't you? Go and have a look at the old church. It's well worth it. The weather looks reasonable. Help yourself to any books – and the TV's all set up for streaming and so forth. There's a list of instructions taped to it. You won't be bothered by any neighbours. They're all off on cruises at this time of year – those that do actually live here, that is. There's some building work on the way up to the church, but they haven't been too noisy up to now. There's a chance my sister will call in. You never really know with her. She's called Imogen Peake. Oh – and she's got a daughter by the name of Kirsty who comes and goes. They take it for granted they can just drop in whenever they like. They only live in Lower Swell, just the other side of Stow. The dogs are very fond of them.

By rights they should be doing your job, but Immy said she couldn't make the commitment. I explained all that before, didn't I? She took our mother's death very hard and still isn't over it. It makes her somewhat unreliable, I'm afraid.' He sighed, as much from impatience as compassion.

Thea frowned as she tried to remember what he had said six weeks earlier. 'Does that mean they could turn up without any warning?' The prospect of sudden unannounced invasions by relatives was somewhat concerning.

'I'm afraid so, although from what Immy said last week, she's very much tied up with her business troubles just now, so it's not very likely. I'm just letting you know it's possible. We're a big family, all very close. It's the Italian influence, still lingering on after two generations.'

'Yes, you said,' Thea told him impatiently. 'And they all live around here, do they?' That struck Thea as improbable. Despite his old clothes and badly kept house, Umberto was clearly middle class – and middle-class families, in her experience, tended to disperse around the world. Or at least around the country.

'More or less. If you want the full story, there's a booklet you can have a look at. My oldest sister's husband, as well as her mother-in-law, does genealogy in a big way. Between them they tracked everybody down and wrote it all up. Victor fancies himself as a bit of a writer, apparently, and he did do a pretty good job, to be fair.' He snatched a slim paperback from the top shelf of a little bookcase standing in a corner. 'This is it.'

Thea took it automatically, trying to process this new twist, while mentally drawing up a family tree that included a sister's mother-in-law. 'Thanks,' she mumbled. She read the title and author aloud. '*One Family Among Many* by Victor Rider. Nice title.'

Umberto shrugged and then gave himself a shake. 'All this is making me late. It's a long drive to Folkestone. Just don't worry about anything. You'll like Immy, if you see her, and Kirsty's mostly harmless. They've got keys but they won't just march in. You'll get a warning at the gate, anyway. You have to buzz people in. That won't be a problem, will it?' He eyed her suspiciously, and she could tell he was wondering whether she intended to pursue activities that unexpected visitors might upset. He might even be suspecting her of inviting unsuitable friends into his house.

'No, no. It's your house,' she said inanely.

'It is, and I'm paying you handsomely to keep it safe, because of the dogs. That's not complicated, is it?'

'Not at all,' she relied firmly. 'Have a good trip.'

And with a departing purr from his van's engine, he was gone.

Boredom was always a hazard for a house-sitter. Thea had dodged it on past occasions by embarking on unofficial and often intrusive amateur investigations into local crimes. The departure of the owners of the various properties she had been in charge of had sparked bad behaviour of extreme proportions at times. She was well known to the police, and had a prominent reputation across the region. She regularly bumped into people she had encountered on previous commissions.

But somehow she doubted this would happen in Oddington. Perhaps if she ventured into Stow-on-the-Wold, only a few miles away, she would see familiar faces. But here, as Umberto Kingly had pointed out, there did not seem to be any people to bump into, apart from some builders. Nobody would complain if the dogs barked or if she played loud music. She could take Hepzie out for short walks and probably not see a soul.

The salukis themselves would have to provide both Thea and her spaniel with entertainment. She had learnt their names and how to tell them apart. Dolly had darker ears than the others; Gina was the smallest and that left Rocket, the affectionate one. The names, Thea realised, had been carefully chosen to sound as different as possible from each other. Umberto had joked that Rocket was in fact rather slow, by saluki standards, but was the one he was planning to use first for breeding. 'She'll be a rather young mother, but I think she'll be up for it,' he said fondly.

The field used by the dogs looked to be two or three acres in size – more than enough to provide space for a good run, but surely very limited as far as variety and interest went. There was something unkind, and definitely unnatural, about keeping these lovely creatures imprisoned here, presumably for fear that they would be stolen if their existence were to be revealed in the wider world. The sturdy wooden fence on two sides was impossible to look through or over, while the other two sides bordered farmland and were therefore less likely to be used by potential thieves – or so Umberto apparently believed. There were thick and well-kept hedges forming the boundary on those sides. Thea imagined drones flying overhead and filming the dogs. Or cunningly disguised felons tramping across a neighbouring field pretending to be farmers or hikers gone astray. She had instructions to take the dogs indoors at night, or if she went out. If it rained, they had a sort of open-fronted summerhouse to shelter in. But her main task was to make sure they exercised, in particular by being organised into races, like greyhounds. This, she had been shown, was associated with feeding time and involved two or three processes in which they had to run for snippets of food.

The presence of Hepzibah was sure to complicate the procedure and Thea had been surprised at Umberto's ready acceptance of her. 'She'll add variety,' he had said, with a grin. Later, Thea had wondered whether he expected the salukis to catch her and tear her apart like a rabbit or a hare. A flicker of chilly humour made the idea credible. Hepzie was going to be kept away from the field unless under supervision, Thea resolved. They would go for sedate little walks around the village instead.

It was only just past ten on a Monday morning. Outside it was June, not far off the longest day. Thea could hear her father's voice telling her not to waste it.

Richard Johnstone had always been acutely aware of the seasons and their rapid passing. He had died too soon, his urgent attitude to life amply justified with hindsight. All his offspring missed him with a perpetual dull ache.

It was not of course necessary to remain indoors. The field behind the house was in fact her primary area of responsibility and she could sit there all day, guarding the precious dogs, reading a book, dozing in any sunshine there might be, ignoring the rest of the world. Her family were reconciled to her absence and need cause her no concern. She had nothing to feel guilty or anxious about. With a bit of effort she could imagine herself on a Caribbean beach, provided it didn't rain.

But there was no way that Thea Slocombe could remain idle for more than about ninety minutes. Even that would probably be a record. There would have to be a project of some kind if she was to remain sane for five whole days. And the only thing she could think of was to organise the dogs into something that would entertain them all.

She went out through the sliding doors, which opened from the living room onto a patio. This was the closest there was to a proper back garden – six stone tubs containing begonias and lobelia and a shameful number of weeds. There was no sort of barrier between the edge of the patio and the field, and the dogs freely gambolled across it and into the house when they noticed the open doors.

'Hey!' shouted Thea. 'You're not supposed to go in

24

there.' Umberto had clearly laid out the rules – dogs in their own room next to the kitchen, and nowhere else in the house, unless one had special dispensation of an evening. 'It goes against the grain,' he admitted. 'But I was forced to the conclusion that three large dogs are too much for any room that wants to stay halfway civilised. I probably wouldn't stick to it if it wasn't for Imogen. She keeps me on the straight and narrow.'

It seemed to Thea that such rules spoilt much of the pleasure in having dogs at all; a thought that must have shown on her face. 'I do sometimes let them onto the couch one at a time,' the man confessed. 'Especially in the winter.'

Hepzie detected the chance of some excitement and began to yap in the mindless way that Thea found particularly irritating. 'Shut up!' she said. 'You'll just cause more chaos.' Hepzie sat down and drooped in a shameless display of pained reproach.

'Gina!' Thea ordered at random. 'Come out of there.' The smallest of the three salukis turned her head, ears up, eyes bright. Thea could see her thinking *This is going to be fun.* 'You heard me. Out – all of you!'

The tone was evidently well chosen and all three good-naturedly trooped through the patio doors, which Thea quickly pulled shut behind them. 'Good dogs!' she applauded. '*Very* good dogs. Now let's go and play outside.' She tried to remember everything Umberto had told her about the doggy games. Then she realised she had left the spaniel in the house, and opened the doors again. 'Come out, you fool,' she said fondly. 'You'll be all right while I'm here.' Hepzie trotted out, avoiding her owner's gaze, and stood watching the salukis. 'You'll soon get used to them,' Thea told her. 'They're really going to be excellent company for us, you see.'

She spent the next hour throwing toys, exploring the various contraptions designed to occupy the dogs, and giving Rocket so many cuddles that Hepzie almost exploded with jealousy. The objects scattered around the field suggested both the gorilla section of a modern zoo and a carelessly arranged circuit at a gymkhana. There were tunnels, jumps, seesaws, a hammock and even a paddling pool, although it was devoid of water. To Thea's eye, it all looked rather ramshackle. She imagined Umberto acquiring most of the equipment second-hand at his auctions, or through an outfit such as Freecycle. She had an idea that he had embarked on some kind of agility training and then quickly abandoned it as too time-consuming or effortful. As far as she could recall, she had never seen salukis in that kind of activity anyway. They probably lacked the right skills or motives. But she saw Dolly wriggling through one of the tunnels, as if the animal simply enjoyed the experience for its own sake.

Thirsty for a mid-morning coffee, she left the dogs to rest and went back into the house with Hepzie. There were clouds gathering and the temperature had dropped to a level that made sitting outside unappealing. She settled down on the couch in the living room and took up Umberto's family history with a lukewarm curiosity.

Such volumes tended to be poorly written and sadly dull.

Neither proved to be the case in this instance. The first chapter launched into a vivid account of a sea voyage to India in 1859, rapidly followed by a detailed description of the birth of a baby who turned out to be Umberto's great-grandfather. Lengthy quotes from letters and diaries gave credence to the narrative, and Thea was hooked. The writing was good and the structure blessedly clear. There was never any doubt as to which generation was being described, despite the hectic pace that rushed from 1850 to 1920, back to 1900 and on to 1960. Themes were followed – seafaring, childbearing and dogs were predominant. The final chapter came all of a sudden, with a summary of how the family stood at the time of writing. Umberto was one of four siblings, with a generous helping of cousins – one of them still in India and several in Italy.

The last lines held her attention most of all.

Ours is a family of violent feuds and sentimental reconciliations, up to and including the present day. I end this volume with the hope that current animosities will quickly be resolved.

Chapter Two

Dogs and antiques were both Cotswolds clichés, to Thea's mind. Especially expensive pedigree dogs. She had already decided that Hepzie's successor, when that time came, would be something of mixed parentage that never crossed the radar of the Kennel Club. The world of antiques was entirely mysterious to her, and not at all interesting. The things only got broken, or caused fights, and ended up at country auctions and car boot sales. Either that or they were bought by rich Chinese and African individuals, who wanted them back, after they'd been wickedly purloined by European colonists. It all made Thea sigh. Even an innocent Ming vase carried overtones of exploitation and dirty dealings. But Umberto's cameras were an exception, to her mind. Although they might technically qualify as antiques, there was something refreshingly practical about them – at least compared to a Ming vase.

What else did the man do with his time? she wondered. He evidently kept in close contact with a good number of relatives – but equally evidently he had no spouse or offspring of his own. A bachelor uncle, then – perhaps with somebody tucked away for occasional intimacies. A married woman, she guessed, since he had seemed to her to have heterosexual instincts. There had been an at-another-time-under-different-circumstances twinkle in his eye when she met him, despite his being older. Thea was pretty – some might even say lovely. Her face had a lucky symmetry that never changed with age; she was small and shapely, with the waist and the bust of a woman a lot younger. Men reacted to her even now, just as they had for the past twenty-five years. She automatically knew what they were thinking and what their bodies were telling them. Umberto Kingly had been no exception.

She scanned the books on the shelves in the living room for clues about him. On the bottom shelf there was a row of leather-bound Victorian novels – Wilkie Collins, Trollope and J M Barrie, but no Dickens. Above them came some more recent hardbacks with their dust-wrappers intact. On the basis of very little knowledge, Thea marked them as first editions likely to gain in value over time. And at the top, on a narrower shelf, came a mixed bunch of paperbacks, in far from pristine condition. D H Lawrence, Iris Murdoch, Ngaio Marsh, Elizabeth Taylor, Doris Lessing, Graham Swift and A N Wilson all caught her eye. No trashy crime or saga for our Umberto, then, thought Thea. Unless he was simply showing off, his taste generally ran to the good stuff. The only author she herself had enjoyed of this lot was

Doris Lessing, but she was in no doubt that they were all admired by those in the know. Then it struck her that the books had probably belonged to his mother, given their vintage, and were of no interest to Umberto. Looking around the room, she concluded that almost everything dated back several decades. Umberto was too young and too male for many of these writers to suit him. Hadn't he told her he had simply moved in with Mama after being part of a shared rota with his sisters? Somehow he had been landed with the caring on a more permanent basis and then naturally stayed on in the house after she died, making very few changes – if any.

The day was passing easily enough. She explored the kitchen and the contents of the small freezer, which she had been told to make full use of. There was fish, three or four ready meals, bread, burgers and frozen peas. In the drawers at the bottom of the fridge were quantities of carrots and green beans, tomatoes and a cucumber. Higher up was cold meat, with cheese and eggs. More than enough to keep her fed for the whole week, in fact. Umberto had deliberately ensured that she would have no excuse for venturing beyond the environs of Oddington – which made her feel more like a prisoner than she had expected.

But it was a big house and Umberto had made no limitations on how she might amuse herself. 'Make yourself at home,' he had said.

'Is it all right if my dog sleeps on the bed?' Normally she would not ask, but simply wash everything on the last day and hide all traces. In this instance, she felt confident there would be no need for subterfuge.

'Don't see why not,' he shrugged. 'I'd have all mine on top of me if I thought I'd get any sleep. As it is, I can't favour one over the others, can I?'

There were four bedrooms upstairs, including the camera room, none of them unduly large. They were simply furnished, with beds, cupboards, rugs and curtains all having seen better days. One had a wardrobe but no chest of drawers, another the opposite. Thea had been given one at the front, which had a duvet on the bed, where the other spare bed had sheets and blankets. She did not venture into Umberto's room. Hers looked down onto the village street – though part of the view was blocked by a copper beech tree that grew inside Umberto's gate. His front garden was considerably better tended than the back. It had a cluster of colourful azaleas in full flower, and a bed of tall gladioli just opening into flower, which spoke of a certain defiance, since they were sure to be deemed common by Cotswolds folk. It also suggested that Umberto – or perhaps one of his sisters – took the trouble to plant corms somewhere around Easter. Thea herself had a great liking for the flower, but seldom managed to find the right moment for planting them. The copper beech was a fortunate element, distracting the eye with its pleasing shape and colour. Further away, on the other side of the street, was one of the oldest village buildings, with fairy-tale gables and a lavishly filled front garden. Umberto had probably felt he would earn opprobrium if he failed to create some kind of floral display to match.

Before she embarked on feeding herself and the dogs, she gave them another twenty minutes of exercise, calling them from one corner of the field to the other, checking to see which commands they would obey. 'Stay!' certainly worked and came in very useful. She left them sitting expectantly in one spot, walked as far away as she could, and then summoned them with a whistle. They flew across the ground as if weightless. Hepzie tried to participate, but got left far behind.

It was fun – more so as she got to know her charges as individuals. Dolly was the quickest, both physically and mentally, always slightly ahead of her sisters. Rocket had been given the wrong name. There was something goofy about her, as she pushed forward for extra attention, gazing at Thea with an adoration that could well be illusory. Gina was the only one who showed any interest in Thea's spaniel, sniffing at her, and then lying down to display her smooth pink undercarriage. All three of them had the untidy flyaway ears that defined the breed. A saluki was never going to be altogether elegant, as a whippet or greyhound was. From what she had seen of Umberto, the choice was perfect. He might be charming and nice-looking, but he was always going to have a subtly raffish dimension, just as these dogs did. 'You're all lovely,' Thea told them. 'Now let's go and get you some supper.'

It was six o'clock before she knew it, the sky still on daytime shift, but evening for all that. Thea listened for returning commuters, half-hoping that Oddington might come to life at the end of the working day. With an idea of catching a glimpse of some neighbours, she went up to her room and stood by the half-open window. When there was no sign of life, she felt a little drop in her spirits. Not so much disappointment as resignation. Perhaps it was better in the sister village – Upper Oddington – where there were some smaller houses, which might belong to more ordinary families.

Then she saw someone. A car had pulled up alongside the pavement, only a few yards from Umberto's gate. A young woman emerged from it, and stood for a moment in the road, first looking up at the house and then along the street, the way she had come. She had her car door open and was standing passively as if waiting for something. Thea wondered whether she was visible, and what the person would think if she found herself being watched. But the sun was shining on the windowpanes, making it impossible to see what was inside the room.

There was no time to continue the thought. Out of nowhere another car came speeding down the street from the same westerly direction as the first car had come. The young woman reacted to the sound of it, but did not try to move out of its way. There was ample space for it to pass her. She left her car door wide open, and appeared to focus on the oncoming vehicle with a look of welcome . . . although Thea had no word for it in that moment. Certainly nothing to arouse alarm; no hint of what was to come.

The impact was horrifying. The oncoming car simply drove parallel to the one that was parked, scraping the wing mirror along it, making a noise that must have been fully audible all down the street. The standing woman and the door of her car flew up into the air like so much balsa wood. Then they landed on the hard tarmac, the metal door clanging and the attacking car accelerating away. It was over in five seconds. Thea blinked, dazed and disbelieving. The body in the street made no movement. Nobody appeared in any doorways. Thea mindlessly tried to close the window, for no reason she could explain, only to leave it swinging open again as she let it go without knowing what she did.

Then she ran downstairs and out of the front door, her spaniel at her heels, thinking this was a sudden walk. Opening Umberto's gates took a stupidly long time, during which she confined her gaze to the small red car a few yards away, now minus its door. It was a Skoda, one little part of her brain informed her, because it was the same as her daughter's motor. The registration plate also implanted itself on her brain, which she later supposed had been a sort of distraction mechanism. A nice innocent harmless five-year-old Skoda, driven by a nice innocent harmless young woman, who was lying shapelessly a short distance away, streaked with blood and half-covered with the crumpled door of her own car.

The body was inescapably dead, its head at a grotesque angle, arms and legs mere lifeless appendages. The car door lay like a very inadequate protective cover, concealing all too little. Having opened the gate at last, Thea went no closer than the middle of the pavement. A man was shouting not far away, and an approaching car had stopped at the sight of something impossible in its way. There was no sign at all of the killer vehicle that had wrought such unspeakable damage.

Thea went on standing rigidly outside the gate. There was nothing she could do or say or even think. Somebody else would take charge any moment now.

It seemed to take a long time before the shouting man came closer, a phone already at his ear. Two more cars drew up, from the other direction. The world was composed of unnatural shapes and alien voices. Nobody seemed to see her. She was not sure of her own reality; the world seemed to have altered beyond recognition.

Her dog brought her back to at least one or two of her senses, when it gave a single bewildered bark. 'Let's go in, then,' she said. Indoors there was a more normal world, where at least you were unlikely to be run down by a speeding car.

Chapter Three

After about ten minutes she recovered just well enough to find her mobile and call the private number she had for Detective Superintendent Sonia Gladwin. Then when her friend responded, all she could do was gibber at her. Her voice was as shaky as her hands and something had gone wrong with her hearing. The impact of metal on flesh kept repeating in her ears, drowning out Gladwin's words. But she forced herself to think, and to utter something coherent. Outside there were people and somebody would have called 999. Thea had burnt through any number of links in the chain by going directly to a senior police detective. 'I *saw* it!' she repeated. 'I saw the whole thing.'

Gladwin took the time to calm her down and then explained that she was unable to drop what she was doing and come to Oddington for at least another hour. 'Speak to whichever officer shows up first,' she instructed. 'It doesn't have to be me. You'll have to have somebody with you, though. You sound completely traumatised.'

'It was *murder*,' Thea wailed. 'Cold-blooded deliberate murder. I *saw* it.' She was never going to dispel the image of the ravaged body in the street, however hard she tried.

'Slow down,' Gladwin repeated. 'She might not even be dead, for all you know.'

'She is,' said Thea with certainty. 'She was crushed between two chunks of metal and then tossed into the road – and probably run over as well. Oh, and an ambulance has just arrived. I can see the blue light.'

'Don't go out,' Gladwin ordered her.

'Why not?'

'For half a dozen reasons that I won't explain now. Just don't. I'll have somebody come in and sit with you. Give me two minutes. And try not to think about it too much. From the sound of it, you might be the only witness, and we need your immediate observations. Not things you *think* you saw.'

Only then did Thea understand that she had not seen anything like as much as she first thought. The attacking car, the body and the mangled door of the smaller vehicle had all disappeared behind the copper beech tree. Only when she went downstairs did she see the results of the impact. By then the murderous car had long gone, with any one of four or five directions to choose from.

'I didn't see what happened next,' she mumbled.

'Okay. Well just sit tight and wait. It'll all get sorted. I'll be there as soon as I can.' Thea could hear frustration and impatience down the phone waves, even through her own hysterics. 'I really didn't need this,' added the detective bitterly, and ended the call.

Neither did I, thought Thea resentfully.

It was humiliating to admit how little she had seen, when the first uniformed police officer came to speak to her. It was a nice-looking woman she had never met before, working conscientiously through the checklist of questions, having first spent ten minutes being kind and concerned and making a mug of sweet tea. It was astonishingly delicious.

'Colour of the vehicle?' 'Size?' 'Was the driver a man or a woman?' 'How would you say it was being driven?' Careful open questions with no suggestion of guidance or pressure. All Thea could say for certain was that it had been considerably larger than the dead woman's little Skoda and some kind of silvery colour. And that it was being driven fast and seemingly with a clear purpose. There had been no sounds of sudden braking that she could recall. 'I would have heard,' she realised. 'The window was open.' She was feeling better for the change of tone. Practical, matter-of-fact, a sense of being useful. 'All I heard was the crash of metal on metal.' Then she remembered the detail of the wing mirror scraping the side of the smaller car, and felt pathetically pleased with herself at having something concrete to report.

The police officer asked nothing about the impact and

its effect on the victim, but still Thea found her head full of images of the impossibly delicate body being crushed as effectively as any wasp between a windowpane and a book. The final flinging into the street was barely relevant after such violence. 'It was going terribly fast,' she choked, turning her face away. 'I've never seen anything so horrible.'

'You'll probably need to talk to someone,' said the woman briskly. 'You'll have symptoms of trauma for a while.'

'Am I the only witness?' Thea asked, already knowing the answer.

'Seems so.'

'I haven't told you anything you couldn't have worked out for yourselves, have I? I may as well just be another victim, for all the help I've been.'

The woman gave her a steady look, with greeny-brown eyes full of calm intelligence. 'That's right,' she said. 'You *are* a victim. It might help to regard it in that light.'

'I doubt it,' said Thea, aware of an inner stirring that felt like resistance. 'That's not the way I like to think of myself.'

'Up to you.' The officer closed her notebook, in which very little had been written. 'Thank you for your time. Have you anybody who can stay with you tonight? You might not want to be alone.'

'It's not my house. I told you that. I can't just invite random people into it.' Hearing her own words, she remembered that she had done just that on another house-sit, not so long ago, and learnt never to do it again. She also remembered that Gladwin had agreed to come – and would be there very soon now. It seemed indiscreet to mention this to PC Green-Eyes.

Outside the street was closed, a white tent erected over the dead body and a growing assemblage of professionals milling about. There would be no skid marks or fingerprints or DNA to identify the aggressor – but there could be fragments of wing mirror, perhaps. Thea couldn't say whether or not it had been broken in the impact, but the vehicle's height and colour could perhaps be detected from its contact with the Skoda.

It was past eight o'clock when Gladwin buzzed the keypad by the gate and Thea fumblingly let her in. The full significance of being barricaded against intruders in such a way only then occurred to her. It was, she had been told, the result of an impulsive purchase by Umberto's mother, eight or ten years ago. It made Thea feel as if she'd carelessly stepped into another world that she was not equipped to deal with. She and Drew often forgot to lock their front door before going to bed.

'Coffee?' she asked, keeping her voice steady with an effort. 'Are you hungry?'

Gladwin accepted coffee and a biscuit, standing close to Thea as she made the drinks. 'You're shaking,' she observed. 'You're probably not safe around boiling water.'

In a sudden unanticipated burst, Thea began to cry. It was as if some quite alien force had invaded her and flicked a tap – it was entirely beyond her control. Gladwin had no need of an explanation. 'It's all right,' she soothed. 'All quite normal. Come and sit down.'

They sat together on Umberto's sofa and Thea took deep breaths. 'That was very weird,' she gulped.

'Shock,' said Gladwin. 'Reality breaking in. Horror. Disbelief. I expect you know the theories.'

'More or less,' Thea agreed, thinking she probably didn't. Probably nobody did. Even when you had every reason to expect something terrible to happen – like in the trenches, with your soldier friends being torn apart in front of you – you couldn't anticipate the effect on yourself. And this was not a war – it was closer to a terrorist bomb going off just as you were in mid-sentence, or thinking about a birthday party. 'Isn't there a poem about it?' she said, idiotically. 'The one about Icarus falling out of the sky.'

Gladwin ignored this. 'Where's the owner of this house?' she asked.

'Somewhere in France, I guess. Driving towards Germany in a van.'

The detective gave the room a slow scrutiny. 'What's he like?'

'Quite nice.' Thea's mind was working sluggishly. 'Why?'

'That girl was coming here, most likely. She's parked just outside this house, after all. They're going to send me her ID any time now. Assuming it was her car, there shouldn't be much trouble over that. All the usual wheels in motion – telling next of kin and so forth.'

Thea could muster little immediate interest in this information. 'I'm looking after the dogs,' she remembered irrelevantly, giving her own spaniel a careless pat as it crouched beside her. 'They're lovely and terribly valuable. Somebody might want to steal them. I've got to guard them.'

'What's in the van on its way to Germany, then? More valuable dogs?'

Thea shook her head. 'Old cameras. He buys them cheap here and sells them to German collectors at a handsome profit. He's not very rich. This was his mother's house. There's a whole lot of stock upstairs. I'm supposed to be guarding that as well.' She was speaking almost at random, her eyes darting from one corner of the room to another, as if looking for something meaningful to comment on.

Gladwin remained perfectly calm, her questions clear and to the point. 'Why the pretentious gate?'

'Everybody's got one around here. Actually, this one was probably the first.' She recounted Umberto's story of the gate's origins.

'It does look quite old. There's rust on it.'

Thea shrugged. 'The whole place is a bit run-down.'

Gladwin's phone jingled and she attended to its

message. 'We've got the DVLA information now, from her car.' She looked up at Thea, and then read, 'Miss Gabriella Milner. Twenty-five. Lives in Burford. No penalty points on her licence.'

Thea grimaced. 'Twenty-five,' she whispered. 'Maybe she deals in cameras as well, and came to talk to Umberto about them.'

'Unlikely,' said Gladwin. 'They're trying to find her parents. All the usual stuff. Somebody's going to have to identify her.'

'They say people look like rag dolls after being hit by a car. It's true. Her arms and legs . . . they were all crooked and limp.'

'There's no quick way round it, Thea,' said Gladwin seriously. 'You'll have those images in your head for quite a while. I'm inclined to think it's best not to fight them. They'll fade eventually.'

'There's a dreadful fascination to them,' Thea admitted. 'I keep trying to make them real, and explain exactly what happened. I mean – to her, physically. Which bones broke, what it did to her brain and heart and lungs. Is that ghoulish?'

'What if it is? There aren't any rules. From what I can see, her spinal cord was snapped, and her skull's quite likely cracked. All the internal organs crushed by her ribcage. A car can do appalling damage.'

'I know that now.' She closed her eyes. 'And it never even paused. I think it must have just accelerated away without a backward glance.'

'There's no sign of sudden braking on the road,' Gladwin agreed. 'But the headlights – or one of them anyway – got smashed. They're collecting slivers of glass out there as we speak.'

'Can you work out the make and model from them, then?'

'We'll have to see. It'll take a bit of time. Maybe enough for the killer to permanently dispose of the vehicle.'

'That can't be easy. Won't there be CCTV somewhere of it driving along all broken?'

'Let's hope so.'

'It was big. And some metallic sort of colour. Silvery.'

'I know. You told Samuelson. She's still out there, doing door to door. Very keen.'

'She did a good job with me. Dodged most of the pitfalls, anyway.' Everything they said came to Thea through a mist, as if a long way off and barely relevant. 'Said I should talk to someone. I assume she meant a therapist.'

'Counsellor. Early days for that. And I'm not sure there's anyone who could fit you in for a bit.'

'I can talk to you instead.'

'You can. And even if I say so myself, I suspect I can be every bit as much use to you. Now – what's going to happen tonight?'

'What do you mean?'

'About staying here. The dogs. You know what I mean.'

'I'll keep going. Might as well. It won't make any difference where I am – I'm still going to have those pictures in my head, aren't I? And I like the dogs. I can't go off and abandon them.'

'You always say that, but what's Drew going to think? This will be headline news tomorrow. Probably hit the nationals. It's got all the right elements. Young woman killed in hit and run in sleepy English village. They'll go mad for it.'

'Are they out there already?' Thea had deliberately avoided even a glance at the street beyond the gate.

'Oh yes.'

'Are you the SIO?'

'For my sins. And I need to get back to it. I'll try and call in again tomorrow.'

'Am I really the only witness?' It was a question that kept returning to her. Every time, she hoped to hear that some keen-eyed villager had seen every detail and even photographed the killer in the very act. And every time she knew that was sheer fantasy.

'So far, yes.' Gladwin smiled ruefully. 'Nobody else about, as far as we can tell. Of all the people in all the Cotswolds, it had to be right outside your door, didn't it? And you're going to say it's all because the house is empty, or you're known to make a bit of a mess of watching out for people's dogs. That it's really not a coincidence at all.'

For the first time, Thea felt a flicker of fear. 'You think they'll come back for the dogs?'

'Absolutely not. We're leaving a vehicle just across the street, with two very fit young PCs in it. They'll be here all night, if that makes you feel better.'

'Poor things,' said Thea. 'I'll take them some tea in the morning.'

'Don't you dare. Unless it's of vital importance, I think your best bet is to stay inside until we've got a better handle on what's what.'

'I was going to anyway,' said Thea with a sigh. 'Although I did think Hepzie and I might at least do a quick tour of the village. There's a road leading up to an old church that we should have a look at.'

'Leave it another day or so,' Gladwin advised. 'It's going to rain tomorrow, anyway.'

When Gladwin had gone, Thea sent her husband a text. They had agreed that there was no need for nightly phone calls. He was going to be comfortably occupied with two funerals and other business matters, and his children were going to be at school all week. Fiona Emerson, wife of Drew's partner Andrew, had agreed to prepare meals with Stephanie's help. The Emersons had recently taken on more of the funeral work, expanding the services on offer and helping to generate a larger income. Fiona was proving to have a variety of hidden talents, which included wholesome cooking, filing and maintaining the burial ground. The long summer grass vanished under her ministrations, where both Drew and Andrew had neglected to keep it under control. She had also trimmed back a hedge and organised a load of stone chippings for the gateway. Plans were well advanced for a building where mourners could gather, and extra space for cars to park.

Thea's text read, 'The dogs are lovely. Nasty accident in the street outside. Plenty to keep me occupied indoors tomorrow, if it rains. Hope all's well at home.'

It wasn't altogether honest, she acknowledged to herself, but there would be time enough for a full report in the coming days.

She took the salukis for a brief run to the end of the field and back, letting them veer off as the mood took them and rewarding them with nibbles when they trooped into their palatial night-time quarters. They were proving blessedly easy to handle, apparently unfazed by a new person and contented with their lot. There was much to be said for the life of a dog, Thea concluded.

She closed the lounge curtains, to block out any sight of the street, and looked around the room as Gladwin had done. The walls were painted an unimaginative magnolia, the furniture showed little sign of having been carefully chosen. There was a bland rug covering about a quarter of the solid parquet flooring that was the best feature of the room. The fireplace at one end was obviously not used, but had been made a focal point with its Cotswolds stone surround and a hand-stitched sampler hanging above it. A closer look showed the sampler to have been worked in 1877 by a child called Mary Harrison at the age of nine.

On the wall to the left of the fireplace about twenty framed photographs had been hung, in two uneven rows that suggested a somewhat careless process. The frames were all different, as were the methods of hanging. Some showed string or wire where they hung from a nail in the wall; others did not. They were, however, in a kind of date order. They could mean little to anyone outside the family without somebody to explain and identify them. Thea had no doubt that Umberto's mother had arranged them, in a sequence that she had devised herself. If anybody had been looking for clues as to her character, they might arrive at *careless, sentimental,* and perhaps *old-fashioned.* Not many people stuck pictures like this on their walls any more, as far as Thea was aware.

It did, however, confirm the impression that this had never been an affluent household. The photographs had mostly been stuck into cheap mass-produced frames. The wall behind them was showing signs of grubbiness that shouted for a fresh coat of paint. The skirting boards were even more in need of attention. Thea remembered that when Umberto had first approached her and given his address, she had instantly assumed he must be rich. He was, after all, prepared to pay her handsomely.

That was an anomaly, she now concluded. It must be coming out of a 'dog fund' of some sort. A sort of essential insurance payment because the salukis were an investment, as well as loved for their own sake. But it did occur to her to wonder where the money for their initial purchase had come from.

But for lack of anything else to do, Thea began at the beginning and slowly inspected each picture in turn. The first one showed a couple at their wedding, circa 1905. There followed studio portraits of men and women in their best clothes. One man sported a pipe, and one woman wore a hat with a feather. There was a baby, and about halfway along, a cluster of four children, one of whom might be Umberto at the age of about ten. The display finished with two graduation photographs, in colour, both featuring a female student. One had distinctive curly brown hair and looked to be of rather short stature. The other, Thea realised with a jolt, was the girl she had witnessed going to a violent death only a few hours ago. There was not a single label to identify any of the people in the pictures.

She stood transfixed in front of the two last pictures. The girls were surely cousins, probably of a similar age, each bringing pride to the family with their academic accomplishments. One of them was now dead – and she found herself wondering how that would affect all the others on the wall who were still alive.

The family history book was still lying close by. With a feeling that it would now make more sense, she took it up and turned again to the final pages, with the oddly ominous final lines. The chapter that it concluded was devoted to bringing everything up to date. There was Umberto's familiar name, his mother and three sisters, the eldest of whom was called Penny. It was her husband who had written the book. With a nice sense of life going on, future generations to be born, the story never really coming to an end, the author listed every family member. There was Imogen, with her daughter Kirsty plus two sons who were briefly listed as 'dedicated Europeans resident in Vienna'. And the youngest sister, Theresa, who had a son named Jacob and a daughter.

The daughter's name was Gabriella.

Chapter Four

Thea's first instinct was to call Gladwin, and save her team the bother of tracing the connection through online databases. But then she paused. Chances were that some diligent constable had already worked it out, sending someone to the door to tell Theresa and her husband the terrible news. They would tell the rest of the family – Imogen, Penny, Umberto. The news would fly around the world – to Vienna and Berlin. What had at first glance appeared to be a tightly clustered group of siblings, now felt looser. The younger generation had at least partially spread their wings. Attendance at Gabriella's funeral might well involve long flights and complicated arrangements.

The immediate effect of her discovery was to banish the worst symptoms of her trauma. Already she was experiencing a glow of embarrassment at her reaction. That, she suspected, would get worse before it got better. Other people had far greater reason to collapse into shock and despair.

The victim now had an identity and the glimmerings of a story. Her photo was there on the wall of

Umberto's living room. She had surely been coming to visit her uncle, perhaps after work, not knowing he'd gone away. Some enemy had followed her, intent on homicide. Perhaps she had been sleeping with somebody's husband, or cheated them in some way. *Perhaps* repeated itself in all kinds of hypotheses. A stalker, driven crazy by rejection. A driver, full of rage at the way she had just overtaken him on the road out of Stow, following her in an insane fit of male pride. The owner of a dog she had carelessly killed the previous day. The exercise was therapeutic, if nothing else.

Outside it was at last fading into darkness. She could see the sky at the back of the house, through the kitchen window. The salukis were quiet in their bedroom, and Hepzie nestled comfortably in one corner of the couch. Umberto had left written instructions for setting the nighttime burglar alarm and locking all the doors. With very deliberate care, the paper in her hand, Thea went around the house doing as bidden. Where she would usually feel a kick of irritation at such paranoid behaviour, this evening was different. It was comforting, and even rather sensible, to erect defences and bar the house against crazy stalkers or ferocious jealous wives. Granted that their victim was well and truly destroyed, there could still just possibly be a residual malice, an urge to slaughter poor Gabriella's entire family for good measure. And Thea might be mistaken for a cousin fully deserving of attack, given that she was in the uncle's house.

She and the spaniel retired to bed at half past ten, unsure about the prospects of sleep. The night was cool and evidently the exercise with the salukis had been beneficial, because they both sank into oblivion two minutes after switching off the light.

Tuesday morning started early. Umberto had mumbled something about letting the dogs out 'first thing', which in June could easily mean 5 a.m. In fact, it was six-fifteen and there was no sound of life from downstairs. The sky was pale grey. A bird was singing somewhere.

Memories and images came back in clumps. The two policemen in a car outside; the emptiness of Oddington; the long day stretching unpredictably before her – and only then the violent shock of the main event. Cautiously, she inspected her own inner workings. The shock was definitely fading, with no more shakes or tears. If anything, she felt rather brisk and business-like. Gladwin – or perhaps Detective Sergeant Caz Barkley in her place – would show up and share confidential police findings with her, as they regularly did. Thea would perhaps share some of her less fantastic speculations and together they would tease out connections and histories and probabilities.

Getting dressed took very little time, even on a cool June day, and then she and Hepzie went down the wide staircase that ended in the generous hall. Space had never been in short supply when this house had been built, she concluded. The ceilings were high, the walls thick. Some rich wool merchant had done his best to vaunt his success. Or had she got the dates wrong? The house was a lot later than the seventeenth century, when it was easy to make a fortune from your sheep. Perhaps its first occupant had owned cloth mills or needle factories. Most of the industry of the time would concern the basic necessities – clothes or food, horses or houses.

The salukis greeted her with a well-bred nonchalance, before trooping outside to assess the weather. Hepzie followed them slowly, unsure of her status in this sudden pack. Her normal routine of walks along country lanes and footpaths had apparently been abandoned, and running about in a field was a peculiar substitute. Admittedly there *was* a field at home in Broad Campden, but she mostly ran straight across it, to get to the other side, not foolishly round and round it for no reason.

Thea threw some toys and noted the use of the toilet area and found herself relentlessly haunted by the events of the previous day, despite the initial effects having worn off. It felt somehow risky to be here at the back, instead of keeping the village street under observation. She might be securely locked in, but somebody could come to the gate and want her. There might be an overlooked clue to the crime somehow lodged in Umberto's hedge. There might even be a distressed ghost hovering in the air just outside, desperate to convey something to Thea, as the only witness to her slaughter.

Umberto's instructions gave details of the dogs' breakfasts, which she followed with care. Then she went into the kitchen to make herself coffee and give Hepzie a handful of biscuit. It was only a few minutes past seven o'clock. Nobody was going to come for hours yet. The day became suddenly ominous, with acres of empty time and hardly anything to do. She could not expect Gladwin or Barkley to divert their attention away from such a high-profile murder investigation just to keep a house-sitter company, however traumatised she might be. And the honest truth was that she now found herself very much less traumatised than people might think.

But she had reckoned without her husband. At twenty past seven there was a phone call from him, much to her surprise. 'Hit-and-run killing in Oddington,' he said without preamble. 'Is that what you call a nasty accident in the street? How far was it from the house you're in?'

'Why are you checking news headlines at this time in the morning?' she countered without answering his question.

'I'm not, but Stephanie is. She found it five minutes ago.'

'But why?'

'Why do you think? She's taking an interest, trying to visualise where you are, hoping you're all right.'

'I am all right.'

'But it was no accident, according to the news. The police are looking for a large silver or metallic car with broken headlights and probably other damage.

A woman died. If I remember rightly, Oddington is extremely small. If I know you, you'll already be involved.'

'Yes, but I am all right,' she admitted. 'Gladwin's the SIO and she left two uniformed officers here all night, just in case.'

'Just in case *what*?' His voice rose with concern.

'Nothing specific. Tell Stephanie it's nothing to worry about. The dogs here are lovely and it's a very nice house. And it's only till Friday.'

'Thus speaks my eternally over-optimistic wife,' he said. 'I suppose I should be used to it by now.'

'Yes, you should. And honestly, Drew, think of what he's paying me. My whole focus has got to be on these dogs. I'm not even supposed to leave the house in case somebody steals them.' An alarming thought entered her head as she spoke, but she had the sense to keep it back. 'I won't be able to get involved at all this time. I'll be more likely to die of boredom than anything else.'

'Very funny,' he said with a sigh.

Thea changed the subject to the children's school day, the midday funeral that Drew was conducting, and the options she'd left him for that evening's meal, in the absence of Fiona Emerson's assistance. Thea had provided one or two ready-cooked meals, to cover sudden emergencies, although Stephanie had protested that she could easily do any cooking that might be required. But the girl was very young and had year-end exams, and no way of doing any shopping. 'This will be easier, and you still have to peel potatoes, and get everything coordinated, even if you use my casseroles,' Thea had assured her. 'You'll be sick of even that much by Friday.'

The girl had shrugged. 'I can do potatoes and defrosting isn't very difficult,' she said.

'You might be surprised,' said Thea with a laugh.

Drew ended the call with a reluctant agreement that he would refrain from worrying. He was well aware that Thea would go her own way, do her own thing, whatever he might be feeling. He accepted that this was better than if she let him control her with his own anxieties and weaknesses. That would be unhealthy and destructive – or so she assured him. 'You knew what I was like when you married me,' was often her finishing thrust, and he had to concede that it was true. He had seen quite a lot of her house-sitting at close quarters, and even shared a few of her adventures in their early days together.

Afterwards, Thea found herself annoyed with Stephanie for checking up on her. She acknowledged that it was well-meant, and the child was a born diplomat in most ways. But telling Drew about events in Oddington felt like an act of mild treachery. Stephanie would know perfectly well what the result would be, and that it could do no good. Surely it would have been wiser and kinder to simply leave Thea to herself for a week, and get on with their own interests?

The next hour trickled by with more coffee, a check

on the weather forecast, straightening her bed and thinking. It was interesting the way thinking could pass the time. There were plenty of things to speculate about, after all. Did Umberto know by now what had happened to his niece outside his house? Would he be desperately upset? Would there be a gathering of his sisters and their offspring before he came home, and would Thea have to make tea for them? Would she get to meet some neighbours?

It was still early when at least a few of her questions were answered. Her phone warbled and proclaimed 'Umberto Kingly' as the caller. Thea was still not convinced that this piece of cleverness was to her liking. It removed any little thrill there had once been at not knowing who was phoning.

'I've had the police onto me,' he began. 'Are the dogs all right?'

'They're fine,' she said stiffly. *Never mind how* I *might be*, she thought crossly.

'It's completely beyond belief,' he went on. 'Literally impossible to accept as real. It must have been an accident, whatever the police might think. Nobody would deliberately kill Gabriella. She's a fine girl. Not a nasty bone in her body. She had everything going for her.' His voice was thick and quiet. She could tell how stunned he was. She was also beginning to notice the way he appeared to think well of almost everybody in his family. Whatever mild criticisms he had made were well seasoned with affection. Both Kirsty and Gabriella had been given a good character by him.

'I know,' said Thea meaninglessly.

'Well, listen. You will stay on, won't you? For the dogs. There's nobody else. I've been trying to get hold of Imogen, but her phone's off. God knows where she is. And Theresa must be so completely shattered, I don't like to bother her. She's Gabriella's mother,' he added helpfully.

'Yes. I found them in that book you gave me.'

'Oh – Vic's book, yes. So you know about Penny as well, then.'

'Um…?'

'My other sister, married to Victor Rider. She's a civil servant and thinks family history is bunkum.'

'Right. Yes – she's there as well. I mean, in the book. And on the wall, I suppose.'

'Pardon?'

'The photos. Dozens of them, all family portraits,' she prompted.

'Oh – right. I barely even notice them any more. Well, maybe you'll get to meet some of them. It's possible. My money's on Penny. She's the eldest, you see.'

Thea did see, even if her own eldest sibling was male.

'Can't ignore Penny,' Umberto said, as if to himself. He sounded remote, detached. Thea felt she had raised a completely irrelevant topic when referring to the photos. Which was a shame, because she found herself suddenly wanting to know a lot more about the family and its own special dynamic. Everything would shift with the violent death of one of its number, in ways that were impossible to predict.

'I'm just glad my mother's not here to see it,' said Umberto, in a stronger voice. 'That's one thing to be thankful for.'

'Mm.'

'But – oh Lord, I still can't believe it. I had no idea Gabriella would seriously take it into her head to come and see you. When I told her I was going away she said something vague about coming round, but I never thought she'd do it. She's got a demanding job and a splendid boyfriend. She's been all wrapped up in him for a year or more now. Nice chap . . .' Again he seemed to be drifting away.

Thea's close encounters with police murder investigations meant that bells inevitably rang. The *nice chap* would already be near the top of any preliminary list of potential killers.

'I see there's a lot about your mother in the book,' she offered, thinking the woman was looming quite large in Umberto's mind.

His laugh was bitter. 'You could say that. My mother was a woman about whom there was always a great deal to say.' The formal syntax did nothing to conceal the feeling behind it. Without even thinking about it, Thea had learnt that Mr Kingly had not always felt kindly towards his maternal parent.

'Oh,' she said. 'She must have been still alive when the book was published.'

'She died a week or two after it was printed.'

'Did she get to read it?'

'Oh yes. Some of us even think it might have been what killed her. Splurging family secrets and all that. It's really just Imogen who got herself in a tizzy about it. She never did like poor Victor much, anyway. Mama had a catastrophic stroke – it could happen to anybody at any time. She would never go to a doctor, so nobody knew her blood pressure was through the roof.'

'Oh dear,' said Thea, feeling inadequate.

'Well, no need to go into that now. I'll have to go. I'm already late. I'll see you on Friday.'

The call was concluded with Thea's assurances that the dogs would remain her highest priority, that nothing would be allowed to threaten them. Visitors would only be admitted once they were securely shut outside or in their living quarters. 'I need your absolute commitment to that,' he insisted. 'They've been known to make a dash for it if they see an open door.'

Hard experience had taught Thea that where dogs were concerned, a careless moment could spell disaster. 'Don't worry,' she said. 'The dogs will definitely come first.' And she meant it.

All of which quickly led to another prolonged session outside playing with the salukis, devising variations with a deliberate concentration that blanked out everything else. She experimented with the orders they did or did not understand. 'Stay!' worked perfectly, and 'Fetch!', but very little else. Even that was enough for some enjoyable games. Each dog answered unhesitatingly to her own name, which meant they could be despatched individually to different corners of the field by means of throwing a toy and then ordering the animal to stay. Then Thea stood in the middle and called each one to her. It was ridiculously satisfying when it worked. Hepzie added an unpredictable element by randomly allying herself to one saluki after another, and staging competitive races, which only she found interesting. Salukis, it turned out, could run very much faster than spaniels.

By ten o'clock everyone was comprehensively exercised, and it was raining. 'Now what?' said Thea, anticipating by about three minutes the next visitor, buzzing to be admitted through the inhospitable gates.

'It's me again,' said Gladwin. 'Let me in.'

After a careful check of the doors, Thea opened up. Tired and contented as the dogs might be, she was still mindful of her responsibilities and the need to be alert. Her own behaviour, so different from earlier occasions, gave her a little glow of self-satisfaction. This time she was really going to get it right.

She led the way into the kitchen and made two mugs of instant coffee. They did not sit down, but began a somewhat purposeless ramble around the ground floor of the house, carrying the drinks.

Gladwin had, as expected, found the link between the murdered Gabriella and Thea's employer. 'He phoned me just now,' Thea said. 'He's stunned, poor man.'

'Did he tell you she was his niece?'

'Well, actually, I knew already. It's in the family history book. I only found it late last night, so didn't phone you about it. I assumed you'd figure it out soon enough.'

'I'm not sure how to take that. People's family trees aren't posted on the Internet as a matter of course, you know.'

'Okay, but once you knew her name and address, you'd find her parents, and they'd fill you in. There's a whole lot I don't know, if that's any consolation. What was her job? What about her *life*? Friends, hobbies, qualifications . . . Umberto says she didn't have a nasty bone in her body. Those were his actual words. And he said she had a boyfriend.'

'Yes. She was living with him. He's called Ramon Rodriguez. He's Spanish, but has lived here since he was about three. He's a teacher. She worked as a freelance interpreter and translator. Fluent in French, Spanish and Italian, clever thing. Does that fill out the picture for you?'

'Very much so,' Thea said.

As before, Gladwin was giving the room a close inspection. 'There's something a bit sad about this house, don't you think? It feels neglected and unloved.'

'I know. It's typical Cotswolds in that way, even if it's much more shabby. I mean – they all have a kind of *temporary* feel to them. With the others it's the value of the property itself that matters. Here, it's the dogs. It's not so different, really.'

Gladwin frowned. 'He *is* unusual, though. We've had a quick look at him, given that the incident happened outside his house. His activities in Germany came up on his website, and it really isn't anything to get excited about. All rather small-scale, in fact. Just a lot of stuff about old cameras.'

'I think he's pretty keen on the cameras in a geeky sort of way – lenses and film sizes and all that. Although he doesn't seem to care much about the end product.'

'Sorry?'

'The photos. You'd think he'd want to show off what the cameras can do. It seems a bit lacking to just bother with the contraption and not the photos it can take,' she finished vaguely.

'It probably isn't unusual. Those old cameras are lovely in their own right. Precision tooling and perfect lenses – that sort of thing.'

Thea was reminded of her neighbour in Broad Campden, who collected old glass, just because he loved it. Umberto didn't seem to be that sort of enthusiast. 'I think it's more dogs than cameras that gets him going,' she said. 'But he's probably got lots of contacts, and collectors who'll pay through the nose for an original 1924 Leica, or whatever. I dare say you can still find them in house clearances and so forth. Car boot sales. Auctions. I don't know,' she finished irritably. She sighed, her attention lapsing. Gladwin gave a little cough.

'Sorry,' said Thea. 'I lost it for a minute. So why are

we talking about Umberto? He's got a very good alibi.'

'Because it happened *here*,' said Gladwin, insistently. 'I said that already.' She tapped an impatient finger on the window sill, where they had automatically gone to stand and look out on the street. 'So tell me about the dogs.'

'What about them?'

'If he breeds them, every puppy can sell for thousands. Although there are laws to limit how many litters he can produce each year.'

'He hasn't bred any yet. It's all part of a plan for the future. And he said he'd only have one lot a year, with the girls taking it in turn.'

'How would that work financially? I bet he'll give in to temptation and go in for a lot more than that.'

'It's probably not a very reliable market. And he does love them for themselves, not just as breeding machines.'

'Okay, so he makes a fairly basic living with buying and selling antique cameras. I can see there's a bit of profit to be made if he's canny, but it won't be many millions, will it? How does he pay his council tax, for a start?'

'Maybe his mother left a handsome bank balance for them all to share.'

Gladwin's attention was wandering. 'I expect you're right that it's not important, anyway,' she said. 'He was definitely out of the country when it happened, so unless he paid a hit man, he's in the clear.'

'Gosh! I never thought of that,' grinned Thea. 'What

if he did? That would make pretty good sense.'

The detective closed her eyes for a moment, as if recalibrating something. 'Would that fit with what you saw last night? Just a gut feeling, a subliminal impression – anything?'

Thea leaned back, trying to clear her mind. 'For a start it doesn't fit with Umberto. He really seems to like all his relations. He says nice things about his nieces and gets along with his sisters.'

'So let's go over what you saw yesterday, one more time,' Gladwin urged.

'All right. You saw for yourself from upstairs – it's all at a funny angle. I saw the car roof, and the way the wing mirror scraped the little car, which must have taken about half a second before it hit the girl and the door, all in one ghastly crash. It was going terribly fast.' She shuddered. 'It must take enormous force to wrench a door right off like that.'

'Apparently not as much as you might think. Cars are pretty flimsy these days.'

'Does that mean the killer's car will be badly damaged?'

'Not necessarily. Once it had bashed the door off there was nothing to get in its way – not like running into a brick wall, or even an oncoming vehicle. We've been running simulations,' she explained, with a rueful expression. 'Which isn't too good for a person's peace of mind when you know there was a real victim caught up in it.'

Thea merely shook her head sympathetically.

Gladwin persisted with her questions. 'You didn't see the driver at all? Not a tiny glimpse? No reflections?'

'There's no way I could have done. I was watching the girl.' Again she tried to clear her mind. 'She saw the car coming, I think. She was turned a bit sideways, maybe because she heard the engine. She might have been worried about the door of her car being open and getting in its way.' She paused. 'But she didn't look worried. I'm not sure, but I even think she might have been smiling.'

'As if it was someone she knew; somebody she was glad to see?'

'That's possible,' said Thea.

'Which would mean it wasn't a hit man,' said Gladwin.

Chapter Five

'Where did Gabriella and the boyfriend live – did you say?'

'Burford. Not too far from here.'

'Nice. I wonder what they thought of Umberto and the way he's treating this house.'

Gladwin shrugged. 'Who knows? They probably didn't even think about it.'

Thea scratched her chin thoughtfully. 'I bet they did. How could they not?'

'I don't follow. What are you trying to say?'

'There's something not right about this house. There's not enough *stuff*. The old mum died last year, suddenly. She wasn't ill, and yet the family kept a close eye on her, actually *staying* here with her, taking turns, because she hated being on her own. For some reason Umberto seems to have taken root here, not long before she died, and just stayed on, claiming the house by default. Something like that, anyway. But it all feels very odd. That's not how it usually works, is it?'

The detective shrugged again. 'What's wrong with it? And how on earth do you know all this, anyway?'

'He told me most of it yesterday, before he set off. He seemed quite relaxed about it, as if everything was perfectly normal. But none of it fits properly. It's like doing a jigsaw with pieces from two different sets.'

'I still don't follow. I need detail, Thea. Not all this impressionistic stuff.'

'It's been helpful before,' said Thea mulishly.

'I suppose so.' Gladwin's attention was still not wholly on Thea. She had drifted out of the living room and was now walking around the kitchen fingering the contents of the cup rack attached to one wall, opening the fridge and cupboards. Thea followed her, wondering whether she should offer more coffee or something to eat. 'Very ordinary things,' said Gladwin. 'Reminds me of my family home, in a way. Nothing fancy. Good solid pots and pans. I can't see anything wrong with it.'

'I didn't mean *wrong*, exactly.' Thea stopped herself, aware that she was verging on another round of *impressionistic stuff*. 'Give me another day or two, and I might have put my finger on it. It isn't likely to have anything to do with poor Gabriella, anyway.' She found herself glad to have a reason to say the name of the dead girl. It felt good not to be avoiding it or using euphemisms. You had to do that with death – stare it down, voice the terrible truth, ride the waves of pain and horror. Anything else left you even more damaged and afraid, in the long run. Drew Slocombe knew that, which was the single most wonderful thing about him.

'And yet it might,' said Gladwin. 'So I have to take

notice of this house and everything about it. Gabriella was coming here yesterday and was killed before she got to the gate. Did she know he was away? How often was she here? He hasn't got any children, so was she like a daughter to him?'

'Ask Ramon. What's he like?'

Gladwin spread her hands. 'I haven't seen him. Barkley went round last night with a FLO. Not surprisingly he's in a state of shock, suffering agonies of grief and all the other stuff that goes with it. Caz asked a few basic questions, but didn't get very far.'

Thea sat down at the kitchen table trying to construct an overview of everything surrounding the death of Gabriella Milner. 'Where do you start?' she said helplessly. 'You're going to have to unearth every aspect of her life, only to discover that it was a fit of road rage, and nothing to do with her work or friends or family.'

'If that was it, we're most unlikely ever to know. It'll be an unsolved case for ever.'

'You've got me,' said Thea warmly. 'At least you've got some idea of what the vehicle was like, thanks to me.'

'More a matter of what it's *not* like,' said Gladwin.

Thea could think of nothing useful to add, since the detective seemed liable to dismiss random details about the Kingly family. That struck Thea as a mistake, but she knew better than to say so. There were matters of process and protocol in a police investigation that she knew she would never properly grasp.

'Was there anything else about Umberto's phone call?' Gladwin eventually asked, with a sharp glance at her watch. 'I really do want to get back, you know. Is there anything you think might help?'

Thea felt pressured, doing her best to come up with something helpful. 'Oh – er … we went through some of the family connections. He wanted me to reassure him that I would stay here as arranged. He cares more about the dogs than anything else.'

Gladwin subsided. 'Is that all?'

'Can't remember anything else. He wasn't in any fit state for idle chat. He's completely fixated on family and dogs.'

'Are they Italian? I mean – with a name like Umberto they must be, surely?'

Yet again, Thea picked up the book about the Kinglys and flicked through it, more as a way of directing her thoughts than to acquire fresh information. After a minute, she said, 'His grandmother was. Mother's mother.'

'I'm assuming she's long dead,' said Gladwin drily. 'She'd be about a hundred and ten otherwise.'

Thea's laugh was brief and insincere. She riffled again through the pages of the book, increasingly convinced that the answers to most relevant questions lay there to be found.

The detective sighed impatiently. 'I doubt if any of this is the least bit significant, but we'll have to at least check where all these relatives are and what sort of vehicle they drive.' She paused to think. 'They must have a high opinion of themselves, to put it all in a book.'

'Not really. It's obviously self-published, just to keep a printed record of who everyone is. I think it's nice – although I have a feeling they don't all like it, from something Umberto said. I haven't found any black sheep or outcasts. They all seem to live reasonably close by, even the younger ones. It is a bit ominous at the end, though.' She read aloud the final lines about animosities.

Gladwin groaned. 'I can't even begin to get it all straight. I don't suppose I could take the book, could I?'

Thea felt oddly reluctant to part with it. 'It's not mine to lend,' she said, holding it close to her chest. 'And I haven't read it properly yet. Look – I'll draw you a family tree instead, starting with the Italian granny. I'll take a sheet of A4 out of Umberto's printer.'

She quickly did as promised, checking the book for everyone's ages and full names. 'Here,' she said, when she finished.

'At least two missing husbands,' the detective muttered. 'I wonder where the money came from? This house was never going to be cheap, was it? Not even two hundred years ago, or whenever it was built.'

'Stone,' said Thea. 'They quarried stone. First in Italy, then here.'

'Ah,' said Gladwin with a nod. 'That makes sense, I suppose.'

A buzzer interrupted them. 'Somebody at the gate,' said Thea with a grin. 'Doesn't that sound grand!'

The intercom announced Detective Sergeant Caz Barkley, which gave Thea a thrum of pleasure. She really liked Caz. 'And I've got somebody with me,' added the newcomer.

Thea met two people at the front door and ushered them in. 'This is Mr Milner – Gabriella Milner's brother,' said Caz quickly. 'He's come to see where it happened.'

A tall man in his late twenties held out his hand. 'Jacob,' he said, holding out his hand. 'Also known as Jake.'

Thea took the hand and met his gaze. He had hazel eyes, light-brown hair, and not a trace of Italian ancestry. He was quite obviously distraught. Thea immediately deleted him from her mental list of suspects. Glancing at Gladwin, she could see that the Senior Investigating Officer was not intending to listen to another half-hour of family history, however relevant it might turn out to be. 'I'll be off,' she said, having led Thea outside, away from the others. The village street had not yet been reopened to traffic. The white tent had gone, but there were two police vans parked further down the road towards Upper Oddington. A TV van was sitting obtrusively outside a house across the road. 'Why do you let them in?' Thea asked. 'And what do they think they're going to see?'

'That's nothing. There were *four* of them here last night. As long as they keep their distance, we've no reason to object. News is news,' she finished with a sigh. 'You soon learn to ignore them.'

'I think they're parasites,' said Thea.

'They have their uses. It's all part of what they like to call a free society.'

Thea accepted this with poor grace, turning her back on the van.

'Oh, well, back to the rock face. It's all forensics and nit-picking today.' Gladwin went on. 'Not that there's much evidence – but we have to gather what there is as quickly as we can. The locals will want their village back.'

'Lucky there's an easy detour around this bit of the street,' said Thea. This was true – the village street formed a loop parallel to the main Stow to Chipping Norton road, which was the A436. Closing a section of it created very little inconvenience to anybody.

Gladwin departed and Thea went back into the house, where Barkley and Jacob Milner were hanging about awkwardly in the hallway. 'Are the dogs all right?' the man asked, the moment he saw Thea.

'They're fine,' she assured him. 'We've had a good romp today already.'

'That's good. Uncle Umberto is terribly fond of them.'

'They're lovely,' Thea said in all sincerity. 'I can see why your uncle's so keen to keep them safe.'

Jacob Milner grimaced. 'We all think he's a bit paranoid about it, to be honest. The chances of them being stolen are tiny, in reality. They'd be too obvious.'

Caz pursed her lips. 'They'd be shipped off to Ireland or the Isle of Man before you'd noticed they'd gone,' she said. 'And used as breeding machines for the rest of their lives.'

'And as soon as they tried to sell the pups, somebody would be onto them,' Jacob flashed back. Apparently, thought Thea, his distress about his sister could be set aside when it came to any talk about dogs.

'I'm terribly sorry about your sister,' she said, in the belief that the real issue ought to be faced.

Instantly, he went pale and his eyes seemed to sag. 'Thanks,' he muttered. 'They tell me you saw it happen.'

'It was very quick,' she said, thinking it was probably rarely the case that these words could be so true. 'She can't have known what was happening.'

'She must have seen who did it, though?'

Caz intervened. 'It might be best not to go into too much of the detail,' she cautioned. 'And remember it was traumatic for Mrs Slocombe as well.'

He gave a thin smile. 'It must have been. Although you don't look—' He stopped himself too late. It was obvious what he had been meaning to say.

'I got over it quickly,' she nodded. 'But I must admit I'm dreading the dreams I might have in the next few weeks.'

'So – can I ask? *Did* she see who it was?'

Thea hardly hesitated, ignoring Barkley's intervention. 'I think so. Perhaps only for a split second – whatever that means. She didn't have time to react at all. Not that I could see. I was upstairs – it was all at a funny angle. And the tree got in the way of most of it. But I think she was going to smile, as if she recognised the driver of the car.'

'That's ridiculous!' the man snapped. Then he softened his tone. 'I can't believe anybody would do that on purpose.' His words were stale, as if he'd said them many times already. 'I can't see how it could have been planned in advance. So that surely means a stranger – road rage stuff. Gabriella was quite a careless driver. She might have cut some macho bloke up and he went berserk – followed her into the village and slammed into her.' He looked at the detective. 'Surely?'

Caz looked at Thea, eyebrows raised, apparently resigned to some uncomfortable sharing of details.

'It doesn't really fit,' Thea said reluctantly, but determined to get as close to the truth as she could. 'It was the way it never even slowed down. Just swerved into your sister and her car, then off and away without touching the brakes. I keep thinking about that and I can't make it fit with anything accidental, or even spur of the moment.' She sighed. 'Sorry. I'm not sure that's what you wanted to hear.'

Jacob rolled his lower lip out in an exaggerated expression of scepticism. 'Don't worry about that. It's what I'm here for. I want to make a case for it being a stranger if I can. Just because it happened here, at Umberto's house, doesn't prove anything.' His frankness endeared him to Thea. He was close to admitting he had his own agenda, and that he was going to do his best to make the police see things his way.

'I understand,' she said. 'But I wouldn't say you're very likely to make that work.'

He became more animated, his eyes widening. 'It's ghoulish, I know, but I tried putting myself in the person's shoes. I discovered I'd closed my eyes in the last second. You'd be scared of flying glass, airbag, all that stuff – wouldn't you? So when you opened them again and found the car still worked, you'd be desperate to get away, for all sorts of reasons.'

'Well, maybe at first. But then you'd stop and think. Probably before you got out of Oddington.' It was Caz speaking. 'That's assuming the car windscreen wasn't broken, or the radiator smashed. And even then – maybe more so – you'd stop and get out.'

'Who can say?' said Thea. 'None of us knows how we'd react. If it *was* planned, the person might have rehearsed it over and over, factoring in all the possibilities, and done just what they'd practised.'

Caz was thinking. 'Airbag,' she said slowly. 'It would have gone off with the impact. So that means – possibly – that the driver had disabled it in advance.' She gave Jake a considering look. 'Which would make it very carefully and deliberately planned.'

'Which would also make the person a complete monster,' said Jake, his eyes bulging. 'Somebody insane.'

Barkley and Thea let his words hang in the air, both knowing how unlikely they were to be true.

The visitors stayed another ten minutes, wary of saying the wrong thing in case emotional floodgates opened.

The dead Gabriella floated invisibly around them, her character, relationships and lost future all subjects too large to be broached. Summaries would sound like platitudes; anything more detailed might take all day. Caz avoided empty promises about police wizardry and Thea made it clear that her first duty was to the salukis.

'Can I see them?' Barkley asked.

'Of course you can.' The reply came from Jacob Milner, not Thea. 'I want to say hello to them anyway.'

They trooped out to the garden, followed by Hepzie, and the three resident dogs greeted their owner's nephew with an effusiveness that Thea had not previously seen. 'Gosh – they certainly love you, don't they!' she said.

'I've always been good with dogs.' He was on his knees, cradling one silky head after another, burying his face in Rocket's accommodating neck. Jake sniffed damply, and Thea wondered just how badly he was suffering. After all, his grandmother had died not so long ago, almost as unexpectedly as his sister.

'Well, I'm making sure they're all okay,' she assured him. 'You've no need to worry on that score.' The words echoing in her own ears sounded as if they'd come from someone else entirely.

'Thanks.' The man stood up and brushed at himself. 'I should go.' He gave Caz a helpless look. 'If that's all right?'

'Of course,' she said heartily. 'I'm at your disposal.' She turned to Thea. 'I'll be back before long. It was good to see you again.' Then she winced. 'Although . . .'

'I know,' said Thea quickly.

They trooped back through the house and down to the gate onto the street. 'Silly bloody thing,' said Thea, wrenching at the catch to open it. 'All this is to safeguard the dogs,' she said to Caz. 'As far as I can make out.'

'It's not Uncle Berto's idea, you know,' said Jake Milner unexpectedly. 'It was all like this before he moved in, before there were any dogs here.'

'Oh?' said Thea, wondering why this came as such a surprise. 'We did think the gates looked as if they'd been here a while.'

Jacob sighed with a gust of irritation. 'Nonna had them installed ages ago, when Gruntie died. Our grandfather, that is. She got rather paranoid about living here on her own.'

'Yes, I gathered that from Umberto. The family all rallied round to make sure she was okay – right?'

'Something like that,' said Jake, with an odd little grimace. 'Except she wasn't, was she?'

'She died suddenly, he said.'

'She did. And we all feel guilty about it.'

Chapter Six

Thea was left alone again with four dogs and a lot to think about. There was a fine balance between assuming that Gabriella had been killed by a maniac who hadn't liked her style of driving, and envisaging some carefully planned murder by somebody who knew her well. The latter was gaining ground and in the process connected itself to Umberto, dogs and a large close-knit family. There had been recent changes, probably sparked by the death of Umberto's mother – Gabriella's Nonna. Change did strange things to people. It threw up old resentments and new disagreements. Why had Umberto got the house? What about his sister Imogen, who he had mentioned to Thea as a potential visitor? Had she expected to inherit it instead of him? And what did any of it have to do with Gabriella?

The family history book was of limited help. Its opening chapters concerned Italian ancestors dating back four generations, quoting from a diary written between the wars, and the turbulent family fortunes of those times. It then followed Umberto's grandmother to England and her life as the wife of a successful quarryman in the years following the Second World War. There were two pages about Cotswold stone and its impressive history.

But this was all long ago, and therefore hardly relevant. The current generation, comprising Imogen's Kirsty and Theresa's Jacob and Gabriella, were given only cursory attention. But then Thea found a small paragraph, tucked in as a kind of afterthought and out of place. It should have been in the final chapter, where the present-day family was summarised – although she had to concede that the 'two sons' had been included anonymously. The real facts were mingled with a brief account of Imogen's education at a minor public school in Bristol, where she had shown great promise. 'Imogen's two older children, Christian and Stefan, born of her unhappy relationship with her Austrian lover, are no longer in contact with the family.' The clear implication was that the Austrian lover had scuppered her prospects, careerwise.

Briefly, Thea contemplated this intriguing information before dismissing it as little more than gossip. The Austrian sons had been included in the interest of completion, their existence dutifully recorded, and left at that. The only lingering question in her mind was whether or not they were twins.

If there were any clues to the motive for Gabriella's

murder, they were deeply buried, and only a much greater knowledge of the family members could ever hope to reveal them.

She was seeing the dogs in a new light, since their display of adoration towards Jake Milner. It became clear that they were simply being polite with Thea, going through the motions for want of anything better, but with their hearts not really in it. She sympathised whilst feeling somewhat slighted. Their midday romp was muted, partly due to the weather, but mainly because it was only Tuesday and they all had to muddle through another three days of compromise and confusion. Even Hepzie was quiet and unsure of herself.

'We'll go for a walk,' Thea told her. 'Just up to that old church and back. You'll get wet, but that won't matter. I've got boots in the car.'

Wellington boots in June made Thea think wistfully of warmer climes, where summer was reliably summer and rain behaved according to a proper schedule. The waterproof jacket only added to her frustration. She remembered that Timmy's sports day was due soon, as well as Stephanie's school trip to Stratford. Both would be dreary if it rained. Sports Day might even be postponed. There were village fetes, dog shows, gymkhanas, sheepdog trials – all reliant on sunshine for success. The occupants of Cotswold villages did not often get together, and it would be a shame if weather further reduced their opportunities to be sociable. There would sometimes even be a scattering of second-homers showing up to the fete if the day was nice.

She got the gate open, and closed it again behind her. The TV van had vanished and everything was quiet. The way to the church was signposted, giving a distance of half a mile from the main street. A pathetic little walk, then, but given that she was not supposed to leave the salukis unattended for a moment, it was probably just as well.

The little road quickly became quite rural, with some actual cattle in a field – which was more than could be said of Broad Campden most of the time. On the left-hand side was a very large property with a very large garden and the inevitable unwelcoming gate with its keypad. Opposite it something was being built, involving several workmen on ladders and piles of materials. It was unclear what the eventual edifice would be, but it looked rather large for a house. The workmen were chatting quite loudly and ignored Thea and her dog. She faintly recalled the days when as a teenager she would have been whistled at. Now, if there were to be a whistle, it would probably be aimed at the spaniel and not her, because at last the message had got through that most women found it unpleasant.

The half-mile was, if anything, an exaggeration. Beyond the large property was a small patch of woodland, made up of mature beech trees. They seemed somehow too big for the land, as if they were a forlorn vestige of some great forest – which she supposed they probably were. There was a stout fence all round it, with two or three small gates in it, all firmly fastened shut, with 'Private' notices for good measure. *Typical*, thought Thea crossly. Small as it was, it would have made a perfect place for Hepzie to have a run. Instead, the dog had to stay on the lead, giving her a very unsatisfactory level of exercise.

Thea's first impression of the church was favourable. The trees were gathered around it like a protective hood, with an untidy little graveyard on the further side. There was space for cars, and a sensibly worded sign on the gate. Evidently this once-abandoned Church of St Nicholas had been comprehensively rehabilitated and restored. Visitors were welcomed – perhaps the only place in Oddington that could make such a claim.

Inside, one whole wall was covered with an ancient painting. But before giving it an inspection, Thea's eye was caught by a notice hanging to the right of the door, depicting in the most vivid colours how the wall painting would have looked when new. Its symbolism was explained and missing sections filled in. After that, the real thing was rather insipid, which was probably not the intention. It was certainly big and might well have been intimidating to medieval churchgoers in its time – which was given as 1340. The subject was 'Doom', which felt ominous even in the heathen twenty-first century. Information boards and a leaflet conveyed the basic facts that during the 1850s the church had been abandoned and became derelict. Nobody seemed to know the reason for its rejection. Vague suggestions came to Thea's mind – which included the unconvincing hypotheses that it was too far to walk from the centre of the village; that the vicar might have alienated his congregation somehow; or that there was some kind of curse put on the place, which even in the nineteenth century was powerful enough to drive everybody away.

Outside again, she went to sit on a damp wooden seat at the far side of the graveyard and continued to muse gently on this oddity of history. Somewhere on one of the information boards she had seen a suggestion that plague might have sent worshippers away – which seemed wrong to her for a number of reasons. There had to be a better story than that. In 1850, people were rapidly losing their superstitious beliefs and there was little chance that plague was a problem in leafy Gloucestershire in such relatively recent times. Perhaps they were just sick of the gloomy picture on the wall. Perhaps there had been schisms and fatal disagreements about what to do with it – cover it up, or restore it to its original technicolour. It had not taken them long to erect a substitute church closer to the cluster of houses in Upper Oddington, and start all over again. Except that the graveyard had obviously been used continuously, up to very recent times, regardless of the abandonment of the church itself.

She had released Hepzie to run around the graves and have a good sniff. There would be rabbits and squirrels and possibly pheasants to chase, if the mood took her. The sign by the gate had instructed visitors to keep their dogs on a lead, but Thea was never very good at obeying that sort of order. Her coat was long enough to sit on, but there was a creeping sensation of wet skin, even so. 'Come on, then,' she told her dog after about ten minutes. 'Better get back.'

At the gate she met two women, who gave her a rather rude inspection. 'Are you Umberto's dog-sitter?' the older one asked. 'He said you'd got a spaniel.'

'Oh – yes, I, am actually. I just popped out to have a look at the church.' She felt ridiculously guilty under the two accusing stares.

'We come here a lot,' said the younger one. 'We've got family buried here.'

'Recently?' asked Thea, before realising it was a slightly impertinent question.

'Very. Old and new, covering nearly two hundred years.' Again it was the younger one speaking, with a distinct air of pride in her family credentials. Thea was slowly developing a theory as to who these women must be.

'I often come across people doing the same thing,' she said, still sounding daft in her own ears. It was also an exaggeration, because the only instance she could actually recall had been in the little village of Barnsley the previous year. 'Tracing their ancestry through old graves, I mean.'

'We're not doing that. We already know everything about the family. We're here to *honour* them, and to check the . . .' Her words petered out, and Thea understood that Gabriella Milner was to be buried here with her relatives, if that could be arranged. Because these were undoubtedly her aunt and cousin.

'Let me guess – you're Umberto's sister Imogen and niece Kirsty. Is that right?' She gave them a muted version of the scrutiny they had given her. The older one appeared about sixty, tall, short wiry hair, dressed in a pair of faded trousers and a quilted sleeveless jacket over a shirt. Her daughter – if such she was – wore a more formal dress, which fitted her closely and emphasised her nice figure but also showed hints of having been worn for a long time. She had the same thick hair, carefully cut to highlight her good cheekbones. On her feet were white trainers, which had streaks of mud on them.

Both faces grew stony. 'How do you know so much about us?' the older one demanded. 'Who have you been talking to?'

Thea laughed uneasily. This was not going well. Why were they here? Had they followed her without her realising, after trying to gain access to the house? Why weren't they huddled in grief-stricken prostration at home? 'Umberto gave me the family history book – the one your sister's husband wrote,' she explained. 'Everybody's in there.'

Imogen made a sound of exasperation. 'That bloody book!' she spat. 'Telling the whole world our business.'

'Calm down, Ma,' said Kirsty. 'He only had fifty copies printed. And Umberto's the only person who takes it seriously – and then not very much.'

Thea took a deep breath and gave herself another moment in which to consider these people. Imogen had skin a shade darker than Umberto's and she stood awkwardly as if just remaining upright was painful. Her daughter looked to be in her mid-twenties. Both had brown eyes and wide mouths. Thea found herself thinking they looked somewhat anachronistic in newly affluent Oddington. Only ten or twenty years earlier they would have fitted in perfectly, with their hints of make-do-and-mend. They would have had an automatic air of belonging, because they had roots and stability with family in the churchyard and no need to show off. Now they looked shabby and conspicuous. Imogen ran some sort of business that wasn't doing so well, Thea suddenly remembered. Kirsty's line of work had not been mentioned. Thea felt a kinship with them, in her wellies and scruffy mackintosh.

'Are you coming back to the house, then?' she asked.

There was no direct answer to this. 'The police have

been to see us, asking about our cars, if you can believe it. Seems to me they've jumped to entirely the wrong conclusion about what happened to poor Gabriella yesterday. It can only have been an accident. Nobody would do such a horrible thing on purpose.' It was Imogen speaking, emphasising every word as if saying it could make it true. 'I had a friend, as it happens, who was killed in exactly the same way, on the M4, a few years ago.'

'This is hardly the M4, is it?' said Kirsty impatiently. 'And normal people stop after they've done something like that.'

Thea nodded in agreement. 'Come and have some tea,' she invited lavishly. 'I expect the dogs will be pleased to see you. They're obviously very much part of the whole family, to judge from the way they greeted your cousin this morning.'

'Cousin?' Kirsty repeated sharply. 'What are you talking about?'

'Jacob. Gabriella's brother. He wanted to know . . . well, he wanted to . . .' She faltered to a halt, lost for the right words. 'You know. I suppose it's the same for you two.'

'Jake's an idiot,' said Imogen, with barely a hint of fondness.

'A harmless idiot,' her daughter corrected her. 'Trust him to pile on the agony for himself, for no reason at all.'

'His mother's the same. She'll be over here too, I shouldn't wonder.'

Theresa, Thea mentally noted, refraining from showing off any further family knowledge. It had been unwise the first time. But Theresa was Gabriella's mother, as well as Jake's, and it would make perfectly good emotional sense for her to view the scene where her daughter met her death. And what were Imogen and Kirsty doing here, if not the very same thing? She was also struck by the word *harmless*, which echoed a remark that Umberto had made about Kirsty herself. It felt potentially significant that two members of the family had felt the need to make this point.

As they walked, Thea became aware that the older woman was struggling to keep up. Not exactly limping, she was clearly having to put real effort into every step. 'Where's your car?' Thea asked.

'Just beside the little green,' said Kirsty. 'We thought a little walk would do us good. Exercise,' she added vaguely, with a glance at her mother. 'We should do it more often.'

'So what about a drink?' Thea offered again.

But no, they did not want tea – or coffee or anything else. They were planning a late lunch at the pub, they said. They had just wanted to get a look at her, since she had been a witness to their relative's terrible death, and was interesting for that and other reasons. Imogen disclosed these truths with little hesitation. 'Umberto can be a bit ditzy at times,' she said. 'We thought we should check you out, just in case.'

Just in case what? Thea wondered. *In case I*

accidentally let his dogs die – or do they think it was me who smashed into Gabriella?

'Where's *your* car?' Kirsty asked, as they reached the junction with the main street. Her tone implied that Thea's question had been uncalled for and here was her turn to be interrogated.

'Just down there,' she pointed.

'So only a few feet from the crash?'

It had not occurred to Thea until then that she ought to have worried about her vehicle's welfare. Ever since she and Drew had come to the conclusion that they needed a second car, all logistical worries about who would be mobile when had evaporated. On earlier house-sitting jobs, there had been great complications and dilemmas associated with the car. Now Drew had got his own Volvo and the only problem remaining was how to squeeze it into the limited space outside their house. Only thanks to Stephanie's friendship with the man over the road had it been resolved. 'Mr Shipley says you can leave one of the cars in his driveway,' she had reported. 'He says there's plenty of room.'

Which there was, and they used it gratefully.

'I suppose so,' said Thea now. 'I don't think it was actively involved, though.'

'I'm not suggesting it was,' snapped Kirsty. 'Only that you were lucky it didn't get damaged.'

Yet again, Thea ran the sequence of images through her mind's eye. Gabriella had parked between Umberto's gate and Thea's own car, which was a little way further down the street. It was still just as she had left it when she first arrived. There was no remaining trace of the ruined Skoda.

'I suppose so,' she agreed again. 'If I'd been on the other side of the gate it might have been different.'

'What?' Imogen interrupted. 'What do you mean?'

With a sigh, Thea tried to explain that any vehicle to the left of the impact – as seen from the house – might have been hit by flying debris – or even a flying body. As it was, that stretch of street had been empty of any parked cars for some distance. 'They've all got garages, or secure spaces inside their gates,' she finished. 'Not many people seem to leave their cars on the street.'

'Okay,' said Imogen slowly. 'So the thing that killed Gabriella came from that direction.' She pointed towards Upper Oddington, to the west of where they were standing.

'Right,' said Thea. 'And it kept on going that way.' She waved towards the east, where the road went round a sharp left-hand bend beside The Fox pub. 'It didn't even slow down, as far as I could see.'

'That tree must have obstructed your view,' said Kirsty. 'The copper beech.'

'It did,' Thea confirmed. 'I actually couldn't see very much at all.'

'You probably saw enough to give you a few bad dreams, all the same,' said Imogen with a sudden flash of kindness. 'It must have been horrible for you.'

'Yeah,' mumbled Thea, swallowing back the infuriating tears. 'Do you know the neighbours?' she asked abruptly, desperate to head off the disabling sympathy. She could also see that Imogen needed a moment or two of rest before finishing the walk and collapsing into a car. They were all noticeably damp from the continuing drizzle.

The older woman leant against a house wall and took a few breaths before replying. 'What? Oh – well we *did*, of course. We grew up here. We knew everybody then. But it's all different now. Although I do see familiar faces at the garden centre now and then.'

'Oh?' said Thea quickly. 'Is that your business? A garden centre?'

Mother and daughter both looked down their noses at her, the two faces suddenly identical. 'She's just like they told us, isn't she?' said Kirsty. 'Always asking questions.'

Imogen made a sound that was as much amused as annoyed. 'Umberto's going to be kicking himself.'

Thea's heart was thundering, but she managed to say, 'Why?'

'Oh, he had some notion that you'd be the perfect person to cope with his dogs, because you knew how to look after yourself. In his mind you're some sort of superhero. Didn't he tell you?'

'No,' breathed Thea. 'I don't think it's true, either.'

'She's exaggerating,' said Kirsty. 'But Umberto

thought it would be fun to ask you to do it. He kept saying, "What could possibly go wrong?"' She pulled a face that was full of complex emotion.

'Oh. Well . . .' Thea tried to think of something to say that would salvage some of her dignity.

'Don't let it upset you,' said Imogen. 'It's not your problem.'

Thea tried to recapture some of the former quality of their exchanges. There had been a growing warmth, at least from the older woman. 'You were saying there were still people around here who you knew,' she said.

Imogen appeared to be relieved. She nodded. 'There might be two or three families in the Oddingtons that we knew when we were young. But it was forty years ago. Nobody stays in the same place for that long.'

'Umberto did,' said Kirsty. 'And Nonna, until she died.'

'So we're the exceptions. We always were. They all called us "the Italians" because our mother cooked with garlic and was fussy about which olives she used.'

It struck Thea that she had shifted at some point from the impossible quest for the identity of Gabriella's killer to a deepening interest in her family for its own sake. The obvious implication that one of them might be a killer had been pushed aside in favour of working out relationships and how it had all evolved over the past generations. The presence of an ancestral home, with its associations and anecdotes, along with a cast of relatives who could give first-hand accounts of it all, was fascinating. The very emptiness of the house raised numerous questions. Even the very long dead ancestors in the churchyard would have stories that might be compelling. Plus, of course, the churchyard itself was interesting in a number of ways.

They were still standing in the street, all three of them aware that there was a lot yet to be said. But they were also all three hungry, since Thea had somehow overlooked the matter of lunch. She was on the verge of inviting herself to join them at the pub for lunch, when a voice came from behind her. 'Thea Slocombe – is that you?'

There was no vestige of a possibility that some old acquaintance would be strolling through Oddington on a Tuesday afternoon. She turned and saw Detective Inspector Jeremy Higgins standing on the pavement beside her car. Her first thought was – *Blimey, they've brought in the whole team for this one, then.*

'Hello, Jeremy,' she said.

They had last met only a few months previously, in Northleach, where Stephanie had been involved, and Drew had been reproachful and people, as usual, had behaved badly. Caz Barkley had been working quite closely with Higgins, Thea recalled. Perhaps it was not so surprising that they and Gladwin should all be mobilised for this highly publicised and very unpleasant hit-and-run slaughter of a fine young woman.

Higgins looked at Imogen and Kirsty and kinked an eyebrow. Thea said nothing. Her spaniel took over, and pulled at her lead until Thea released her and she went to jump up at the detective's knees. 'She remembers you,' said Thea.

'We're old friends.' He fondled the long ears and gently returned the dog to its rightful place at his feet.

'We have to get on,' said Kirsty. 'They'll have stopped serving food at this rate.'

'We'll be lucky to get more than a sandwich, anyway. It's half past two,' said her mother. 'I don't know where the time's gone.'

They went along the street towards The Fox, without waiting to be introduced to Higgins. He and Thea watched them go in silence. When they were safely out of earshot, Thea said, 'Have they seen you before? Do they know who you are?'

He laughed. 'I hope not. Come to that, I have no idea who *they* are.'

'Aunt and cousin of the girl who was killed. I must say, they don't seem to be especially affected by it. Except the mother looks rather ill.'

'Not devastated, as the media would have it,' he agreed. 'But it takes people in funny ways. The older one doesn't look as if she's brushed her hair today.'

'That's Imogen. Her brother lives in this house. The daughter's called Kirsty. I know quite a lot about them,' she realised wonderingly. 'Surname is Peake. I think the mother runs a garden centre – something like that. I guess they live somewhere fairly local. I told Gladwin how they all relate to each other.'

'Of course you did,' he said with a sigh. 'Dare I ask how long you've been here?'

'Oh – ages. Must be about twenty-nine hours now.'

'Typical,' he said. 'And I see you witnessed the actual incident, with your very own eyes.'

'I did. It was awful.'

'She wouldn't have suffered. Her whole torso was crushed. Massive damage. Just shows what a car can do.'

'Not to mention *two* cars, with you sandwiched between them. That poor little Skoda, just minding its own business.' She found her voice was rising and the things she was saying came from some odd part of her brain.

Higgins kinked his eyebrow again, and made a kind of purring sound. 'Easy,' he murmured. 'Let's go in for a bit, shall we? They tell me there are dogs.'

'There are. And I'm not supposed to leave them unattended. I've been out for nearly an hour, heaven help me.'

'Come on, then. You can make me some tea.'

Chapter Seven

DI Higgins had never been as forthcoming about police investigations as DS Gladwin was in her conversations with Thea. 'We're drawing diagrams,' he said, over the mug of tea. 'Trajectories, velocity, force and all that. Trying to decide whether it could have been an accident. Mind you, not stopping after a fatality is a serious crime in itself.'

'It matters, doesn't it?' said Thea. 'If it was an accident there's no motive. It wasn't an accident, though.'

'No,' he agreed. 'Not unless it was some boy racer, high on cocaine or something. That's not impossible.'

'If there was some sort of blockage on the main road, people might drive through the Oddingtons as a diversion and be in a great hurry – but there wasn't, was there?'

He shook his head. 'We checked all that sort of thing.'

'So why are you here? You're the third detective to visit me in one day.'

'The Super thought you might have remembered a bit more. Impressions. Details.'

'I don't think I have. The trouble is, anything I think I remember now will probably be dreamt up out of my imagination. Like the look on her face. I know I've embroidered that, based on pretty much nothing. There wasn't time for any real expression, and I was too far away to see properly. But I did think there was something – maybe she only lifted her head slightly, or her eyes changed. But it struck me that she knew the driver of the car. That her very last thought must have been that there was no reason to be frightened because this was a friend. Somebody she liked. It's a dreadful idea – the betrayal doesn't bear thinking about.'

Higgins chewed his lips. 'Embroidery is right,' he said. 'You can't possibly have any real grounds for believing that.'

'No,' said Thea. But when she tested the strength of the idea, she found it stubbornly persistent. 'And yet . . . would a stranger be so determined, so unswerving and *lethal*? A stranger wouldn't plan it and carry it through like that. There had to be some very powerful emotion behind it. And the practicalities – getting rid of the car. *Obtaining* the car in the first place. There had to be a risk that somebody – or a camera somewhere – would take note of the registration number, or the make and model at least. So where is it now?'

'You took the words out of Barkley's mouth,' he said. 'She thinks exactly the same as you, and said so at the briefing this morning.'

'There you are, then,' said Thea. 'More tea?'

'No thanks.' He turned a distressed face to her. 'I sometimes think I'm not suited to this line of work.

What you said just now – that Gabriella might have known and *trusted* the person who killed her. It's right. A betrayal like that is too ghastly to contemplate.'

She thought about it. 'You could say that all killing is a betrayal, unless it's in a war. Every time a cow or pig is sent for slaughter, it's betrayed by the people it knows and trusts. And murder breaks some sort of unwritten assumption that we're essentially all brothers and sisters, and have agreed not to end each other's lives.'

Higgins smiled weakly. 'That's why it's the worst possible crime. And it's why the motives so often turn out to be banal or inadequate, or just really stupid. I can hardly think of one I've heard that made me think the person might have had a tiny bit of justification. It's often protecting their own reputation or self-image, which was never seriously under threat in the first place.'

'Or somebody was in their way. Or their feelings have been so badly hurt they can't rest until they've taken revenge.'

'Or they feel betrayed, which is where we came in.'

'I think revenge explains a lot, in many cases. And you might say that comes from a strong sense of justice. You just can't let somebody get away with what they've done. I can think of a few where I've had some sympathy for that sort of motivation. I was talking about all this with Stephanie a little while ago, and she actually said she could imagine killing somebody in revenge for some horrible thing they'd done.'

'How old is she?'

'Nearly thirteen.'

Higgins sighed. 'As I say, I often have a suspicion I'm missing something when it comes to this sort of thing. I'm fine with collecting evidence and spotting details, but the other stuff just scares me.'

'And so it should,' Thea said warmly. 'It's the scariest thing there is.'

When Higgins had left, Thea went to inspect the salukis, thinking she should have shown them to the detective inspector. They were comfortably loafing in their indoors quarters, showing little inclination to run around outside in the damp. Dolly was scratching her neck with an intensity that rang a mild alarm bell in Thea. She remembered that Hepzie had been scratching herself more than usual, especially first thing in the morning. Stephanie had muttered something about fleas, which Thea had ignored. To her mind, the occasional flea was nothing to worry about, and the expensive chemical treatment supplied by the vet was only resorted to once or twice a year.

If Hepzie had infested Dolly – and no doubt the others too – with fleas, what would Umberto say? Would he laugh and blame himself for failing to apply the medication, or would he be outraged by Thea's careless behaviour? Either seemed entirely possible. The prospect of the latter made her feel impatient and rebellious. What was the world coming to, when a few little bloodsuckers caused such hysteria? Even Stephanie had been annoyingly insistent about it, claiming she had been bitten on her legs and was suffering as a result. And now it seemed the season was upon them again and action would have to be taken.

But what action? Where was the nearest vet, or pharmacy that would produce the right stuff? And what if she applied it to the salukis only to discover they were allergic to it and it killed them? She glared accusingly at her spaniel, and said, 'This is all your fault.'

She could hardly contact Umberto about something so trivial – while at the same time she could not ignore it, either. By Friday there could be flea eggs lurking in every surface of the house – carpets, cushions, bedding – and nothing short of wholesale fumigation would destroy them. And it would indeed all be Hepzibah's fault. Thea would have failed, despite her strenuous efforts to do a perfect job for once.

Umberto had left a list of instructions, mostly about food and exercise, with the phone number of a vet at the bottom. When he had handed it to her, he had flicked a finger at this final line and said, 'I'm not expecting you to want this,' as if it would be a serious dereliction of duty to need such assistance.

But he did love his dogs, for their own sake and for their potential value. He probably didn't want them to be itching and restless. Something would have to be done and quickly.

First, she pulled Dolly close to her and commenced a close examination of her coat. The hair was not particularly dense, and the skin fairly easy to see. No small black insects came into view. Perhaps it was all a false alarm after all. But then a speck of something jumped onto her bare arm, and then jumped again back onto the dog, and the problem was confirmed. Dolly had fleas, damn it.

'Come outside, all of you,' she ordered. 'Go and run about while I change your bedding.' Knowing it was futile, if only because Hepzie had been roaming freely all over the house, she bundled the dogs' fleecy rugs into the washing machine and set it as hot as she dared. Rummaging through the small wall cupboard where Umberto had vaguely told her there was all the dog equipment, she found a small white comb with very finely spaced teeth. *A fine-tooth comb* she thought to herself. Or was it a fine toothcomb? In any case it looked useful, and she started to deploy it on her spaniel who she called in from the garden.

It worked beautifully. In fact, *too* beautifully, because when she inspected it, she saw five quite large wriggling fleas caught between the teeth. 'Oh God,' she said.

At four o'clock she was still obsessively combing dogs and squashing fleas. Her own skin was crawling with imaginary parasites and the dogs were beyond the point of endurance. The bedding was transferred from washing machine to tumble dryer, since the weather was not going to co-operate with the process. There was a sense of having at least arrested the onward march of the infestation for a day or so, while she considered what to do next. On reflection, it had been a rather soothing interlude. All around the world, people – and apes – were dealing with fleas, ticks, lice on themselves and their fellow creatures. It was basic and real and mindless. There was no morality attached to it, no betrayal or viciousness, no violence or malice. It just was what it was, and there was something grounding about it. Here in the Cotswolds, where money ruled supreme and non-human species existed to serve or entertain homo sapiens, the disgusting basics still lurked just below the surface. As the hour went by, Thea found herself almost relishing the subversion of it all. These handsome locked-up houses would be chemically treated to repel ants or mice or silver fish, rendering them sterile and pristine – to what end? In her musings, Thea envisaged the inevitable invasions that would take place one day. It was a war that humanity could only win by destroying everything, themselves included. Pockets of the country had quite recently come to understand and accept this as true – but not yet here in the heart of Gloucestershire.

Food began to acquire ascendancy over everything else as she noticed how empty she felt. Lunch had been a slice of cheese and a small pot of yoghurt from the fridge, which Umberto had invited her to raid. The variety of food on offer was a source of pleasurable anticipation. There were also two bottles of white wine and some beer. 'I've ordered you some milk for Wednesday,' he said. The prospect of old-fashioned bottles on the doorstep made her smile, even though they would in fact be outside the gate, on the pavement where people could knock them over.

An early supper of cold chicken, coleslaw and tomatoes assuaged her hunger, and she opened one of the bottles which turned out to contain a very pleasing Sauvignon. She noted the label specially, so that she'd be able to tell Drew about it.

Outside, as on the previous evening, the sun was no more than a faint glow, shrouded with dense cloud. At some point the rain had stopped, but it could hardly be termed a fine summer's day. 'At least we managed a little walk,' she told Hepzie. 'That was plenty of excitement after yesterday.'

Yesterday's 'excitement' was still very much present, the trauma fogging her brain and making her slow. She did not want to think – not just about the murdering car, but about *anything*. Her frank conversation with Higgins had not been therapeutic, it seemed. Only his steady gaze and endearing humility had persuaded her to turn her thoughts to the ghastly events. When he had gone, she shut it all down again.

Now there was a lengthy evening to get through. Television was the only viable entertainment, and she juggled the remote controls until a showing of an old James Stewart film turned up. In fact, there was a whole night of James Stewart films, starting with *Vertigo*, followed by *Anatomy of a Murder* and *Winchester '73*.

That would take her through to well after midnight, if she chose to stay up for them all. The last one did not greatly appeal, but the first two would do nicely.

It felt decadent to be huddled indoors on a June evening, but that did not greatly trouble her. Whatever plans she and Drew might have for the long days – walking over the wolds, strolling beside a river or canal, simply sitting outside with some Pimms – they almost never came to fruition. June would fly by, mostly cloudy or cool, and then July would be upon them, perhaps with better weather, but much of the gloss of early summer expectations rubbed off. This year, after lengthy discussions, there was to be a family holiday in August. They would all go to Penrith for a week, taking kites, books about fell walking, sketchpads and indomitable optimism. Of them all, Timmy was by far the most excited.

Vertigo was not one of her favourite films. She had seen it in her twenties and found the plot entirely impenetrable. The loss of a moment's concentration was all it took to turn it into nonsense. But now she gave it full attention. How, she kept asking herself, had poor Jimmy Stewart ever got down from that collapsing gutter, hundreds of feet above the ground, where he hung in the opening moments of the film? The subsequent story was gripping and distracting, but the question never went away. At the end, there he was on another high ledge, perhaps about to fall or jump off it. The events in between had all been a dream, then? Or a sort of avoidance of the inevitable awful death that was certain to befall him from the outset?

She made herself a large mug of coffee before the next film started, and went on reviewing the convolutions of *Vertigo*. Too late, she caught up with herself, and the slippery way her mind had linked it to what had happened to Gabriella Milner. Had *her* imagination constructed an entire fantasy in that single second between realisation and impact? Or had her brain died much more slowly than that, giving her ample time to relive her whole life and conclude that she had been most cruelly betrayed by somebody she trusted?

James Stewart – the character in the film never quite detached himself from the actor – had been betrayed most comprehensively. Deliberately and with infinite care, he had been duped. His emotions had been exploited and used against him. Nothing was as it seemed. It struck Thea as rather horrible that real life – and death – could run so closely parallel to something in an Alfred Hitchcock movie.

True to form, she had left her phone in the kitchen, where she couldn't hear it. When the film finished, she remembered it, and found a text from Drew had been sitting there for over an hour. 'Hello? Are you receiving me? Everything fine here – hope you're alive and well? With a generous dollop of love, Drew.'

She smiled and replied. 'Sorry – got immersed in a Hitchcock movie. Love you too.'

He might be waiting for a proper call, but would settle

for a text without complaint. After a number of such wifely absences, leading to entanglements with police investigations and no guarantee of personal safety, Drew had eventually learnt to accept that it was never going to change. He had been slow to redefine marriage with this second wife who possessed very few of the traits of his first one. Thea was a poor cook, a disinterested gardener, a sloppy housekeeper and a somewhat detached stepmother, although the last was evolving into something warmer and closer than Drew had initially feared. Stephanie and Thea now had a bond that seemed set to continue through the girl's oncoming adolescence. Timmy had slowly relaxed into the new family life, after the hard lessons of loss and neglect he had suffered while his mother sickened and died. Karen – the first Mrs Slocombe – had been ideological, sociable, and a very devoted wife. Why, Thea sometimes wondered, had Drew ever thought he could possibly replace her? As it turned out, she concluded immodestly, he had really done rather well for himself.

At ten-thirty, having failed to immerse herself in *Anatomy of a Murder* she abandoned it before the end and took the dogs out for their bedtime routine, watching all three of them as they squatted in the further reaches of the field, and concluding that they were tolerating her and Hepzie pretty well, whilst refraining from any undue enthusiasm. They were essentially a self-sufficient pack in everything but food. She found herself idly wondering how long they would survive if a great apocalypse removed all the people. No time at all, if they were left in this big green cage, was the conclusion. By the time it occurred to them to try to climb over the fence to freedom, they would be too weak to accomplish it.

Ten minutes later, they had settled down meekly in their indoor quarters and Thea took her spaniel up to bed with her.

But she found herself unable to sleep, which was something that happened so rarely that it caused panic after twenty minutes or so. She put the light on and fumbled for the book she had brought with her. It had been a careless choice, and when she began it, she found that it was both set in a historical period and written in the present tense – a transgression to her mind that could not be borne. She liked her stories to follow the 'once upon a time' format. This happened, in the past – it is not happening *now*, for heaven's sake. Her irritation only served to make her more wide awake.

Downstairs there were small sounds familiar in any house on a summer night. Things expanded and shrank, shifted and settled, with their little creaks and clicks. There were no bumps or thuds, nothing to suggest an intruder – and yet Thea's volatile imagination envisaged a felon tiptoeing up the stairs holding a machete or even a pistol. She would hide under the bed or in the wardrobe, she decided – but what would become of her dog? Impatient with herself, she repeated inwardly that of course the salukis would bark if anybody came into the house. And besides, the fortifications were more than adequate to prevent such a thing happening.

Thea Slocombe was very much not a nervous person. She had found that by imagining every kind of horror she could address it and then put it away. She had just witnessed a real death caused by extreme violence, bones crushed and organs destroyed, life utterly extinguished. Nothing could be more horrifying than that. Playing with childish notions of axe-wielding burglars was simply a diversion, born of the night and the alarm at being unable to get to sleep. Smiling at her own nonsense, she sank back into the pillow and let her thoughts flow into fairy tales from Grimm and the magical mutations from *Spirited Away* and other Ghibli films so beloved by Stephanie and Timmy.

And then she was finally asleep and before long she was dreaming. In the dream a girl was being thrown out of a high window, and as she fell, Thea could see it was Stephanie. She watched the frail body land on concrete far below, and when she peered closer, it had become her own daughter, Jessica, as she had been at about fifteen. The dream continued, with Thea trying to reassemble the body, breathe life back into it, tears streaming down her face.

She woke up gasping for air, her cheeks wet. The spaniel twitched irritably at the foot of the bed. The sky was not completely dark, and when Thea consulted her phone she found it was just after midnight. 'Post-traumatic stress,' she muttered aloud. 'So this is what it's like.'

She put the light on, got out of bed and went downstairs to the kitchen. Wondering idly as to whether the lights had been noticed by anybody outside in the village street, she made herself a mug of tea, and added two biscuits. There was a rustling from the dogs' room, but no more than that. The dream took a long time to fade, merging with what she had seen on Monday and reminding her that awful events could not always be tidied away and forgotten.

Chapter Eight

Wednesday morning came as a relief. Despite the broken night and minimal sleep, Thea was awake and getting dressed well before seven o'clock. The sky was blue for once, and there were birds chorusing energetically outside her window. You did not waste a June morning, any more than you wasted an evening. All that lavish daylight was there to be enjoyed. So had said her father, first husband and now Drew. It was obviously a cast-iron axiom.

The first hour or so proceeded as the day before had done. Contented dogs, undisturbed house, nothing much going on outside. 'Only three more days,' said Thea. 'We can probably manage that, don't you think?' Her spaniel blinked at her non-committally.

The gate buzzer went off at a quarter to eight, and Thea assumed it would be Gladwin, Higgins or Barkley. It crossed her mind that she might be taking their attentions for granted in making this assumption, but could see nothing wrong in that.

A man's voice came through the intercom. 'Hello? Is that the house-sitter? I'm a neighbour. Can I come in?'

Everything about this idiotic gate arrangement hit her at once. If this person had simply come to the door, knocked, been seen in the flesh and either invited in or not, that would have been a normal human interaction. Being forced to judge on the basis of a disembodied voice was ludicrous. He could easily be the murdering figure from her night-time fantasies. Or a friendly old codger offering a sympathetic ear to a traumatised female. How was she supposed to know?

'I'll come down to the gate,' she said.

And of course, as soon as she was out of the front door, she could see through the bars of the gate well enough to assess the acceptability of her visitor. The distance between door and gate was roughly twenty yards – just enough space for Umberto's van and a small car, although not enough for them to turn around. Approaching, the man's features came into better focus, and first impressions were cautiously favourable if only because of the colour of the hair.

'Hello,' she said. 'I'm Thea Slocombe. I assume you know Umberto?'

The gate was still between them. A young woman passed, wheeling a toddler in a buggy. A large truck came from the eastern end of the village and turned up the road to the old church, presumably heading for the building work up there. There were still birds singing here and there.

'I'm Clifford Savage. People call me Cliff. I live a few houses along – that way.' He pointed towards

Upper Oddington. 'I would have called by yesterday, but everything seemed a bit . . . *raw*, if you see what I mean. At least they've opened the road again – that was a bit unnerving.' He had a strong Birmingham accent, stressing the final *g* of his last word.

'You didn't see it happen, did you?' Sudden hope flared at the prospect of somebody to share the trauma. 'On Monday.'

He shook his colourful head. 'Sorry.'

He was early thirties, shorter than average by two or three inches, slim, very pale-skinned and blue-eyed. But his hair was by far the most distinctive thing about him. It was dark ginger or red in common parlance. In reality, it was starkly and unarguably *orange*. The colour of Christmas satsumas, or Sevilles waiting to be turned into marmalade. And there was plenty of it – wavy and thick, it sprang from his head in a glowing tumult. The thought flashed through Thea's mind that this man could not have been driving the killer car on Monday – because surely there would have been some flash of memorable colour somehow perceived in a reflection or vanishing down the street?

He was certainly not at all typical of a Cotswolds-dweller. 'Pity,' she said. She wanted to ask his business, still unsure about opening the gate to him. It began to seem slightly odd that he should even want her to. 'These gates are an abomination,' she said. 'Don't you think?'

He laughed, not so much amused as contemptuous. 'I

114

do, absolutely. It's a sort of contagion – one person gets them and everyone else just follows. A status symbol, in fact. You can't afford to be the only property without them.'

'So you've got them as well, have you?'

'The house has, but it's not mine. I'm here on a two-year let, and there's only a few months still to go. I'm from the east Midlands, where this sort of thing hasn't yet arrived. We're hoping it never does.'

'It is very weird,' she said distractedly. 'Can you tell me how I can help you? I mean . . .'

He gave her a direct look, somehow implying that she was at risk of being rude. 'Oh, sorry,' he said slowly. 'Okay. Yes. I can see it must seem a bit funny, me turning up like this. The fact is, I had a visit from one of the police people yesterday, and it turned out I know her slightly, by coincidence. Caz Barkley? She was at college with my sister, and they were pretty good mates for a while. Anyway, she told me about you and how you saw the whole horrible thing, and said you might be glad of a friendly face. The trouble is, I've got to be off by nine, to get to work.'

'What a coincidence about Barkley,' said Thea, thinking that life was full of such connections. 'Is your sister in the police, then?'

'Actually, no. She was for a bit, and then she dropped out and took up truck-driving instead. Says it's the best decision she ever made.'

'I can see why Caz would like her, then.' Caz Barkley

would have made a good truck-driver too, in Thea's estimation. 'Well, come in for a bit. You've got nearly an hour to spare, from the sound of it.' Somewhere in her chest was a small flicker of unease. The words *friendly face* repeated themselves, and carried a degree of reassurance. The man had Barkley's endorsement, after all, and Thea Slocombe never rejected the chance of a useful chat with a neighbour when she was looking after someone's house.

'If you're sure. Thanks.'

She operated the annoying gate mechanism and took him into the kitchen. 'Have you met the dogs?' she asked. 'They're out in the garden. And this one's mine.' Hepzie was at her side, having been with her down to the gate and back. The newcomer was only of marginal interest to her.

'I used to come in, before Mrs Kingly died. I never got to know Umberto very well, though, or his dogs.' He was standing in the hallway, looking around. 'It's changed a lot since then.'

'Oh? How?'

'You sound surprised. It was full of a whole lot of stuff. She was one of those hoarders, especially upstairs. Old magazines, knitting patterns, ancient toys, boxes, scrapbooks of cuttings – the list is endless. All gone now.'

'Oh,' said Thea again. 'I had no idea.'

'They couldn't wait to clear it all out. Umberto's sister – Penny, I think she's called – came with a rented

116

van and took it all to the tip. I helped her to load it up. And there was a bonfire out at the back that went on for weeks. They only kept the furniture, and not all of that.'

'That seems a bit odd. Although I suppose Umberto wanted the space for his own things.'

'Probably,' said Savage carelessly. 'He wasn't really involved in the decisions. He just sat in there,' he indicated the living room, 'and stared into space. The sisters came and went and worked around him. There were the nieces as well. They were relentless – and there were a few disagreements along the way. Umberto tried to grab a few things to save, and I nabbed some books and old postcards, but almost everything just went. Their poor old mum would have been distraught.'

'Turning in her grave,' said Thea, still not thinking very clearly. 'Although there are books and pictures that must have been hers.'

'They weren't all as keen as the big sister was to chuck it all away. She was the real sergeant-major.'

'Penny,' Thea nodded, to show that she was keeping up. 'Did you know Gabriella, then?'

He pulled a face and shook his head. 'Awful thing,' he mumbled. 'I did meet her a time or two, that's all.' He gave her a close look. 'And you? Are you all right? Did you say your name was Thea?'

They were both still standing in the hallway, as visitors tended to do. 'Do you want coffee or something?' she asked. His reason for being there was still not entirely clear. She found herself wishing he would go.

'No, thanks. Better not. I'll have to go soon.'

'What sort of work do you do?'

'I'm teaching at the University of Gloucester, for my sins. It's an offshoot of the main university. History. I'm officially an archaeologist, but I'm between operations, as you might say. Everything's very hand-to-mouth these days, and it suits me to fill in with some teaching now and then. I'm not very good at sticking at just one thing.'

Thea looked at him more closely, wondering about the vibes that she was picking up. He was glancing around with sharp eyes, looking into the living room, one hand scratching at the opposite wrist in suppressed agitation. There was a sense that he knew very much more than he was saying. His revelations about Umberto's mother felt like the tiniest tip of a substantial iceberg.

'Isn't it rather a long way from here to Gloucester?' she said.

'I'm based in Cheltenham, actually – which is an easy drive most days.'

The conversation was superficial and unemotional. Perhaps that was deliberate, Thea thought, but she also wondered whether there was something else going on. There were questions hanging in the air, which she was waiting for him to ask. It made her feel chafed and off-balance. It was still a few minutes before nine. He would soon go of his own accord. Meanwhile she could not miss the opportunity to learn a bit more. In a clumsy attempt to keep the conversation going, she said, 'History was always my favourite subject, and there's a lot of it in this area. My stepchildren find it all very interesting, but we've never gone into anything in much depth.'

He was looking towards the back of the house, as if able to see through the solid wall into the garden. 'Are the dogs out in the garden? It's funny the way he never takes them out where we can see them.'

'They're too precious, apparently. They can have a good run in the field, which seems to keep them happy.'

He answered with a sudden glint on his eye. 'They're extremely ancient, you know. We found skeletons in Iraq when I was on a dig there. The original feral dogs in that region are almost exactly like present-day salukis. They're supposed to have amazing stamina and speed. I very much doubt that one small field is enough for them.' He frowned his disapproval. Thea felt helpless. 'But I don't imagine many dogs in this country get to express their essential natures any more, do they?' he concluded.

'Lapdogs do, I suppose. And collies – unless some fool tries to make them live in a city.'

'Right.' He smiled sadly. 'I miss her, you know. Umberto's mother. She never should have died when she did.'

'Oh. What was she like? Apart from being a hoarder.'

'Incredibly old-fashioned. She was brought up by nuns, apparently, and never lost that strict moral code. Her mother was Italian, which probably explains some of it. But she was fun to talk to. She used to go for long walks, all the way over to Bledington, and I went with her now and then.'

'She wasn't very old when she died, was she?'

'Late seventies, as it turned out, but perfectly fit and healthy. It was a stroke while she was here by herself. Umberto was away. Kirsty found her, by pure luck, and got her into hospital. By the time Umberto got home it was all over.'

Thea struggled to unravel this new tale. 'I thought he was living here with her at the time.'

Savage shook his head regretfully. 'He was, in theory, but he'd gone off on one of his buying trips for a day or two. She was on her own here – which she always hated. I actually came round the evening before she died, to keep her company. I might have been the last person to see her alive.' He gave her a careful look. 'Which makes me think we might be deliberately avoiding the subject of the girl who died?'

Thea heaved a sigh. 'I think we are. But I suppose we shouldn't. *I* shouldn't, anyway. But I can't see very much hope of them ever finding who did it. There's so little to go on.' Almost too late, she stopped herself from revealing any details of the police investigation. Again, she looked at the vibrant hair and wondered about its implications for its owner being a potential killer. Anyone seeing him in his car might recall such an unusual head. But then, she realised, he might have been wearing a hat. Or a wig. If the murder had been carefully planned in advance, that would be a detail to take into consideration.

He spread his hands in a gesture of ignorance. 'I have nothing helpful to contribute, sorry to say. The fact is, I'm only here because Caz suggested it. I can't honestly say I know very much about the family. Mrs Kingly was a character and quite lonely, I think. Even though all her children were still nearby, it was obvious that they only took their turns staying with her out of duty. Basically, they slept here, but went their own ways during the day. It was a crackpot set-up, to my mind. She didn't belong to any clubs or anything, as far as I know. Her father was disgracefully rich and that bothered her, I think. She had a thing about money and the obligations that went with it. She said it could blight a family if you let it.'

'Have you seen the photos of her in the living room?'

'Are they still there? I thought the sisters would have chucked them out as well.'

'Come and see. You might know who some of them are. Have you got time?'

'Only a minute.' He glanced at his watch with a little frown.

She took him to the wall of framed portraits, and

he lingered over the last one of Jocasta. 'This captures her exactly. Everything so prim and proper, but that look in her eye. Do you see? She's got a whole lot of feeling behind those eyes. From what I've seen of them, the whole family has a special spark. They're all of them real characters.' He walked slowly along the wall, examining the earlier photographs. 'Here she is at about my age. She must have had four children in their late teens or thereabouts by then. A busy life, with all those worries and responsibilities, and she looks impossibly serene.'

Thea was intrigued. 'Where was her husband?' she asked.

'Oh, he was there. They lived together in this house until only a few years before she died. He was a bit older, and he got septicaemia from a bite – something like that. Nobody realised how serious it was until too late.'

'Which one's him, then?' She indicated the pictures.

'She took him down. Said it made her cry to see him.'

Thea felt a sliver of mistrust. How did this man know so much? Could it all be gleaned from a few country walks? How could she be sure he was who he said he was? Had he perhaps invented the whole connection with Barkley, in order to win her confidence? If so, it could easily be checked, and if she discovered he'd been lying, then what? Wouldn't it throw suspicion onto him for the killing of Gabriella? Wouldn't any rational person living so close to a murder go out of his way to be scrupulously honest? 'That's sad,' she said, with a pointed glance at the mantelpiece clock.

He quickly caught her drift. 'Oops – time to go. I'm late already. It was great to meet you. Sorry if I've wasted your time. Maybe I can see you again before you go?'

'Maybe,' she said, with another flicker of unease. The moment he was gone, she was going to call Barkley and ask her if the man could be believed. She let him out of the gate, firmly clicking it closed behind him, disgusted with herself for the sense of security it gave her. The very word 'security' annoyed her, as a rule. It was all too easy to persuade human beings to crouch securely in their little nests like timid field mice, shunning the terrifying world outside. No way was she ever going to be like that, she vowed to herself at regular intervals.

Barkley did not answer her phone, so Thea left a short message. 'A man called Clifford Savage showed up at eight o'clock this morning, saying you know his sister. I'm not sure I should thank you for that. I hope I'll see you soon.' She had exaggerated the time – it had been twenty past eight, at the earliest.

The man had left her in a discordant state, with his inconsistencies and subtle air of knowing more than he was prepared to tell. She went back to the wall of family pictures, wondering whether she was using them to avoid confronting the harsh reality of murder, or whether she believed there could be a clue to the killer. The latter seemed foolishly unlikely. As far as she had been able to judge, the whole clan was close-knit and harmonious. Imogen had criticised the book about them, but in a tone of mild irritation rather than genuine anger. Kirsty had looked gaunt and shocked, as would be expected after that terrible death of her cousin. Jacob likewise had been all over the place. And – she now remembered – Imogen had called him an idiot, apparently in all seriousness. Was Imogen the odd one out, then? Perhaps even the black sheep, with her two oddly absent sons called Christian and Stefan? There was a photograph of the whole Kingly family as it must have been thirty years ago or so; six of them arranged on a lawn, the children holding toys – a Barbie doll and a big plastic object that Thea recognised as a Transformer. She had owned one herself at the age of about ten. There were the three sisters, with their brother in their midst, sitting on the grass, the parents standing behind them. Penny was obviously the eldest of the children, probably about sixteen, dark and thin. Then Imogen, recognisable from her thick unruly hair, perhaps three years younger. Umberto looked to be nine or ten, wearing short trousers, his hair neatly parted. And then came Theresa, mother of Jacob and Gabriella, the baby of the family, with a collection of Care Bears on her lap.

Thea performed the rapid calculations which came naturally to her when working out family connections. Coming from a large tribe herself, with a dozen cousins and eight nieces and nephews, she kept track without undue effort. Drew's funeral business also demanded a firm grasp of the way relatives were linked to the deceased, and who took precedence. That was Thea's favourite part of the enterprise by far. She would encourage him to recount all the ramifications of first wives and resentful in-laws, relishing it all.

It was after ten when the gate buzzer went for a second time that morning. Again, the palaver with the intercom and the necessity of walking down to look at the person before letting them in. Because this time it was *two* persons, man and woman, husband and wife. 'I'm Penny Rider, Umberto's sister, and I've come with my husband,' she said succinctly into the grille at the gate.

Chapter Nine

'Oh,' said Thea. 'I'll come.'

'Just press the button thing and let us in,' the woman ordered.

'No, I'll come,' said Thea obstinately. More than most, she disliked being given orders, especially by a complete stranger.

The people at the gate plainly resented her impertinence. 'I grew up in this house,' said the woman imperiously. 'When there was none of this foolery with gates. I tried to stop Mama from installing them, but she just went ahead anyway.'

'I'm sorry,' said Thea humbly. 'I feel the same about them as you do – but with everything that's happened I just thought—'

'Yes, yes, all right. It's not your fault. Just let us in, will you? Or do you think you need to call Umberto first for permission?'

The situation was a repeat of Clifford Savage's visit, which only made it more ridiculous. Thea opened the gate and stood back. Mr and Mrs Rider marched up to the front door and went straight into the house. This was the author of the family history, Thea reminded herself, feeling curious to get to know him.

'That's your dog, is it?' Penny demanded, glaring at the spaniel.

'Yes, that's Hepzibah. She comes everywhere with me.'

The woman sniffed in an old-fashioned expression of disdain and said nothing. Her husband was standing passively just behind her. 'Coffee?' asked Thea.

'All right, then.' Penny Rider gave her a very close inspection. 'You're pale,' she observed. 'Didn't get much sleep, is my guess.'

Thea nodded, dreading a rush of sympathy which was bound to make her cry. Even worse, she wanted to lay her head on this woman's broad breast and let her take over. Dogs, house, murder, police – Penny Rider seemed capable of dealing with all of it, leaving Thea to let everything go. Instead, she went into the kitchen and put the kettle on. Without waiting for an invitation, the couple settled themselves in the living room.

Victor Rider was holding the copy of his family history when Thea joined them with coffee and biscuits on a nice inlaid tray she had found. He waved the book at her. 'Swotting up on the family, are you?' he said with a slightly unpleasant smile. Thea suddenly recalled the final lines referring to feuds and animosities. Was the answer to Gabriella's slaughter right there in the pages, if only it could be deciphered?

'Umberto suggested I have a look,' she said. Other remarks were coming back to her, made in the final flurry of Umberto's departure: Penny was his oldest sister – the bossy one.

'You're wondering why we're here,' Penny said. 'You seem rather at a loss.'

'Well—'

'We were all extremely fond of Gabriella,' said Victor Rider, suddenly. 'Proud of her, doing so well. A good, clever girl with a strong sense of family loyalty. For someone to kill her here, right outside her uncle's house, is devilish. A piece of absolute wickedness. An abomination.'

The Victorian language made Thea wonder if the man was a vicar, but he wore no distinguishing garment to that effect.

'Yes,' said his wife. She patted his arm. 'When something like this happens, words can be so inadequate. I keep quoting that speech from *Macbeth* to myself. You know – "it is a tale told by an idiot". Everything seems so pointless.'

Thea was silenced by this resort to literature. It made normal everyday feelings seem childish and thin, while at the same time casting doubt on the genuineness of these people's emotions. She looked at them – a middle-aged couple from the comfortable heart of England, cosily wallowing in family connections and memories, sufficient unto themselves. Penny had the same physical shape as her sister Imogen but was

128

slightly shorter. She looked confident that anything she wanted could be obtained. Her husband was not so much cowed by her as fully accepting of his role as supporter and provider.

Umberto was the only one with the Kingly surname, but he was childless, a mere uncle. Had that given him a reduced status with his sisters? Or did he retain the time-honoured perks of being the only son? Victor had spoken of 'loyalty' which felt significant. It also had to be relevant that they all lived within easy reach of each other. And Victor had written a book about them.

'I have read your book,' she told him. 'You obviously have a very strong feeling for family. I would have liked to have met Mrs Kingly – she seems to have been a strong woman.' She looked at the photograph of Jocasta where she was somewhere in her seventies.

'We all thought she'd live another twenty years,' said Penny, readily diverted. 'I still can't quite believe she's gone.'

'We knew it would happen, of course.' Victor spoke with the same suddenness as before. 'Not Nonna, of course. I mean Gabriella. Something very nasty, anyway. When that robin came into the house on Sunday, we both said – something terrible's coming. We even put it on the Facebook page.'

Thea waited for his wife to chastise him for talking nonsense, but instead, Penny just nodded grimly. 'It's always true. Anyone will tell you.'

'I've never heard it in my life,' said Thea. 'Isn't it just a silly superstition?'

'You can't say that when it turned out to be true,' said Victor with total certainty.

Thea gave up all efforts to argue. What difference did it make? She glanced at the clock, as she had done with her earlier visitor. The morning was far from finished; she may as well make the most of these people and be glad of the diversion. 'More coffee?' she asked, feeling that she had made considerably more of the beverage than was reasonable in one morning.

'If there's any in the pot,' said Victor with unconcealed sarcasm.

'No pot – just instant,' smiled Thea. 'Sorry about that.'

'Stop it, Vic,' his wife reproached him. 'You know Umberto wouldn't have any sort of coffee machine.'

'Despite his Italian forebears,' sighed the man. 'And no, I don't actually want any more, thank you.'

Thea let it all flow past her, content that nothing was being required of her beyond a rudimentary social interaction. Gabriella Milner's death was somehow receding into the background; a tragic and incomprehensible occurrence that could not bear too much discussion. Whatever had motivated these relatives to drop in on a Wednesday morning it did not appear to contain any malice. They were mildly curious about her, she supposed, and equally mildly concerned about Umberto's house – although they had not yet mentioned the dogs. At such times, Thea had discovered, people did gravitate towards the physical location of the event, especially if it was murder. They needed to convince themselves of the reality; share in the sense of occasion; voice at least some shreds of how they felt. Complete strangers would show up at the scene of a violent death and just stand about looking helpless. Some perhaps were hoping for a television crew to come along and ask them to express their shock in the same hackneyed words that people always used. At least the Riders had managed to avoid 'devastated' – so far.

'You're not afraid to stick around, then?' Victor said, in another of his sudden remarks. 'Here all on your own.'

'No – why should I be?'

'Don't be naive. It's common knowledge that you witnessed the whole thing. Don't you think there's a chance the killer will come back and try to stop you from saying too much?'

Thea huffed a scornful syllable. 'It'd be a bit late for that. I've already talked to any number of police people, telling them everything I saw.' Then she backtracked. 'What do you mean, anyway? How is it common knowledge?'

Penny intervened. 'He's exaggerating. It's only the family who knows about you in any detail. And Ramon, I suppose.'

Gabriella's partner, Thea reminded herself. 'The police are keeping a protective eye on me,' she said, with a small thrill of self-importance. 'I know most of them as friends, actually.'

'Bully for you,' said Victor, which Thea admitted was perfectly justified.

Penny was stirring, plumping her bag off her lap and onto the arm of the chair, leaning forward. She was sitting in a somewhat saggy armchair, too deep for a quick exit. A big woman, stronger in the legs than the arms, she had to rock herself slightly before she could stand up. 'Time we were off,' she said.

Her husband was at the door ahead of her, looking out towards the back of the house. 'Should we have a look at the dogs?' he wondered.

'Don't see why. It'll only get them excited. I'm sure they're quite all right.'

'They are,' Thea promised her, pushing any thought of fleas out of mind. 'They seem very fond of your nephew.'

'Really?' Penny's eyes narrowed slightly. 'You mean Jacob, I suppose? Gabriella's brother. Yes, he told us he'd been here. Apparently, the police brought him, which I thought was a bit peculiar.'

'They do that sort of thing these days,' said Thea confidently. 'He seemed very upset.'

'We're all upset,' said Penny tiredly. 'As you'd expect.'

'And we're all showing up here, by the sound of it,' said Victor. 'Must be trying for you.'

Thea smiled. 'Not really.' She was tempted to

explain her theory about the need people have to visit the scene of tragedy, but doubted whether she would get a patient hearing. 'And it's not as if I had anything else to do.'

'No. Well . . .' he said vaguely.

'We ought to be off,' Penny announced again, sounding like a more powerful version of her sister Imogen. 'I'm meant to be giving a report to a meeting this afternoon, for my sins. And you're taking that woman to hospital, don't forget,' she told her husband. 'He does voluntary driving,' she informed Thea. 'Mostly to and from the hospital.'

'And you?' Thea asked.

Penny's chin went up. 'Me? I'm what they laughingly call "a highly paid consultant" in the civil service. I have a particular expertise that people value, and they call on me to give advice and guidance. It concerns a small area of economics that would not interest you.'

'Futures,' said Victor, incurring a bad-tempered glance from his wife. 'In the world of animal husbandry.'

Thea nodded and gave him a grateful smile. 'Oh,' she said. 'I like the sound of your hospital driving. I might think about doing that myself, when the kids are a bit older.'

'Last week's woman vomited in my car,' said Victor, and Thea quickly changed her mind.

They loitered on the way to the street gate, looking all round themselves at the front garden, the copper beech and the road beyond. Then Penny turned back and looked up at the first-floor window where Thea had been standing on Monday afternoon. 'It all feels very *neat*,' she muttered. 'You were watching – I assume from up there? Gabriella parked just where you could see her. Nobody else in sight.'

'So?' said Thea, sensing an accusation.

'Nothing. I'm only trying to reconstruct it all. Jacob came round last night, talking it all through, even drawing diagrams.'

'Did he?' She wondered why that hadn't been mentioned sooner. Was it merely confirmation that the Kingly family was unusually close-knit? There was a faint implication that Jake's aunt and uncle were somehow vouching for him, making it plain that nobody could imagine he had any hand in his sister's death.

'All futile, of course,' Penny went on. 'What difference does anything like that make? It's all very well for the police to be measuring angles and velocities and that sort of thing, but for the family, all we need to know is that she's gone. Imogen must be feeling wretched.'

Thea did a double take. 'Why her particularly?' Where was little sister Theresa in the story? she wondered. A name that was seldom mentioned.

'Gabriella was always her little darling. The two little cousins – Gabby and Kirsty – were inseparable when they were small. We used to go off for weeks together in

134

the summer – the whole family. Dogs as well, of course. That was before . . . well, before everything got spoilt.'

'Before your mother died,' said Victor, with a sympathetic little smile.

'It must have been nice,' said Thea, thinking that a holiday with her brother and sisters and their offspring would be horrendous. 'The holidays, I mean.'

'It's worse for Theresa than it is for Imogen,' said Victor, into the pause. 'Don't you think?'

'Oddly enough, that probably isn't true,' said his wife. 'Imogen's a lot more maternal than T, for a start. And with all her other troubles, I dare say she's in quite a state. That daft garden centre alone would be enough to make her ill.'

They were finally at the gate, and Thea let them out before she could give in to the temptation to ask more questions. They stepped onto the pavement and again scanned the street, as if looking for bloodstains. Thea did the same, wondering about angles and velocities and how it could have been that she saw as much as she did of the impact. She also marvelled at the efficient cleaning up that had been done. Tiny slivers of glass and metal, human tissue, perhaps oil and other fluids must have besmirched the road. But it had opened for traffic only twenty-four hours after the event, and now looked just as it always had.

As Penny Rider had done, Thea turned and looked back at the house. It sat there serenely impervious to human drama, comfortably shabby, the wooden window frames at the end of their useful lives, the roof dotted with moss. 'It's a nice house,' she said inanely. Looking at the road had engendered a sort of dizziness that made her feel like crying. She wanted Gladwin or Caz to be there, with their sensible understanding.

'And it's all Umberto's now,' said Victor heavily.

'Don't start that,' said his wife, and they walked away. Thea watched them get into a Volvo parked fifty yards up the street. *Don't start what?* she wondered.

Chapter Ten

One thing about visitors, they certainly passed the time. The dogs had been neglected, Thea was hungry and still there had been no word from any of the police people. With any luck it would be teatime before she knew it. Her trauma was proving to be entirely manageable, despite dreams and sudden strange panics. All she had to do was keep her nerve and assure herself that it was all a necessary part of the process.

She played with the salukis as before, throwing toys for them and watching them run. Gina co-operated very agreeably with a few jumps over hurdles, pretending to be a greyhound in a steeplechase. It was altogether enjoyable and soothing, and Thea felt waves of love for the pretty creatures, who understood nothing of horrible human behaviour going on outside their gate. The encounters with so many of Umberto's relatives had given rise to undercurrents of curiosity as to how they would be affected by the death of Gabriella, and what their various motives had been for turning up in Oddington – but it remained at a low level. She automatically reviewed all their names and instant assessments of their characters, reminding herself of the details. It was a lifelong habit, which had been reinforced by her frequent encounters with the police, who were often intensely interested in her observations. She found herself most intrigued by Imogen, who gave an impression of acting a part, standing tall and wary, as if expecting an attack. *Prickly* seemed a good word for her. And her daughter, Kirsty, following her like a watchful collie, both subservient and protective. The images that remained in Thea's memory carried associations that she had learnt not to dismiss. If everybody in the family could be compared to a kind of dog, then Jacob was probably a Labrador, and Penny Rider a mildly mistrustful terrier. Her husband was obviously a setter with an uncertain temper, hampered by inadequate brain power, but loyal. After all, he had written that book about Penny's family, which had no real connection to himself. That suggested a sort of selfless fidelity that was very doglike. But Imogen – what breed was she? She really wasn't easy to pigeonhole. Intelligent, but showing signs of defeat in life's constant struggle, probably rather brave, and yet difficult to read. Thea found herself hoping that she would meet that particular relative again.

And there were still one or two gaps. Theresa Milner, for one. And Gabriella's boyfriend, Ramon, for another. The two people most likely to be drowning in shock and grief and in no state to come visiting the scene of the crime.

Playtime over, Thea went indoors to construct

something substantial for lunch. Her dog sat beside her as she ate, looking unusually dejected. 'What's the matter?' Thea asked her. It took a while to work out that Hepzie had actually enjoyed much less exercise than usual. She found the salukis intimidating and had not joined in their games. While they were left to gambol outside, and then put in their indoor room together, the spaniel had simply hovered on the sidelines, and then followed her mistress into the parts of the house from which the resident dogs were banned. The theory seemed to be that if they were glimpsed by a passer-by they might be stolen. Or if the front door was accidentally opened, they might rush through it and leap over the gate into the street. Living invisibly at the back of the house was the more secure strategy, apparently. Thea refrained from casting judgement on this, and simply made every effort to abide by the rules.

But Hepzie was accustomed to freedom, with long walks and individual attention. 'All right, then,' said Thea. 'We'll risk half an hour or so, same as yesterday.'

They had done it many times before – exploring a new village, trying to find someone to chat to, asking questions and making silent criticisms of the worst aspects of Cotswolds life. The undercurrents had become more and more visible as Thea became more experienced. House-sitting had led her into the darker realities of these picture-book settlements with their dubious histories and artificial lives. As she and her dog set out to walk the short distance from Lower to Upper Oddington, she gave close inspection to every building they passed. A reasonable grasp of local history informed her that the older houses had been built mainly by affluent merchants two centuries ago. There had been shops, thriving schools, four pubs, a malthouse and a Post Office over the years, all gone now except for the pubs and one of them did not appear to be functioning. The reasons for this exodus were connected in Thea's mind with the abandonment of the medieval church. Large social forces, combined with poor judgements, the twists of fortune and human greed probably explained it. They thought they'd be better off somewhere else, so they had betrayed their comfortable little village and left it an empty shell of a place, where material value transcended all else, with electronic gates to prove it.

Most of the houses had substantial gardens tended by paid freelancers who mowed the grass and pruned the roses. A preliminary glance at the Oddington website a few weeks earlier had revealed a small handful of 'local businesses', chief of which was a garden service. She could now admire the fruits of this person's labours at first hand. The gardens were almost all immaculate. There were occasional ornamental ponds, garden swings, even a tree house – created for children who were almost certainly at private schools in or near London, and were brought to this pseudo patch of countryside during their holidays for some fresh air.

Strolling along the pavement, Thea indulged in sour fantasies about this unnatural way of life. The harsh realities of nature would be intolerable to these people. They would spray insects and weeds with chemicals, complain of being woken by dawn chorusing, interfere with the struggling lives of hedgehogs, and shy away from any field containing cattle. They probably couldn't distinguish blackberries from deadly nightshade, and simply believed all wild fruits to be poisonous. If an ant or two ventured into the house, they would call an exterminator.

These notions developed until quite out of control. She caught herself up at the point where she was imagining the hysterics caused by glimpsing a mouse in the house, aware that she was guilty of outrageous stereotyping, and she wasn't especially keen on the idea of mice in her own kitchen, come to that. She was also irrationally intolerant of both spiders and earwigs. It was all part of being human, she admitted sadly. Other species were never going to get fair treatment.

As usual, there were scarcely any people to be seen. The weather was cool and cloudy, but dry. Two or three delivery vans went past, and one car. It was easy to imagine that an apocalypse had taken place overnight and almost the entire population wiped out. And yet – that poor young Gabriella Milner had been pursued and slaughtered right here in this ludicrously quiet village, one Monday afternoon in June. Thea found herself again applying the word 'betrayal' to that terrible deed. It had betrayed every expectation of what might possibly happen here. And if Thea's momentary assumption that the victim knew and liked her killer was correct, then what other word could more accurately describe the act?

Treachery was inevitable, she supposed. Trust was so often misplaced, through wishful thinking or misunderstanding. Human beings were frail and corrupt and put their own interests before those of others. They lost control of themselves. They lashed out when their feelings were hurt or when their self-image was threatened. Her initial hypotheses about the reason for Gabriella's killing returned to her, fitting comfortably with these thoughts about human behaviour and Cotswold villages.

The big gap in all this theorising was Gabriella herself. What had she really been like? You couldn't judge by what her relatives had said in the first shock of her death. Nobody was going to cast aspersions on her character at this point, however much they might have disliked her. It was taboo to speak ill of the dead – especially the very *recently* dead. It was callous, unwise and probably unlucky. It reflected badly on the speaker. It was ungenerous. And if the person had been murdered, it might make the police suspicious of you.

Another gap was the boyfriend, Ramon. Whilst knowing there was very little realistic prospect of ever meeting him, Thea wished she could, if only to further flesh out the picture she had of the family. She assumed that the police would be paying close attention to him, as the person most likely to have some insight into what might explain Gabriella's death. And experience would suggest to them that he was himself very near the top of any list of likely people to have done the deed.

She and Hepzie had reached the 'new' church, built sometime around the 1860s to replace the one the people of Oddington had abandoned. It was handsome enough, close to the village hall, with houses on all sides. Perhaps the lazy folk of the 1850s had merely wanted a shorter walk on Sunday mornings and decided they could afford to start again with their not inconsiderable wealth. It looked as if Upper Oddington had more actual residents than its neighbour, and it was admittedly a fair distance up to the old church. Its pub was thriving while The Fox to the east looked as if business might be rather thin or even non-existent. In short, the whole focus had shifted westwards, leaving the Lower half to slowly disintegrate. Although she suspected it was much less simple than that. The 'new' church did not appear to have a graveyard, which explained why there were so many recent burials at St Nicholas. It also added a further twist to the mystery of exactly why there had ever been a need for a second version.

Before she could explore this notion further, perhaps

143

by going into this newer church for a look round, a car horn tooted discreetly at her and she located Caz Barkley sitting in the driving seat of an ordinary-looking vehicle a short distance ahead of her, watching her and her dog. She had drawn up beside the village hall in a lay-by intended for buses. Thea walked over and greeted the detective. Here was the final element in the day's agenda as she had predicted it some hours ago. She smiled and said, 'I was hoping you might show up.'

'I see you don't need much pastoral care.' Caz eyed the spaniel. 'Are the prize mutts all okay?'

'Absolutely.' She had been about to say *fit as fleas* when she remembered that this might not be altogether appropriate. She did not want to think about fleas. It was a problem she had pushed to a corner of her mind. 'It's nice to see you,' she added. It was not the first time Barkley had tracked her down in a Cotswold village, and she wondered whether she would one day start to feel ever so slightly persecuted by the habit. After all, everybody was very readily located these days, thanks to their phones, which were essentially unceasing tracking devices, monitoring every move and every penny spent. Presumably the identity of the person who killed Gabriella Milner was sitting on a giant Big Brother computer somewhere, if only there was a clue as to where to begin to search for it.

'What are you doing?' Caz asked. 'Exactly.'

'Walking the dog. She was feeling mopey.'

'Poor thing,' said the detective with very little feeling. 'Can we talk? You could get in the car.'

This too had happened before. 'I suppose so,' said Thea without enthusiasm. 'Though I can't see very much point.'

'Don't be like that. I'm willing to bet you've had visitors, and phone calls and ideas that we'd find interesting.'

'No phone calls,' said Thea, and got into the passenger seat with Hepzie on her lap. 'Aren't we a bit conspicuous here?'

'Does that matter?' Caz thought about it. 'Are you scared of reprisals?'

'Reprisals,' Thea repeated thoughtfully. 'That's a good word. You mean – if the killer sees me talking to the police, they'll worry that I'm telling you who they are, so they'll come round in the night and kill me.' She laughed without any humour. 'That's what Penny Rider said this morning, and my reply's the same. Surely it's a bit late for that? Didn't we cover it days ago now?'

'So what's the problem about being conspicuous? And who's Penny Rider?'

'Umberto's oldest sister. I don't think it's a problem. Just that it might make someone curious, I suppose. This place is so empty, and yet most of the houses probably have CCTV cameras, and they'll be paranoid about strange cars parked in the street. That sort of thing.'

'We've done door to door, you know. More than half the properties are empty during the week, a lot of them much more than that. If they were as paranoid as you say, the occupied ones would have the entire incident recorded in detail and our job would be simple. The law decrees that private CCTV cameras are not permitted to film beyond the boundaries of their own property. And, as it happens, there aren't any within fifty yards or more of Positano. What a name!' She deviated for a moment from her subject. 'Positano. What does it even mean?'

'It's a place in Italy. On the side of a cliff, with a beach. They say it's lovely.'

'So all these gorgeous cliffs and beaches in the Cotswolds remind them of it, right?'

Thea laughed with a little more mirth than before.

'Anyway,' Caz proceeded, 'we're now trying to find the vehicle. Strenuous efforts, as the Super says. Every repair shop from here to Birmingham and beyond is being questioned for broken headlights and wing mirrors. You wouldn't believe how many there are.'

'Needle in a haystack,' said Thea sympathetically.

'It's hopeless, to be honest. Any remotely sensible killer would just shut the vehicle away in a barn somewhere and fix it themselves. We've checked for stolen vehicles, obviously, and there's a reasonably short list of possible candidates – but again, if the whole thing was pre-planned, they'd have nicked it some time ago, probably two hundred miles away, and then kept it out of sight until Monday.'

'In a barn somewhere,' nodded Thea. 'Or they could just have used their own car, trusting that there wouldn't be any witnesses.'

Caz ignored this daft idea, as it deserved. 'The trouble is, this is a perfect area for that kind of thing. Everybody's got a garage, securely locked up, not causing any concern or curiosity. Remember those poor pangolins that were sitting in a place like that, nobody suspecting a thing? And these garages can be huge. You could house whole families of illegals inside them if you wanted to. If you ask me, there should be a law that they all have to have a big window with nothing covering it, so we can see what's inside.'

Despite a degree of resistance, Thea found herself drawn into renewed speculation about the murder. The tiny slivers of evidence that she had been able to provide had turned out to be a large proportion of what the police had to go on. 'Penny Rider came to visit,' she disclosed, going back to Caz's question. 'She's aunt of the deceased. I assume you've interviewed her, and the other two.'

'Other two what?'

'Sisters. Aunt and mother of the deceased. They're Umberto's sisters. I know even more now about the whole family than before. His mother's interesting.'

Caz gave a small moan. 'Here we go. Just like the Super said you'd be.'

'Is that a bad thing?'

'No, but it's exhausting. And yes, the whole family has been seen by the police, with no significant result. More a courtesy than anything, to be honest. It's hard to imagine a relative doing such a horrible thing. They all say Gabriella was much loved and an integral member of the family. Stuff like that.'

Thea pulled a sceptical face. 'They would say that, wouldn't they? They're not going to admit to the police that there were ferocious feuds going on.'

'Were there?'

'I don't know. Victor's book hints that there might have been. I showed it to Gladwin.'

Caz merely shook her head helplessly. 'So what's this about their mother? Where is she?'

'Dead, less than a year ago. She lived here. It was her house and apparently she left it to Umberto and he was able to get his dogs, since he had plenty of space for them here. That might be a bit strange, seeing as how she's got three daughters as well. That he got the house all to himself, that is.'

'People still leave stuff to sons and not daughters,' said Caz with a hint of bitterness.

'Do they?'

'Was she Italian?'

'Half.'

'There you are, then. What does this have to do with anything?'

'Probably nothing. But actually, I think it could well explain the murder. You get more high emotion in a

148

family than anywhere else, don't forget. Besides, I like delving into the backgrounds of families. It's always fascinating.'

'You're lucky to have one.' Caz Barkley had grown up in the care system, apparently without anything resembling attentive parents or siblings. It was the first thing Gladwin had told Thea about her new sergeant.

'Well, the Kinglys are remarkably close-knit, it seems to me. They all live around here, and the old mother must have been a real old-fashioned matriarch. Your friend Cliff Savage knew her. They used to go for walks together.'

'Not so much my friend – but I did recognise him when I happened to get his door to knock on yesterday. That hair . . . it's still as bright as ever.'

'He does stand out,' Thea agreed. 'I wasn't sure what to make of him. Did you ask him about his connection to the Kinglys?'

'Obviously. He told me about the old lady and how he was here when she died.'

'He thinks he might have been the last person to see her alive.'

'Don't get complicated,' Caz said warningly. 'That all happened last year and there was nothing a bit suspicious about it.'

'I never said there was. Look – I *know* the mother's death is not likely to be relevant, but I've got to have *something* to think about.'

'Who says it's not relevant?' asked Caz, to

Thea's surprise. 'Relevance isn't the same thing as suspicious.'

'Oh!' Thea tried to fathom this observation. 'So you think it does connect to the murder, do you? How *could* it?'

'I'm hoping you'll help us answer that,' said Caz. 'Now tell me about all your visitors. It sounds as if you've had quite a lot.'

When the detective finally let her go, Thea proceeded on her walk, feeling a need to use her legs and clear her head, despite a nagging sense of obligation to the salukis. The bus shelter had three or four shelves of cast-off books inside itself, presumably free for the taking. Beyond that there was a stretch of large houses with generous gardens, and the ubiquitous gates. She saw a stone set upright on a verge, which looked old and interesting. The house beside it was called 'Silver Birches' and had dragons on the corners of its roof. 'Finials?' she muttered to herself, uncertainly. Quirky roof decoration was something she had seen before in the area. Still there was no sign of life – not just a human silence; there were no birds singing, either. There had been a path for pedestrians for much of the way, which could be termed a pavement at a slight stretch, but it disappeared when the road narrowed. She knew there was a pub around another bend or two, but decided it was well past time for turning back. The encounter with Caz had been reassuring, for the most part, despite throwing her back into speculations about Gabriella Milner's death. There was nothing Thea could contribute regarding the ownership of the killer vehicle, other than improbable theories. Police forensic work would be much more likely to yield evidence that would pin down the make and model, size and weight of the thing. Everything depended on the motive, as far as she could see.

The sky remained cloudy, but the afternoon was reasonably warm. The salukis should definitely be outside, with proper supervision and attention. The matter of the fleas raised its ugly head again, with no clearer solution than before. It would be rash to buy chemical remedies without consulting Umberto. Such short-haired dogs were unlikely to get seriously infested, she believed. But if Hepzibah was the culprit, there would surely be recriminations. Wild remedies occurred to her, such as acquiring a neat-fingered monkey, who would comb efficiently through the dogs' coats and eat the offending parasites. Watching them groom each other in various zoos had been one of Thea's favourite entertainments as a child. She remembered wondering just what a flea might taste like.

Everything at Positano seemed just as she had left it. The gate was still locked; her car still in the street outside; windows closed and no smell of burning. None of these things could be taken for granted, in Thea's experience. There had actually been an occasion where someone tried to set fire to the house she was supposed to be guarding.

She had left her phone in the house, and did not think to check it for at least twenty minutes after she and Hepzie got in. First, she let the salukis out and then made herself a mug of tea. The information that she had missed three phone calls came as a surprise. There was something slightly hysterical about the way the device shouted the news at her, reproaching her for neglect. When she listened to the messages, she conceded that it might have a point.

Chapter Eleven

The first message was from Stephanie, delivered breathlessly and sufficiently arresting to make Thea forget that there were two more calls sitting in her phone's impressive memory. 'Thea? Is it right that you're in the place where Miss Milner was killed? Do you remember she came with us on the school trip last term? Her boyfriend is Mr Rodriguez who teaches Spanish at school. They told us about it yesterday. I sat *next* to her on the bus. We talked about a whole lot of things. She was *nice*. Dad says he'll bring me over to you after school if I want, so we can talk about it. Would that be all right? I don't have to stay long . . . oh, this is too much voicemail. Call me back, okay?'

The girl must have phoned during the lunch hour, just as Thea was setting out on her walk with the spaniel. By some magic an hour and a half had passed, and Stephanie would be leaving school for the day at any moment. Thea called back.

'Hi,' came the young voice. 'Did you get my message?'

'I did. Sorry it took me so long. I was out without the phone.'

'As usual.'

'Right. Sorry.'

'It's okay. I'm on my way home. Fiona said she'd fetch me, but I like walking. You notice things.'

'And it's good for you.'

'Mm. So – can we come and see you? Before supper, Dad thought. He's not busy today.'

Thea hesitated, realising that she hadn't known what she was going to say when she returned Stephanie's call. 'It's not my house to just invite people in. Not *my* people, anyway.'

'Who's going to see?'

'Good question. Yes, come, then. What about Timmy?'

'He says he'll stay and amuse himself. Fiona's here.'

It was eleven miles from one door to the other, a drive that might take as much as twenty-five minutes given holiday traffic and country roads. 'Your supper's going to be late,' Thea observed. 'Unless you only stay a very little while.'

'We've been having it later, anyway,' Stephanie reminded her. 'Now it's summer.'

The whole Broad Campden household felt a long way off, with Stephanie's suggestion of bridging the distance oddly unsettling. The revelation that Stephanie had met the dead woman had yet to be processed. 'I didn't know your Mr Rodriguez was connected to what happened,' she said awkwardly. 'You like him, don't you?'

'He's *wonderful*,' sighed the girl. 'And now he'll be so sad. We had a bit of a cry about it this morning, me and Emily and Deely.'

'Oh dear.' Thea felt thoroughly inadequate. Was she going to disclose that she had seen the actual moment when Gabriella Milner had died? To date, she had kept that detail back from Drew, who had cheerfully accepted the whole thing as just another of his wife's adventures. Had Stephanie somehow acquired better quality information? It would not be impossible.

'It happened so close to where you are,' the girl went on. 'Have the police talked to you about it?'

'Oh yes,' said Thea. 'Plus a whole lot of friends and relations. This house belongs to her uncle, you see.'

'Yes, I know,' said Stephanie.

It was almost half past four when Drew and Stephanie arrived. Thea glimpsed them crawling along the village street looking for the name 'Positano', as she stood at the living-room window. She could only see the top half of the car and the heads inside. They went past and she ran out to open the gate and wave, hoping Drew would be checking his mirror. He was not, but turned round at the small oddly shaped patch of village green and came back again.

Thea and Hepzie were waiting by the gate, thus

avoiding the necessity of intercom and all it entailed. Drew found a spot to park a short way down the street and Thea admitted him and his daughter as quickly as she could, nervous of watching eyes. 'You seem a bit . . . distracted,' said her husband, after she had given him the most minimal of kisses. He looked up at the house, and Thea was suddenly transported to a moment in Cranham, soon after she and Drew had met. She had been house-sitting and he had come to see her there. There was the same look in his eye – incomprehension, and a kind of deference, as if to say he knew he would never properly grasp what was going on and was happy not to try. 'Nice,' he said now. 'If a bit run-down.'

Umberto's house was far from being the oldest or most handsome in Oddington, but it held its own where size and quality of the stonework were concerned. 'They're all nice,' said Thea, rather tiredly. 'Come on in.'

'Where are the dogs?' asked Stephanie, having been greeted ecstatically by Hepzie. 'I thought there were dogs.'

'They stay out at the back. They've got their own quarters, like horses.' She heard her own words. 'Actually, they're a bit like horses, I suppose. They've got fleas.'

Stephanie laughed. 'Did Hepzie give them to them?'

'Probably. I suppose it'll get me into trouble. I daren't put that stuff on them without asking.'

'Horses don't get fleas,' said Drew prosaically.

'True,' Thea agreed.

'Can we go in there?' Stephanie asked, pointing to the sitting room and the open door to it. 'I want to look at all those pictures.'

'Feel free. Don't break anything.'

The girl went ahead, leaving Drew to whisper, 'She's been nagging me to bring her since last night. I'm not at all sure it's a good idea.'

'Nor me,' said Thea. 'What does she *want*?'

'To play detective, I imagine. She's getting worse.' He clearly had more to say, but contented himself with a reproachful sigh that amply conveyed to Thea that this was all her doing and he did not much like it.

They joined Stephanie, who was examining the family portraits with eagerness. 'There she is! That must be Miss Milner's granny. She told me all about her, how she kept the family together, and was like somebody from another age, and what an awful thing it was when she died. That wasn't very long ago. She lived in this house. I checked the electoral roll. So – did her son inherit it from her?'

'How could she tell you all that?' Thea was sceptical. 'And why would she?'

'We were on that coach for *hours*, going to Chatsworth, remember? She asked me something about my mother, and when I said she'd died, that set her off about her granny.'

'Why was she sitting with you, anyway? Why not

with her fiancé, or whatever he is?'

'He was at the back, keeping the boys in order. She was only there because they had to have the right number of adults. And she said she'd always wanted to see Chatsworth.'

'But you found it boring,' Drew interposed. 'I said at the time it was a daft place to take a school trip.'

Wife and daughter both ignored him.

'This is *her*,' Stephanie persisted. 'It must be.' She moved along the wall to a group photo showing three generations. 'And here's Miss Milner again, a bit older,' the girl pointed out, with a finger that shook slightly. 'Her hair's longer here, but I can recognise her.'

Thea peered at the small face surrounded by those of relatives. 'I thought it must be. That's her brother, Jake. He came here yesterday. That seems ages ago now.'

Stephanie was counting. 'Nine people. Do you know who the others are?'

'That's Umberto. His sister Imogen and her daughter Kirsty. The other couple are Mr and Mrs Rider. She's his sister as well. They came here this morning. The other woman must be Theresa, Gabriella's mother.'

'So where's her father?'

'No idea,' said Thea, still checking the numbers and wondering how much she ought to reveal to her stepdaughter. 'Imogen doesn't appear to have a husband either.'

'They've all been here, have they?' Drew asked. 'Is that how you know everybody?'

'Most of them,' she admitted. 'They wanted to see where it happened. Actually, the only one I haven't seen is Theresa, now I think about it.'

'That's amazing!' Stephanie was stunned. 'I can't believe it. Have you talked to the police as well?'

'Oh yes. The whole set – Gladwin, Higgins and Caz.'

'And there we were thinking you'd be all lonely and neglected,' said Drew, with a hint of bitterness. 'We should have known better.'

'Dad! We didn't think that at all. Don't be silly.' Stephanie was on tiptoe, partly to get a better view of the pictures and partly from excitement. 'Don't you think one of these people must have killed her?' She looked at Thea with shining eyes.

'Um . . .' Thea met the adolescent gaze and tried to think. 'Actually, not really. It's such a devoted family – they all seem fond of each other, and terribly upset about Gabriella – Miss Milner.' She kept back the reference to 'feuds and animosities' in Victor Rider's book, which she had still not decided to take seriously.

'Couldn't it have been a ghastly accident?' Drew asked. 'That street's quite narrow. It would be easy to hit something parked at the side. Isn't that what happened?'

'Yes, but . . .' Again Thea hesitated. 'It wasn't an accident,' she finished flatly.

'Because the person who did it didn't stop,' Stephanie

said emphatically. 'That's a crime in itself. It was *obviously* murder.'

Some ghostly presence sowed the same thought in both Drew and Stephanie at that moment. 'You *saw* it,' said Stephanie.

'Didn't you?' said Drew. 'That's what makes you so sure.'

'Was it really really horrible?' asked the girl. 'What did you do? I mean – what was the first thing you did?'

'It was horrible, yes. I went to the gate, and opened it, but I didn't go very close. The door of her car was torn right off. She must have died instantly. I phoned Gladwin.'

'Good God,' said Drew, and pulled her to him. 'Bloody hell, Thea.'

She rested her cheek on his chest and breathed him in. 'Yes,' she said.

'I don't think I should have brought Stephanie here. I didn't want to. But she kept nagging at me . . .'

'I expect she'd have found a bus or something if you'd refused her.'

'I would,' said Stephanie.

'But *why?* It's not the sort of thing somebody your age ought to be involved in.'

'D-a-a-d,' she said in a long, exasperated syllable. 'Why can't you understand? This is where the whole thing is *real*. Thea knows what I mean – don't you? And you should as well, because of the burials and families and actual *death*. We're special, all of us.

That's why you and Thea go together so well.' She was turning from one to the other, drawing them together as well as urging them to include her in the embrace. 'When did you get so *conventional*?' she concluded, with an expression that included a very adolescent reproach.

Drew had gone very still. His women watched him as he pulled away from Thea and stared out of the window at the street outside. 'I think it must be because I'm scared,' he said at last. 'You two are both much braver than me. My funerals try to make it honest and genuine – facing death and the effect it has – but most of the time I keep it away from my own inner thoughts.'

'Because of Mum,' said Stephanie with devastating wisdom.

'Because of Mum,' said Drew.

Thea squared her shoulders. 'Come and meet the dogs,' she said. 'They need their supper, and then another run round the field.'

Stephanie sighed, and gave another long look at the family pictures on the wall. 'You know – if one of these people did kill Miss Milner, that would be the most terrible betrayal. It would be like Auntie Jocelyn killing Jessica, or . . . or . . .' She smiled. 'At least I've got so few relations, it's not likely to happen to me.'

Jocelyn was Thea's younger sister; Jessica her daughter, Stephanie's stepsister. And unusually she also thought of her other sister, Emily, who had become very much detached from the family some years earlier, but who might well have shared many of the feelings around the death of Gabriella Milner. Thea found herself uncomfortably linking the permutations of her own family to those of the Kinglys. 'Maybe they're not as close as they seem,' she speculated. 'Perhaps there are second families.' She held up a finger. 'Imogen had two boys before Kirsty – very likely by another father. Christian and Stefan. They're not in any of the pictures.'

'Where are they, then?' asked Stephanie.

'Somewhere in Austria.'

'The police will have to find them,' said the girl confidently. 'I bet one of them did it.'

'Stephanie, stop it,' said Drew, ineffectually.

Again, Thea saw the look on Gabriella's face, a microsecond before her death. 'It was somebody she knew,' she said. 'I could see it on her face.' She told Stephanie all about it, as she led the way to the back of the house and the neglected salukis.

Left alone again, hungry and restless, Thea regretted her own urges and instincts which repeatedly sent her away from her perfectly good home. The blatant irony of her stepdaughter's determination to ensure that the marriage between her and Drew would survive and prosper made her feel humble. It ought not to be down to Stephanie to identify parental strengths and weaknesses; she should be focused on her own affairs and interests. Except, of course, the stability of the domestic setting *was* her affair. And her brother's. Timmy's well-being was also central to the girl's thinking. He had been the person most damaged by Karen's death and Stephanie was never going to let anybody forget that.

There was an obvious connection between the death of her mother and Stephanie's increasingly passionate wish to be involved with Thea's adventures. Since Christmas, this had become more and more overt. Christmas itself had been overshadowed by a neighbour's death, and another incident in Northleach had cemented her determination to get involved in solving crimes. She had shown considerable maturity and good sense, while at the same time being exposed to adult behaviour that might well have caused lasting trauma. Drew might be right to worry about this, Thea acknowledged. Stephanie's oncoming teenage years might well become alarmingly untypical if her interest persisted. Thea found herself speculating on how the children would have turned out if their mother had lived. Karen herself had been a campaigner, with a wide social circle. She had probably also been a devoted and protective parent. It was an uncomfortable subject to contemplate all on her own, where it was too easy to plunge into gloomy analysis of her own shortcomings. For Thea there was always a lurking sense that she really wasn't a very nice person, and that people were eventually sure to find this out for themselves. Much easier, then, to revert to a less gruelling consideration of the death of Gabriella Milner.

Again, the word 'betrayal' kept floating up. It stemmed from that look on the victim's face, which Thea thought she had glimpsed. Perhaps she was now exaggerating it, finding much more in it than there had actually been. After forty-eight hours, she knew her memory was not reliable. It would be overlaid with emotion, speculation, all sorts of embellishments. Whatever she had told the police on that first evening was as accurate as it was ever going to be. Since then, it had become tainted and corrupted to the point of uselessness.

But she stuck with the idea of betrayal. The worst examples must surely lie within families. Truly terrible treachery could only come from somebody you had always known; somebody you felt you belonged to and could rely on completely. And if that trust was broken in childhood, you'd be scarred for life, never daring to let another person close enough for such hurt to happen again.

Her thoughts were becoming scattered. Much of her thinking was sinking into platitude – the upper-class British men who never got over being sent to boarding school at eight. The devastated wife learning of her husband's twenty-year affair. The sycophantic children plotting to secure their inheritance from an unloved aged parent. Drew, with his sympathetic manner with newly bereaved people, heard countless stories of this kind. His customers felt a need to summarise and explain the life just ended, sometimes blaming themselves, more often bringing up bitter resentments against a treacherous relative. Not long ago he had heard two separate tales that cast considerable doubt on the wisdom of conferring Power of Attorney onto anyone at all. 'You can't trust relatives,' he had concluded. 'Most of the time, they put their own interests first.'

Thea gave herself a shake. This was what happened when you had too much time on your hands. You got into fruitless meditations that led all over the place, and were all too liable to be depressing. Nobody in her family had behaved in this sort of way. They helped each other out when necessary, but all lived separate lives. Nobody had any unrealistic expectations. Everything was going along pretty nicely, all things considered.

But not for Umberto and his relations, she reminded herself. For them, a very terrible thing had happened, and the ripples had spread all the way to Stephanie Slocombe and many other pupils at her school. Gabriella Milner had a boyfriend – a partner – and his pain had affected them all.

She found herself wishing she could meet Ramon Rodriguez. He was the most obvious missing link, who had known Gabriella best, perhaps. He would be of interest to the police on several levels. The chief suspect was generally the partner, and failing that, he would have the best insights into what lay behind the crime. In theory, anyway.

The early evening was thinly occupied with finding something to eat, exercising the dogs, and wondering whether her walk up and down the village street would be enough to ensure a decent night's sleep. She felt reasonably tired, but knew better than to retire to bed early. Much better to hold out until she was really sleepy.

Before that, she had a long text from Stephanie.

'I googled Jocasta Kingly – the granny who died – and found a few things about her. There was an obituary in the local paper. I'll send it in an email if you like. She must have been very old-fashioned, from what it says. Dad was good to bring me, wasn't he! He had two new funerals when we got back. Fiona said the phone just kept ringing. We were only gone about two hours!'

Sweet girl, thought Thea fondly.

Then it occurred to her that there had been two further messages on her own phone that she had never listened to. The one from Stephanie had thrown everything else aside, and only now, with this text, did she remember. The phone was in her hand, a living thing nagging her to stay alert and pay attention. There was no escape. With a mild sense of trepidation, she retrieved the recordings.

'Thea – sorry I've neglected you. Not that there's anything much to say. Barkley tells me you're bearing up. I'll try to come over tomorrow, maybe in the afternoon. Knowing you, there'll be some local gossip that might

166

crack the case – as they say. Hope so, because we're not getting anywhere this end.'

Thea smiled as she listened. Good old Gladwin, always so frank and open, taking everything in her stride. Her Northern origins ensured a healthy scepticism concerning the manicured and cosseted Cotswolds. It sometimes seemed to Thea that the detective rather relished the fact that crime happened here every bit as much as anywhere else. Regardless of security gates and bottomless bank accounts, bad things happened to these self-satisfied people. Sometimes Thea could hear Gladwin thinking *Serves them bloody well right*.

The next message wiped the smile off her face.

Chapter Twelve

'This is for Mrs Thea Slocombe, currently occupying the home of Mr Umberto Kingly in Lower Oddington. A house named Positano, containing three valuable dogs. You should be aware that Mr Kingly is not the legal owner of this property and has no authority to employ you as his replacement. There is considerable opposition to his claim to the house. Your position is therefore tenuous and vulnerable to challenge.'

The voice was male, expressionless and sinister. It was as if a robot was reading a script – but the delivery was a long way from the mumbled calls that came from remote call centres. This was crisp and clear in every syllable. It conjured legal offices and brisk articled clerks.

There had to be a way of identifying where it came from, but the phone stubbornly withheld the information. Gladwin would surely be able to track it down somehow. And was it not threatening enough to justify an evening call to the detective in charge of investigating a murder committed right outside this house? Was this not quite obviously connected to that murder?

Gladwin answered quickly. 'Thea? What time do you call this?'

'Sorry. I've just found a message on my phone. Voicemail. It's a bit nasty. I didn't think I should leave it till the morning before telling you.' The forthcoming night was already beginning to feel much too frightening to endure without help.

'What did it say? Who was it from?'

'It's about the ownership of this house. It said my position was "vulnerable to challenge" whatever that means. It didn't say who it's from. I wish you could hear it. Is there any way I can send it to you?'

'You can't forward voice messages like emails. I'd have to have the actual phone. Look – I can't come this evening. I'm in Leicester, for my sins, following a lead about the murder vehicle. I'm here for a bit longer yet, and by the time I get home . . .'

'That's OK. I mean, this house is incredibly secure. And there are four dogs here to guard me, after all.'

'No, no, I can't let you cope on your own. It's not like you to be panicked. Although . . .' Thea could hear her tapping her fingernails on something hard. 'It doesn't sound like an immediate threat. I would send a car to sit outside, like on Monday, but everyone's got stuff to do. And overnighters have been reduced anyway. Usual story. Just keep your phone charged and have it right beside you – OK? We can have somebody with you in a few minutes, out of Stow, if you call. I'll make sure they recognise your name right away. Is that any help?'

Thea laughed. 'I think I feel quite a lot worse now, if I'm honest. I wasn't really expecting an armed guard or anything. But this does sound as if it's relevant, don't you think? If there's a battle over who owns the house, then Gabriella Milner's got to be part of it.'

'I'll have to think about that. On the face of it, I'd say it would be pretty dim to kill her right outside the house in question, if there's an obvious conflict. And, let's face it, it's a pretty flimsy motive for murder.'

'You think? The house must be worth nearly a million. People have killed for a lot less than that.'

'I know – but who says Gabriella was ever going to inherit it? We haven't found anything to suggest that.'

'Have you looked?' asked Thea.

'Good question. I don't think fights over property have been floated as a motive. I'll get them onto it tomorrow. Meanwhile, lock all the doors . . . you know the drill.'

'I do. But the thing is – I always think it's a bit silly. I mean – anybody who seriously wants to get me could just smash through a window.'

'They never do, though. Double glazing's pretty tough – and it makes a terrible lot of noise.'

'Night-night, then,' said Thea.

She spent twenty minutes with the salukis, combing them and talking to them, trying to assess their state of mind. They seemed to be in the same subdued mood as before, although they ate their suppers hungrily. Perhaps it was just patience they were demonstrating, waiting for their man to come home and play their favourite games with them again. Despite all the freedom they had in the field, it was a very repetitive life, even with Umberto. The plan to use all three of them as 'cash bitches', producing expensive puppies to boost their owner's income struck her as essentially exploitative, however much he might love them. Although she could see plenty of opposing arguments. Puppies would be fun and reproduction was what nature intended. There was little doubt that Umberto would give them lavish attention throughout the process. If people were daft enough to pay thousands for a scrap of canine charm, then you could hardly blame those who fulfilled the desire for such a pet. And yet, to Thea's mind it was all very wrong. Once again, the notion of betrayal pushed its way to the front of her thoughts. The puppies would be born trustingly into the world, their fate a matter of economics and pure chance. They were all too likely to be bought as breeding machines, with a hazardous life ahead of them.

Of course, musing about dogs was subconsciously intended as a distraction from the unsettling telephone message and it did not work for long. Somebody had deliberately gone to the trouble of upsetting her, for some reason. What did they want to happen? Presumably, the hope was that she would run away in terror, leaving the salukis to starve or wander off into the countryside. Except, if Umberto came home on Friday, they would suffer nothing more than extreme boredom for two days. Whether to leave them outside or in would be the biggest question. The intervening door would have to be locked, with the dogs firmly on one side or the other. There would be a lot of mess and distress if they were shut in – but they'd be cold and probably wet if left out all night.

None of which was relevant, because she wasn't going anywhere.

What did the weird anonymous caller know about her, she wondered? Did she not have a reputation for persistence, impertinence, stubbornness – and a few more of such characteristics? The stories that circulated concerning her house-sitting adventures in a dozen different Cotswolds villages all referred to the way she barged in and asked questions and kept the police supplied with vital information.

And why, for heaven's sake, should she care about the ownership of Positano anyway? What difference did it make?

By ten o'clock, her brain was wholly engaged with speculations about Umberto and his family. Over and over again, she assembled everything she had been told about them, arranging and rearranging them into patterns and theories, links and hints that might somehow explain why a young woman of no discernible corruption or immorality should die by extreme violence outside the house in question.

All in vain. The story was too thin, the gaps too numerous, the individuals too shadowy, for anything to emerge by way of a hypothesis. Her final thoughts before sliding into an embarrassingly deep sleep centred on

Stephanie and her enthusiasm for detective work. Was the girl right to infer that somehow Jocasta Kingly was the key to everything? It had been her house, of course, and her intentions about its ownership that were apparently being contested. Great swathes of undiscovered family turbulence were yet to be revealed. If Thea's dreams contained clues to the puzzle, she missed them. They mostly concerned dogs, and telephones and a completely unexpected large ginger cat.

Thursday dawned much as nearly every disappointing June morning had dawned that year – overcast, with a slight breeze and a few defiant birds insisting that it was actually summer, despite appearances to the contrary.

It was half past seven and Thea was thirsty. She made a whole indulgent pot of tea and let the dogs out. Two more days to go. But only one evening, because Umberto was due back in the late afternoon of the next day. It would be strange to see him after what had happened in his absence. And if past experience was anything to go by, there would be further occurrences in the meantime. The air was full of questions, gradually clumping together to form a pattern that might or might not explain the death of Gabriella Milner. Family background still felt important. But there were plenty of other scenarios involving total strangers – which were too frustrating to contemplate. The road rage theory had been pushed aside, but it did retain a degree of credibility. Perhaps less so in the absence of any witnesses coming forward to report a near-collision on the A436, which could have sparked a frenzy of fury on the part of a self-important male person feeling himself humiliated by a young female driver. It would not be the first time. Thea herself had been followed for miles, once or twice, by a hooting flashing car driven by a man consumed with resentment at her driving. On motorways they would overtake after minutes of frustration, revving their engines to an insane level. She always thought it had to be awfully bad for their cars when they did that.

The dogs were as usual, and there was little sign of scratching. Perhaps Umberto kept everything so well fumigated that the beastly little fleas had no chance of surviving for long. Perhaps it had been a false alarm and the salukis were all somehow immune to lasting infestation. Dolly showed a new level of affection, and Thea gave her a special cuddle. They were sweet and easy and Thea knew she should be thankful for this mercy at least. Hepzie was still finding them awkward, however. They seemed to close ranks against her and deliberately exclude her from their games. Like children in a playground, thought Thea. Especially girl children. 'At least you get out to see the world,' she told the spaniel. 'And we'll be going home tomorrow, so just bear with it, okay?'

The borders of the field were starting to look worryingly flimsy after the sinister phone call of the day before. Anybody intent on invasion could quite easily scramble over the fence at almost any point. But first they would have to cross other fields or gardens, belonging to neighbours who might take great exception to trespass. Such an ingress would have to be very carefully planned – and Thea did not have the impression that there was any such intention. The caller had certainly taken pains to alarm and worry her, but the legalistic language had implied something much more civilised than a scramble across fields and over fences to snatch resistant dogs. The dogs, as far as she could tell, were not part of the story at all.

Gladwin arrived at the gate soon after eight-thirty and joined Thea in Umberto's kitchen. With barely a word, she held out a hand for Thea's phone, and listened to the message. And listened to it again. 'Someone wants to stir up trouble,' she concluded. 'But it's not clear why.'

'None of this is exactly clear,' said Thea. 'I keep making all kinds of connections, which are probably completely wrong.'

'Join the club.'

'You didn't find the vehicle, then?'

The detective shook her head. 'The thing is, we could be looking right at it and not be able to prove it's the one we want.'

'Bloodstains? Surely you could prove it was Gabriella's blood?'

'As far as we can work out, there may well not have been any. She was just catapulted into the road, all in a second, and is unlikely to have started bleeding until the car had gone. And even then, her heart would have stopped more or less instantly, so no blood flow to speak of.'

'Spatters?' Thea had watched *Dexter* and knew about spatters.

'Some, but mostly onto her own car and the road, most likely. Unless we minutely examined every silver-coloured four-by-four in the country we'd never find it. A car wash would be more than enough to remove visible traces.'

'And it might not even have been a four-by-four,' Thea said worriedly. 'I'm not sure how reliable I am as a witness.'

'It was. We can tell that much from what we found at the scene.'

'So – this phone message. What do you think?'

'I think we need to get deeper into this family's background. We've been focusing mainly on the boyfriend up to now. His movements aren't totally watertight. He says he left school at four, did a bit of shopping, and was home in Burford by five-thirty. He can't prove the last bit. He tried to call Gabriella sometime after six and twice more in the next half hour. It's technically feasible that he did the deed, in someone else's car. His own motor's a Prius.'

'Any hint as to why he might want her dead?'

'Nothing at all. They seem to have been the perfect couple – which you'd think might be suspicious in itself, but seems not.'

'Stephanie knows him,' said Thea. 'She's at the school where he teaches.'

'Of course she is,' sighed Gladwin. 'Why didn't I cotton on to that?'

'She met Gabriella as well, on a school trip. She feels involved.'

'Uh-oh. What does her father think about that?'

'He's mostly resigned, I suppose. Ever since Christmas, she's been keen to turn detective. Northleach just cemented her interest. She wants to join the police and be another Jessica. Drew's hoping she'll change her mind about that, I'm sure, though he'd never admit it. Everybody knows he's been grooming her to take up as his partner in the funeral business since she was about six months old.'

'And in the end, she'll become a journalist or a market gardener and you'll both be disappointed.'

Thea laughed and reached for her phone. 'So – what about this?' she said again. Gladwin seemed oddly reluctant to stick to the main subject.

'Don't worry – it's brewing in the back of my head. The main question is *why*? Why leave such a message? They'd know you'd take it to the police. So that means it's got to have something to do with Gabriella. It's too much of a coincidence otherwise. They know Umberto's away and you're here.'

'How do they know my phone number?'

'Ah, yes. Basic question.' Gladwin smiled ruefully. 'I almost forgot to wonder about that.'

'I don't give it out much. They must have got it from Umberto. That's all I can think.'

'Isn't it on that old website of yours? Where you advertise as a house-sitter?'

'Yes, but that still says Thea Osborne, who lives in Witney. It's years out of date.'

'And yet there it is. And you've actually only been Slocombe for under two years, if I remember rightly. And you've still got the same phone number.'

'You think they knew Umberto was getting a house-sitter and they googled until they found me? Seems a bit convoluted.'

'Not at all. The work of moments. Now listen. I'm getting some ideas. This is somebody closely connected to the Kingly family, with an axe to grind about the old lady's house going to the wrong person. After all, there were quite a few candidates, weren't there? Shouldn't the place have been sold and the spoils divided equally? Or else Umberto should have bought his sisters out. If he didn't, that gives all three of them reason to be angry.'

'But not with *Gabriella*. Wouldn't it be better to murder Umberto?'

'There must be a whole lot of intervening steps we haven't grasped. And *that*,' she held up a finger to indicate a lightbulb moment 'that must be why they left that message. Somebody has a suspicion, but doesn't dare voice it directly. Plenty of good reasons why that might be so.'

'I bet it's Victor Rider,' said Thea, for no discernible

178

reason. 'The one who wrote the book about the family. He's sure to have a good grasp of how they all relate to each other and who might have it in for Gabriella. But he's married to one of the sisters, so couldn't possibly say anything outright.'

'You've met him?' Gladwin's voice was a trifle faint.

'Yesterday morning. He's Penny's husband. She dominates him, by the look of it. Doesn't let him get a word in. And she doesn't think much of his book, either. That's the impression I got.'

'Okay. Who else?'

'Who else what?'

'Have you met and cast judgement on, and think it might be useful if I interviewed?'

'Nobody I haven't mentioned already. Caz says the whole family has been spoken to by the police, if not exactly questioned. She seemed to think they might feel neglected otherwise. Oh – and we did talk about Clifford Savage, who lives right here. I'm not sure which house it is, though.'

'Who is he?'

'A family friend. Not even that, really. He used to chat to Jocasta on country walks. He teaches at the university in Gloucester. I can't say I liked him very much, but there's nothing to suggest he's a killer.'

'Caz didn't mention him at the briefing.'

'It was only yesterday. Maybe she's planning to speak to him first. Or something.' Thea was beginning to feel she was being relied on just a little too heavily.

She wanted to say something like – have I got to do *all* the work for you? 'I don't know how it works,' she said instead.

'How did you meet him?'

'He came to the gate and introduced himself. That was yesterday, before he went to work. I brought him in and he told me who the people in the photos were. Most of them, anyway.'

'So maybe he's the one who thinks he should have inherited the house because he was nice to the old lady? Did you give him your phone number?'

Thea snorted. 'No, I didn't. He doesn't want the house. He's only here on a temporary contract. I can't see it being him,' she said again. 'Unless there's an awful lot of stuff he wasn't telling me.'

'Which is perfectly possible, surely?'

'Well, yes. But his sister knows Barkley. Did she tell you that?'

Gladwin frowned. 'Really? She should *definitely* have said something, then.'

Thea quailed. 'Am I getting her into trouble? She didn't know until she got his house on Tuesday, doing the door to door. She recognised him from his hair. He's got bright orange hair. And a thick Birmingham accent.'

'Sounds charming,' sniffed Gladwin, still frowning.

'She'll have a good reason for not flagging him up, or whatever you call it. He'll have been in a lecture hall full of students or something, when Gabriella was killed.'

Gladwin nodded. 'I'll ask her. The door to door wasn't

much use, anyway. Half of them didn't have anyone at home.'

'Obviously,' said Thea. 'It's worse than anywhere else I've been in that respect. I mean, most of these villages are dead during the week, but this one is deader than dead.' She giggled at her own words. 'If you see what I mean.'

'You have to wonder what they think they're doing,' Gladwin burst out. 'Hogging all this prime real estate and hardly ever using any of it. There should be a law.'

Thea giggled. 'And you'd be just the one to enforce it.'

'I would,' said the detective fiercely.

'So what happens now? Umberto's back tomorrow and I can go home. I feel completely useless meanwhile. I can't even think of anybody I should barge up to and ask questions.'

'It all comes down to the vehicle,' said Gladwin glumly. 'Without that we've got absolutely no evidence. Don't quote me, but I have a very nasty feeling this is going to be one that got away.'

'Perish the thought,' said Thea sincerely.

Gladwin stayed less than half an hour, pressure of work clearly weighing on her. 'It's not the only thing going on,' she sighed. 'There's yet another of those pop-up brothels to deal with, in Cirencester. If it was up to me, I'd just let them get on with it. I can't see they're hurting anybody. But the neighbours don't like it. Lowers the tone. They all just wish that sort of thing stayed in Gloucester where it belongs.'

'You've got to take me to see one sometime,' said Thea, laughing. 'Preferably before they dismantle everything.'

'It's a lot more ordinary than you might think. Sex is nothing like as glamorous as it used to be. And what we do find is fairly sickening sometimes, I have to admit. I blame the Internet.'

'You just said nobody got hurt.'

'I know I did. I guess there's different sorts of hurt. This latest one sounds fairly innocuous, so far.'

'Well good luck with it,' said Thea with feeling.

The morning had not got much further before Thea's essential nature began to assert itself. Gladwin's pessimism had produced in her a perverse determination to turn over whatever stones she could find in order to identify Gabriella's killer. There were hints and threads and flickering suspicions that she might usefully explore. She wanted to meet with Imogen Peake again and get her talking about the mysterious Christian and Stefan. Imogen had been intriguing and Thea wished she had taken better notice of her. There was also the colourless Jake Milner, brother of the victim and interesting for his very blandness. His appearance so soon after his sister's death now felt peculiar. And again, Thea felt that she could have extracted much more information from him if she'd been in a more alert state. He and Imogen both felt like unfinished business, and the thought of never seeing them again was frustrating.

Besides, following people about and knocking on their doors for no good reason was what she did. She would be disappointed with herself if she gave up on all that now.

It was terrifyingly easy to find people these days. Somebody had said that Imogen Peake worked at a garden centre somewhere in the area and within seconds of some basic googling, Thea found her contact details: more than enough to locate her at any time of day or night, in fact. All Thea needed was the name and address of the garden centre, which came up several times over in answer to the Google call.

'Come on, then,' she said to her spaniel. 'Let's go for a drive.' But first she gathered the salukis and fastened them into their indoor quarters. 'Give me an hour and a half, max,' she told them, scattering a handful of their favourite biscuits randomly into feeding bowls. 'And don't talk to any strangers.'

The garden centre was eight miles away, and considerably smaller than Thea had expected. It had no franchised offshoots selling mowers or wood burners; no 'gift shop' area selling cheap colourful books and jigsaws. There was something slightly ramshackle about it, as if the world had hurtled past it and it had missed its chance to stay abreast of modern ideas. It sold plants of all shapes and sizes, seeds, fertiliser, compost and pots, with outdoor and indoor areas. There was also a small tea room, sharing a space with indoor plants such as coleus, geranium and succulents. Before embarking on a search for Imogen, Thea indulged in a perusal of the wares. There was very little outdoor garden space in their Broad Campden home, since Drew had erected his cool room for the storage of bodies, as well as paving over much of the grass to provide standing for his hearse and other vehicles. But Thea had grown up in a house full of foliage, thanks to her father's interest in unusual plants, and she regularly promised herself to have a go at keeping some herself. When her father had died, many of the plants had quickly followed him, neglected by his widow. Some of his offspring had rescued a few, but with very little long-term success. Thea had a struggling Christmas cactus, which managed a few limp flowers at some point each winter.

So here was a chance to explore options and to ask herself whether she might really make an effort to fill the house with greenery. Stephanie might well possess hidden horticultural talents, given that her mother was so good at it. Besides, now she was here, she really ought to buy something. After ten minutes' browsing, she selected two candidates: a geranium with variegated leaves and a handsome purple coleus that looked reassuringly robust. She remembered that this had been one of her father's favourites, with its vast range of colours and cooperative habits when it came to taking cuttings.

'Is Mrs Peake around?' she asked casually, having paid for her new charges.

'I think so,' came the equally careless reply from the

youth on the till. 'Do you want me to call her?'

'Better just point me in the right direction and I'll go and find her. I just want a quick chat.' His lack of wariness was encouraging, she felt. Imogen had obviously not warned her staff that she did not want to be disturbed.

'Try the office,' he said, pointing to a shed in a corner behind a display of fruit trees. Thea revised her impression of easy accessibility – if Imogen spent her days hidden away down there, she might well not be too pleased at any intrusion. 'If she's not there, have a look in the tea room. She sits in there sometimes.'

The first guess proved to be the right one. The shed was small and far from recent. Its door stood half-open and Thea put her head round it. 'Hello,' she said. 'Remember me?'

The woman looked up and Thea was shocked at her appearance. Her face was grooved and oddly grey in colour. Her thick hair was disarranged, with untidy tufts sticking out over her ears. She showed no sign of having been doing any work. The word *hopelessness* seemed to hover in the air. It dawned on Thea that the boy on the till had been relieved at the prospect of a visitor who might somehow deal with this haggard employer who sat in a shed or a tea room all day. A spectre at the feast, sure to frighten the customers if she decided to show herself.

'You should be at home,' Thea began. 'You need to get some sleep, by the look of you.' Without being invited, she sat down opposite the woman.

Imogen had shown no surprise at being visited like this. She simply shook her head, and muttered, 'Nightmares. It's better when I'm here.'

'I can imagine.' Despite her better feelings, Thea was unable to deflect the thought that this looked a lot like a picture of guilt. Any sane person would suffer terribly after slaughtering a healthy young relative with deliberate malice. It was so axiomatic that Thea sometimes wondered why it wasn't given more prominence in police thinking. Or perhaps it was. What did she know? Nothing except that fictional murderers never seemed to show any traumatic remorse afterwards.

'I mean – *Gabriella*, of all people. I can't get past it. I know she was irritating sometimes, always taking the moral high ground and casting judgements. Just like her mother in that respect. And her grandmother, come to that. But nothing that could possibly warrant *killing* her.' She was addressing the top of her desk, barely glancing at Thea, who was merely serving the purpose of giving an opportunity to voice the thoughts that were obsessing the woman. She could have been anybody. Probably most of her staff had been treated to much the same monologue over the past day or so.

Thea revised her impression of guilt, moving into deeper issues and suspicions. Imogen was hinting at some less-than-perfect family dynamics, echoing the end of Victor Rider's book. Had Gabriella said something that enraged somebody to the point of murder? Not necessarily a relative, who would surely have learnt how to cope with her and shake off her superior opinions about them. Someone she worked with, perhaps? Or . . . it seemed obvious that her boyfriend might be a valid candidate. If Gabriella had told him his faults, pointed out his lack of ethics in some way, might he not have been driven to silence her? The trouble with that was that Stephanie Slocombe was convinced of his impeccable character. Children were poor judges of character, admittedly, but the notion that Stephanie had been in the classroom of a killer was not to be entertained.

All this ran through her head as Imogen kept talking. Then she interrupted, saying, 'My stepdaughter knows Ramon. He's a teacher at her school.'

Imogen stopped in her tracks. 'What?'

Thea said it again.

'He's very popular, I expect. Drives the girls mad with his good looks and romantic accent.'

'Something like that,' Thea agreed with a little frown. 'Although I think it's more that he's a good teacher and keeps them interested.'

Imogen huffed a bitter little laugh. 'I've only met him once or twice. Are you saying I should be feeling sorry for him – that his loss is worse than mine? Or what?'

'Nothing like that. It just seemed rather a coincidence.'

The woman gave Thea the first proper look since she came into the office. 'Who *are* you, exactly? Where do you live? How do you know Umberto? Why are you *here*?'

'I had a phone call yesterday, which wasn't very nice.

187

Threatening, actually. About the house – and the family, at least by implication. I told the police about it.'

'That must have been Stefan,' said Imogen limply. 'What did he say?'

'That the house doesn't belong to Umberto and I'm in a vulnerable situation. Something like that. Is Stefan your son?'

'That's right. He does things like that. Did the person have an Austrian accent?'

'No, not at all. Why should it be him, anyway?'

'He'll have got someone to do it for him. You don't have to worry. Stefan won't hurt you. And don't start thinking he killed Gabriella. Apart from anything else, he's nowhere near clever enough.'

'How old is he?' It was an irrelevant question, but Thea wanted to get some kind of image of this mysterious member of the family, as well as his brother Christian.

'Oh, early forties. I was only eighteen when I had him. I suppose that makes him forty-one, and his brother a year younger.' A strange expression crossed her face – wistful, nostalgic – as if briefly recalling happier times. 'That was another life, another world. I made every imaginable mistake, and the whole family has suffered for it.' The grooves under her eyes visibly deepened.

'It sounds . . . complicated,' said Thea.

'Does it? I must admit I have grown a bit tired of endlessly apologising for what I did. Or didn't, if I'm strictly accurate.'

The flash of defiance gave Thea pause. This woman

had more iron in her soul than was at first apparent. 'Do you see much of them?' she asked.

'Almost nothing. I've got five grandchildren who barely know who I am.'

'And Kirsty's their half-sister?'

'That's it.' Again a vagueness that implied that the whole question was entirely irrelevant. 'She's a lot younger.'

An important question occurred to Thea: 'How would Stefan have got my phone number?'

'Well . . . didn't he use Umberto's landline?'

'No. He called my mobile.'

Again, Imogen shook her heavy head as if to shift some inner sludge. 'Oh, I don't know. Maybe it wasn't him, then. I wouldn't worry about it.'

'So who else could it have been? Why make me the target? I've got nothing to do with anything.'

'For heaven's sake!' Again the flash of steel. 'Don't keep on about it. It could have been someone in the village, who thinks Umberto's got a girlfriend, maybe, with designs on the house. Those people think more of property than anything else. They knew Nonna and probably think the family behaved badly when she died. Something like that.'

It sounded faintly convincing to Thea, who sat back and thought about it. '*Did* the family behave badly?'

'A bit. Penny was noisy at one point. And Kirsty kicked up quite a fuss because she said Nonna had always promised that I could have the house. Trouble is, she never wrote anything down. And she said different things to different people at different times. In the end it was just easier to let Umberto live there with the dogs. He needs it more than the rest of us – though Kirsty wouldn't agree.'

'Why? Does she want it?'

'No – I told you. She thinks it's rightfully mine.' She uttered a sound half-sigh, half-moan. 'And none of it matters a bit, compared to what happened to Gabriella. We're never going to get over it. It'll be the death of me, I can feel it.'

She did look like someone who could die quite soon, Thea realised. 'You do look rather poorly,' she said.

'Oh, well – can't be helped. I expect I'll survive a bit longer yet. I tend to be rather fatalistic about matters of health. I never expected to grow old. I drink, you know.' She gave Thea another rare look, meeting her eye for only the second or third time. 'Enough to shorten my life, I'm told.'

'Oh,' said Thea helplessly. Addiction of any kind alarmed her. She could think of nothing at all to say.

'There it is,' said Imogen in a kind of verbal shrug. 'Now – what else did you come to talk about?'

'I think that's it, really. The phone message was the main thing. It felt very personal and threatening.'

'Poor you.' Thea had no doubt it was meant sarcastically, as was confirmed by the next words: 'An innocent little house-sitter scared by the baddies who thought it was all right to kill a harmless young woman.'

Thea stood up, her heart thundering. A personal attack like this, especially from a woman, was guaranteed to send her reeling. 'Right,' she muttered. 'I'm sorry . . . I'll go . . .'

Outside, she took a few deep breaths. It hadn't been so bad as all that. Imogen had been perfectly civil until that last moment. Sarcasm was not such a crime, anyway. She had probably asked for it, comparing her own little worries to those of a woman crushed under a whole collection of disasters. 'Serves me right,' she muttered, which made her feel better.

A young woman was coming towards her, who she slowly recognised as Kirsty, daughter of Imogen. The recognition was apparently mutual, as Thea received a careless nod. 'Hi,' said the woman. 'It's you again.'

'Your mother's in there,' said Thea superfluously. 'We've just been having a little chat.'

'As you do,' was the odd reply.

Thea was barring the way into the office and held her ground. 'She doesn't look well, actually.'

'I know.' Kirsty Peake did not look too good herself, Thea realised. Pale with shadows under her eyes, she had been moving slowly as if half-asleep. 'It's a horrible time. I've come to take her home. She should never have come into work. I've got two weeks off, and she should too. She can't be doing anything useful in there.'

'You live together, do you?'

'Oh, here we go,' said Kirsty resignedly, which Thea also found odd. 'Mrs Amateur Detective doing her stuff.

Yes, we live together, in Upper Swell, which I'm sure you know is just the other side of Stow. My father left us when I was twelve, and is now somewhere in Cornwall, as far as I know. I never understood why he went – nobody explained anything to me. Usual story, I know. What else can I tell you? You already know Gabriella Milner was my first cousin, two years older than me. We saw quite a lot of each other when we were small. Not so much after that.'

It came out with some force, thrown in Thea's face as if she had pressed a button. She gave a stifled sigh, hoping to convey an artlessness as far as her intentions went. She wanted to make Kirsty feel bad about her aggressive stance, just as she wished she could make Imogen regret her sarcasm. The two assaults had been uncannily similar, at least in their effect: Thea was feeling cowed and wrongly accused of base motives.

'Well,' she said weakly, 'I should be going. Your mother's going to be glad to see you, I'm sure.'

'I'm going to try and make her eat something. She's hardly had anything for days.'

'Oh dear,' said Thea and got out of the way.

She had put the dog in the car along with the plants she had bought, before confronting Imogen. Now she returned to the welcome greeting that Hepzie reliably supplied and started the engine. She was superstitiously determined to fulfil her promise to the salukis, and return within an hour and a half. There was a good ten minutes to spare, if all went smoothly on the drive home.

As she reversed across the modest parking area, another car came in, rather too fast. Automatically, Thea cringed, her subconscious still vividly recalling the fatal impact on Monday. *I'm going to die*, it shrieked, as she jammed on the brakes.

There was never any real risk of a crash. The oncoming car swerved round her and pulled into an empty space with a flourish. It was a medium-sized red saloon of indeterminate make. A Ford at a guess, but Thea was in no mood to worry about its pedigree. She did, however, observe that the registration plate included the letters GNU, which would be difficult to forget.

Without waiting to issue reproaches, since nothing had actually happened, she drove away and was back in Lower Oddington by half past eleven. Everything was as she had left it. She even put the car back in the exact same spot in the street it had been using all week.

Chapter Thirteen

The dogs performed their routine cavorting in the field, with moderate enthusiasm. Thea had the impression that they were all equally weary of the same procedure, day after day. It would come as a welcome change when one of them came into season and got herself mated, she supposed. There would be a litter of adorable little pups joining in the games, at least for a few weeks. She left them to get on with their exercise, after ten minutes of rather forced participation, watching them from the back window of the living room. Without the death just outside the house and the ensuing complexities, she thought she might well have gone crazy with boredom. This was only the fourth day of it and it already seemed like purgatory.

Hepzie shared her restlessness, jumping on and off the sofa, mooching around the kitchen, eyeing the front door with a pathetic optimism. The trip to the forlorn little garden centre had been a sad disappointment to a dog expecting some proper exercise. Her mistress's mood had taken a turn for the worse, too. The salukis were tolerant at best, and hopeless for a proper exchange of canine civilities. They sniffed at Hepzie suspiciously every morning, as if they'd never met her before, and for the rest of the day behaved very much as if she didn't exist. The fact that Thea observed all this and did nothing to help was even more dispiriting. *How much longer is this going to last?* was the question she really wanted to ask.

The pursuit of Imogen Peake had not been in vain, from Thea's point of view. She had learnt a lot, if only she could sort it into a proper shape. And then, from hard facts she could make deductions and theories, which might well begin to form a pattern. Such logical thinking did not come easily to her, unfortunately. She was better at making sudden leaps and guesses, putting herself in the right place at the right moment, and extracting damaging confessions from unsuspecting individuals. At which point the image of Jake Milner floated into her head. The first of the bereaved relatives to approach her, albeit escorted by Barkley, he had left an impression that could well be false. He and Thea had both been functioning below par, knocked sideways by the shock of Gabriella's death. Perhaps a second encounter would throw up very different revelations from the first. Thinking back to Tuesday morning, there were actually no memorable revelations at all. The man was brother to the deceased – he had to know her at least as well as anybody else in her life.

And discovering more about Gabriella felt like a high priority.

But she had no idea of his address, or where he worked, or what his status was in terms of a partner. Even if she did, it would be considerably more difficult to justify descending on him than it had been with Imogen – which in the event had needed no explanation at all.

'Let's ask Caz,' she muttered aloud. Hepzie flattened the tops of her ears in an agreeable doggy smile. It sounded as if they might be going out again, which would suit her very nicely.

Caz answered her phone quickly, but sighed tiredly when Thea broached the subject of having another chat with Jake and therefore needing to know his address. 'I'm really not sure that's a good idea,' she demurred. 'And you definitely can't say it has anything to do with the police.'

'I wasn't going to. It wouldn't be so strange for me to find out how he's doing, would it? He seemed like someone who'd be open to something like that.'

'So when he asks how you knew where to find him, what're you going to say?'

'Um . . . phone book?'

Caz laughed. 'You know better than that, don't pretend you don't. I really can't tell you where he lives. What if he killed his sister, and I send you into his den to get killed as well?'

'He didn't, though – did he?'

'Might have done,' said Caz. 'It could have been just about anybody.'

'No progress on finding the car, then?'

'We're onto the ferries and Shuttle now. Have you any idea how many there are? Channel Islands, various bits of France, Ireland, Isle of Man, Holland – they've all got car ferries going back and forth every day. If I wanted to get my car out of the country without being noticed, that's how I'd do it.'

'Even with broken headlights?'

'Absolutely. It's not a requirement that the thing be in perfect order. Nobody checks. But it might show up on CCTV, which is why we've got a dozen plods trawling through endless hours of the stuff. They'll find it eventually, I suppose.'

'Umberto went on the Shuttle,' said Thea inconsequentially.

'I doubt if that's relevant,' said Caz, before adding, 'Although it might be, I suppose.'

'Haven't you checked his booking and whether he really showed up as scheduled?'

'We have. He was on one that went at something like four o'clock Monday afternoon.'

'And it really was him? He had the right passport, did he?' Thea found herself focusing on precisely how a person might devise a clever scheme whereby it looked as if he was under the English Channel when really he was mowing down a helpless victim in the Cotswolds. 'They do check passports, presumably.'

'Of *course* they do. Haven't you ever been on it?'

'No, actually. I prefer to go on an aeroplane when I leave the country.'

Caz merely tutted impatiently.

'So can I go and see Jake? Just give me a hint as to where I should start to look for him.'

'I can't disclose anyone's address, even to you. See if Umberto has an address book,' came the minimally helpful reply. 'Or see what Google can tell you.'

'All right, then. I'll do that.'

Umberto had no discoverable address book, but he did have a very messy list of phone numbers stuck on the wall by the landline phone. He had printed out a column of names and numbers, down the middle of a sheet of A4, and then scribbled at least as many again on every available inch of blank paper, trying to keep it all vaguely alphabetical. After minutes of close scrutiny, Thea found *Jake M* somewhere in the middle, to the left of the original column. There was a mobile number next to it. Without giving it any further thought, she sent a text to the number.

'Hello, this is Thea at Positano. How are you now? It would be nice to chat a bit more.'

Would he regard that as intrusive, even slightly sinister? That depended, she supposed, on whether he felt guilty. His attitude could be anything from a fierce desire to catch his sister's killer to a terrified paralysis in case he was identified as having done it himself. The

198

latter seemed impossibly unlikely. Jake had been too *limp* to be a murderer. And was there ever a case of a brother hating his sister badly enough to kill her? Undoubtedly there must have been, but Thea couldn't think of one.

Jake replied within moments: 'That'd be great. I'll be with you in 20 mins.'

'Help!' Thea muttered aloud. What had she done? Wasn't there something she should have borne in mind about death and sex? Did Jake think she'd invited him round for a restorative bit of coitus? He was fifteen years younger than her, which might give him pause, but equally well might not.

Or was she being ridiculous?

She could keep him outside, perhaps. Take him for a walk up to the old church, with her dog for good measure. Or sit him out in the field watching the salukis. The weather was barely warm enough for much idle sitting, but it was at least dry. The next rain wasn't due until late afternoon.

Would she have to find him some lunch, was the next worry. Which led to an obvious solution to the various dilemmas. They would walk the half-mile or so to the Horse and Groom in Upper Oddington, find a cosy corner in one of the bars and engage in meaningful dialogue in perfect safety. Again, she reproached herself for entertaining ideas of personal security, with words like 'safe' almost a taboo in her lexicon. When Timmy had once casually stated

'Better safe than sorry', Thea had lectured him on the implications of such a timid attitude. 'Much better take a risk, even if it makes you sorry. Keeping safe is for wimps,' she told him.

After some thought, the little boy had nodded. 'After all, we're all going to die in the end, aren't we?' he said.

'Precisely,' Thea had congratulated him.

'But they say it all the time at school,' he added. 'It's like a sort of *religion*. They would think you're a heretic if they heard you.' Timmy had been watching purportedly educational videos about heretics, somewhere online.

'I'm afraid that might be true,' Thea had sighed.

So now, having allowed herself to worry about an assault from a man who was almost certainly entirely harmless, she gave herself a shake. 'Even so,' she told her dog, 'I think the pub's still a good idea.'

Jake Milner arrived promptly, and she suggested the walk to the neighbouring village and he acquiesced without a murmur. The dog automatically went too. The weather would have graced the middle of March quite adequately, but being June, it was very disappointing. Jake Milner shivered and remarked that he should have brought a coat.

'It's not really that bad,' said Thea bracingly. She was feeling flickers of remorse at having enticed him out for her own not-so-altruistic reasons. 'The pub will be warm, I'm sure.'

He said little as they walked, and winced every time a car went past. The manner of his sister's death had evidently gone deep, imbuing everything with its violence. Thea tried to decide whether this was a sure sign of guilt or innocence, but concluded it could equally well be either. Anyone of even minimal sensitivity would relive the crunching crushing impact of metal on flesh, time and time again for months or years. If he himself had caused it, the reverberations would be immense. If it was no more than imagination, having heard the basic facts, then the wincing would be born of grief and horror and a strong sibling bond. 'You and Gabriella were close, were you?' she asked, sounding fatuous in her own ears.

'About averagely so, I suppose. Nothing special. At least that's what I would have said a week ago. Now I feel as if the person who knows me best has gone, and I'm left all untethered and misunderstood.'

It was a much more lucid reply than she had expected. 'Untethered' she repeated slowly. 'That's a good word to use.'

He threw her a glance that suggested he might feel slightly patronised. 'It's how I feel,' he insisted.

Thea said nothing, giving totally unnecessary attention to her dog for a few seconds.

'Why did you want to see me?' Jake asked, his voice suddenly sharp. 'I thought we were going to have a mutual debriefing session. You asked me how I was, in your text. I'm happy to tell you, but I don't want it to be all about me. You *saw* it, for heaven's sake.'

'Yes I did. But it's hard to explain how it affected me, and how I am now. I can't claim to have lost anything, like you have. I thought I'd cope all right, given that I've been around all sorts of death for a while now. I think for me, it's just shock. Nothing very emotional about it – and it's wearing off already.'

They were walking along a section of road with nothing but grass and trees on either side. Ahead was a bend, beyond which lay the pub. Nobody could hear them, and very little traffic passed by. Talk began to come more easily. 'My main difficulty on Tuesday was *believing* it. That police person was very good about that. She seemed to understand.'

Thea listened hard to every word. There was something about being understood that felt important to the man. 'She's quite special, I think. People like her. *Trust* her, to be more exact. She doesn't seem capable of deception or anything like that.'

'She said she knew you. She said people trust you, as well.'

'Did she?' It had never occurred to Thea to wonder at her own level of trustworthiness. She tucked the thought away for future consideration.

'You sound surprised.'

'Well … it's not something you often hear, I suppose. Anyway,' she changed the subject briskly, 'tell me how your mother's coping. Have you seen her much?' She wanted to add *And what about your father?* And one or two more unacceptably intrusive questions. The hope was that the answers would emerge spontaneously, without direct questioning.

'I saw her one evening. Must have been Tuesday. She's gone all quiet and stiff. They tell me that's not unusual. It's not very helpful, either. I'm assuming she's assessing the way she and Gabriella were with each other and trying to find a way of describing it to herself that doesn't sound too awful.'

'Oh?'

'They never really got on. Gabriella was too intelligent and impatient and *righteous* for poor old Mum. She's a bit dim sometimes. And *not* a person you'd trust with anything important. She loses things and gets things wrong, and tries to get out of pickles by telling very obvious lies. All that made Gabby furious. She'd yell at her to make at least some effort to be a better person. Actually, she seemed to think the whole family lacked moral fibre. She gets it all from our grandmother, of course. I mean got. Past tense.' He sighed.

'Oh?' said Thea again. They were at the pub, walking up the sloping driveway, and past the empty outdoor tables. She hoped the conversation would not be sabotaged by the hassle of choosing a place to sit and ordering some lunch. 'Let's find a quiet corner.'

He followed her and Hepzie into the haphazardly arranged building, and settled without argument into a seat in one of the bars. 'What do you want to drink?' she asked him.

'Beer, I suppose. And a sandwich or something. Let me know what I owe you.'

His passivity was probably the result of shock and grief, Thea guessed; although it might easily be how he always was. It was impossible to know. His descriptions of his sister and mother had been compelling and insightful and Thea was eager for more. There had been all too little information about Gabriella so far. A brother was likely to be an excellent source, if she could keep him on the subject.

She hurried back to him carrying two pints of Doom Bar. Jake drank deeply from his, as if suddenly conscious of dehydration. He exhaled contentedly. 'That's better,' he said.

'Gabriella was younger than you, right?' she prompted.

'Right. Twenty-one months between us. I don't remember a time when we didn't have her. She's always been there to straighten me out.' He looked directly at Thea, who was sitting across the table from him. 'You know the worst thing about all this?' She shook her head. 'The unfinished business. It's as if we were halfway through a conversation, and I had ten crucially important things to say – and now I can't. It's probably the same for Ramon, but he and I never seemed to know how to talk to each other. And her *work*. She was in the middle of translating a book. How can anybody hope to pick that up and finish it now? They'll have to start all over again. And her finances weren't at all straightforward, either. She's been mining bitcoins, for one thing. And getting involved with crowdfunding. I doubt if anybody's ever going to manage to untangle all that.'

'Mining bitcoins?' echoed Thea, who had just about heard those words before, but had no concept of what was involved.

'Don't ask. I expect I'm even more ignorant than you on that subject.' He noticed her expression. 'And no, I don't imagine it has anything to do with her being killed. The police already asked us that.'

'Us?'

'Me and my mother. And presumably Ramon. I got the impression the police don't understand it, either.'

'She sounds as if she was a busy person. Your sister, I mean.'

'She certainly kept herself occupied. She was a sort of hub for the family, keeping in touch with them all and passing news back and forth. Especially fond of Uncle Umberto. Nagging me to find a wife and keep the whole thing going. We're running a bit low on numbers, in her view.'

'I noticed that,' said Thea, thinking of Victor Rider's book.

'Did you?' He frowned. 'Noticed what?'

'That there weren't many in your generation. You and Kirsty, now Gabriella's gone. Is that right?'

'That's what we thought until last year.'

'Christian and Stefan!' Thea remembered. 'Didn't you know about them before that?'

The answer was aborted by the arrival of their

lunch, and Hepzie almost tripping the girl who was carrying the plates. A pickled onion from Thea's ploughman's rolled across the table. Two men came noisily into the bar, followed by a muddy Labrador. Thea forgot her question and Jake did nothing to remind her. 'I could manage another beer, actually,' he said, when the girl asked if she could get them anything else.

It dawned on Thea that he had not yet made any move to pay for his share of the meal, and she wondered what the chances were that he would get round to it. 'We've got a tab,' she told him. Her own beer was still barely touched.

The conversation seemed to have dried up for the moment. They ate in silence until the fresh drink was produced. 'What about your father?' Thea asked suddenly.

Jake looked up. 'What about him?'

'Is he with your mother?'

'Oh – no. Not for ages now. They broke up when I was about twenty. He's got some girlfriend he found on the Internet, who we all pretend doesn't exist. Except Gabriella, who assured us she was perfectly nice. It's always awkward, though, when that sort of thing happens. People don't approve.'

'Do you?'

He grinned, startlingly. 'You have to admit he's done all right for himself. But I know we're not meant to say that. It's beyond my comprehension, to be honest. I can't imagine what she can possibly see in him.'

'She'll be after his money,' said Thea rashly.

'That's what Kirsty says. And my mother, of course. She's got good reason to be outraged, I know. But I'm not so sure. It's lasted quite a while now, and they seem happy enough.'

'And Gabriella liked her.'

He nodded, and gave Thea another close look. This time, she kept her face bland, hiding her suspicions that here could be another clue to why Gabriella had died. She considered Jake's remarks about unfinished business, and how he had already told her about two or three topics on which ongoing discussions might well have been violently interrupted. Had loyalty to the objectionable girlfriend infuriated somebody? Had Gabriella been cheating over the bitcoins? Had she infuriated Ramon somehow? None of these felt especially convincing, but at least there was now a lot more to go on.

'Have you talked about all this to the police?' she asked.

'All what?' He looked genuinely bewildered.

'The family stuff. Your father.'

'I have a bit, as it happens. They just sat there and let me ramble on about cousins and aunts, but I don't think they found it very interesting. I mean – what could it possibly have to do with her being murdered?' He scowled at her as if she'd made an unwarranted accusation.

She shrugged placatingly. 'Good question. They probably automatically want to know as much as possible about her background. It's just part of the normal routine. I expect you were really useful in building up a picture. They can't find anywhere to start the investigation otherwise.'

'They've had three days already. Surely they've made a start by now.'

For the first time she detected a hint of anger. It made her wary. 'Well, yes, they must have. But it's mainly to do with the vehicle, I think. They'll have checked what you all drive and where you all were on Monday.'

He snorted. 'That was just about the first thing they did. My mother was not a bit impressed, I can tell you. She felt they were accusing her of killing her own daughter, just because she said she was lying on the bed reading, and then couldn't remember which book it had been. I mean – after what happened, how could they expect her to?'

Thea cocked her head at him, not daring to ask a direct question.

'And I was driving home. In my small black Ford Focus. I dare say they've found me on some cameras by now.'

He had drained his second beer and was starting to sound slightly slurred. 'I expect they have,' she nodded. 'Are you going to be all right to drive after all that beer? Have you got to be anywhere?'

'Compassionate leave,' he said. 'Two weeks off and whatever day the funeral is.'

'So you don't have to be anywhere.'

'I said I'd go and see Aunt Imogen later on. I saw Aunt Penny one evening. She's actually easier to talk to. Immy's always on the defensive. And Ramon's on leave as well, today and tomorrow. I might pop in. He sounds as if everyone's steering clear of him.'

'He teaches my stepdaughter,' said Thea absently. 'She's very upset on his behalf. She met Gabriella, as well.'

'Small world,' said Jake Milner, equally absently.

'Yes.'

Another silence fell as they each followed their thoughts. Thea was repeating the *small world* remark to herself, wondering how true it was. The Kingly clan made it seem so, clustered as they were in a small area of England. Thea was known to dozens of local people – perhaps hundreds – after her years as a house-sitter and accidental detective. Now she was also the wife of a famed alternative undertaker, her circle of acquaintances had spread even wider. So it was hardly surprising to find that there was a tight network that included the whole Kingly family – as well as her own Stephanie. But there were two notable exceptions, which now came back into view.

'Will Christian and Stefan come to Gabriella's funeral?' she asked.

'What?' Jake's thoughts had evidently not been

209

following the same track. 'I doubt it. Nobody really thinks of them as part of the family, as far as I know. None of us knew they existed until last year.'

'Pardon?' Thea frowned wondering whether she had been particularly dim not to have registered this odd fact earlier.

'No – they were born in Austria and lived there ever since. I don't even know what families they've got, if any. Nobody dares mention them to Aunt Immy. She's ashamed of them, you see.'

'Oh,' said Thea, not at all sure she understood. Her morning conversation came back to her. 'But she talked about them to me only today. There are five grandchildren. She thought Stefan might be the one—' She stopped herself, before revealing the troubling phone message of the day before. There were too many undercurrents swirling about for that to be a sensible idea. 'She said everybody thought she *should* be ashamed of them, but I don't really think she is. I mean – how *could* anybody feel like that about their own children?'

'Hardly children. They must be close to forty.' Jake's thought processes appeared to be slowing, the beer exerting an increasing influence. 'They inhabit a very different world,' he added poetically.

But did they kill Gabriella? Thea wanted to ask. For no logical reason that she could put her finger on, this began to seem a sneakingly credible question. She closed her eyes for a moment, straining to visualise the family tree and all its permutations. 'Did your grandmother never meet them, then?' she wondered.

Jake gave her a weary, bleary look. 'Of course not. As soon as she found out about them, she went berserk at poor Imogen. It was what killed her – getting into such a massive rage.'

Chapter Fourteen

Thea was outside with the dogs when Hepzie barked and she realised there was somebody at the gate. It was Higgins and the time was ten past two. He had missed Jake Milner by about seven minutes. She was shamelessly happy to see him.

'I've been busy,' she reported. 'You can ask me anything about the Kingly family and I bet I'll know the answer.'

'Well, that makes you a better man than I am,' he groaned. 'All we seem to have discovered is what makes of car they all drive.'

'Are you still checking up on the ferries and Shuttle and whatnot?'

He nodded. 'You would not believe how many cars cross the Channel with cracked headlights. There should be a law against it.'

'Cracked? I thought it was smashed to smithereens.'

'Not really. Not past the point where you could make it look reasonably okay with a bit of effort. Even if the actual light doesn't work – and we can't be sure about that – it wouldn't look especially bad. It's June. You can drive all day without needing to use your lights.'

'But most people have them on all the time these days.'

'True. But a lot don't. And Barkley keeps on talking about "hiding in plain sight." We might be looking right at it and never realise.'

Thea had nothing further to suggest where cars were concerned. She found herself preferring not to know the number and position of every CCTV camera in the area, monitoring the movements of every living thing, including the vehicles containing them. It was certain to provoke anxiety or anger or both. Somewhere she felt a sneaking satisfaction at the sheer quantity of work required to trawl through all the footage and find one individual in the great mass of video recording.

But she had underestimated the forces of surveillance.

'Of course, we know the exact time, and direction and general outline of the thing we're looking for,' Higgins went on. 'It must have turned off the main road, probably coming from Stow, but not necessarily. There's a camera two or three miles away that will have caught it if that's right. Coming from Chipping Norton would be more difficult – and going off that way, as well.' He looked at her, as if to assess how much information to disclose. 'And that's the more crucial part – catching it *after* the event, when the light would be broken.'

'When it would be doing its best not to be spotted,' she agreed.

'Exactly. If it went off across country, there'll be nothing to catch it for miles. You could probably get to Birmingham without a camera recording you, if you knew what you were doing.'

Thea tried to conceal how glad this made her feel. It was wrong of her, she supposed, to want life to be harder for the police, and she very much *did* want the murderer to be caught. But somehow the price would be too high, if every mile of every road was under surveillance. What had happened to good old-fashioned detective work, she wondered crossly.

Then Higgins revealed that there *had* been some clever findings in the endless trawl through computer-monitored movements. 'We know that Miss Milner's mother was on holiday in Austria last year, for example,' he said.

'Isn't that where the newfound nephews live?'

'Er . . .' floundered the detective. 'Who?'

'You know. Christian and Stefan. Imogen's sons. Penny's nephews. Gabriella's cousins. Imogen must have had them when she was very young and the family only learnt of their existence last year. They're mentioned in the book.' Too late she remembered that she had not let Gladwin take the book, and she might well have forgotten to include the nephews in her quickly sketched family tree.

Higgins gave her a look from under his unruly hair. He had rather thick eyebrows and a square brow, which made it easy for him to look stern when he wanted to. 'Go on,' he said.

'People keep mentioning them as if they might be important. You know about the phone message I found

214

last night, don't you? I told Gladwin and she popped in this morning to have a listen. When I went to see Imogen later on, I asked her about it, and her first reaction was that it might have been Stefan. It was about the legal ownership of this house. Apparently, Umberto doesn't have any real right to live here. But their mother only died last year, so I suppose that's a bit early to get everything settled.' She was speaking her thoughts almost at random, as new implications dawned. 'It might well not connect to Gabriella at all, but the timing . . . I mean, there has to have been some reason why the person called me. On my mobile,' she remembered. 'That's why Imogen thought it might not be Stefan after all, because he couldn't possibly know my number. Although it is online if you search hard enough.' She chewed her lip thoughtfully. 'I never did understand how people got hold of each other's mobile numbers when there's no proper directory.'

After a valiant effort to listen patiently, Higgins broke. 'Please stop,' he begged her. 'I can't deal with all this, the way you present it. Have you any idea how most witnesses behave? Choking out a few words at a time, needing careful prompting and persistent questions? No? Well . . .' he sighed.

'I'm not exactly a witness though, am I?' she said reasonably. 'I'm your spy, basically. I go where no policeman dares to tread. Today I've been to talk to Imogen at her work, and invited Jake Milner to lunch and let him talk about his sister. That's the same as I always do. All you need to do is let me tell you what I've learnt. Although I must say it does feel a bit as if I'm doing all the work this time.'

'And who's on the agenda for tomorrow?' he asked.

'What? Oh – I don't know. Umberto's due back around five. I know who I *really* want to meet, and that's Theresa. Gabriella's mother. The police have the advantage of me there.'

'Why leave her out?'

'Delicacy, I suppose. She's just lost her daughter. Jake did tell me quite a lot about her,' she reflected thoughtfully. 'I need to think it all through.'

'You need to tell me what he said.'

She shook her head. 'It wouldn't make much sense. I know by now that you have to deal in facts, when it comes down to it. All these undercurrents and tangled relationships just confuse you.'

'Wrong,' he said sharply. 'We are very well aware that it's these tangles that lead to violence, more often than not. We know about simmering resentments and jealousies and damaged reputations. And you know we do.' He scowled at her, and she realised she had taken her teasing much too far.

'Sorry,' she said. 'I got carried away. Maybe we should start back at the beginning.'

'Draw me a diagram, if it helps,' he said. 'It often does when there's a family under investigation.'

She sat back and blinked. For all her ferreting and speculating, she still had no genuine feeling that one of the Kinglys had killed Gabriella. The theories might point that way, and there was obviously no shortage of strong feeling, but that was a long way from actual murder. 'They are under investigation, then, are they?'

'What do you think?' said DI Jeremy Higgins.

'I think it's a horrible idea. What could the poor girl have done to warrant something so horrendous? As Gladwin says, the whole thing seems to have been meticulously planned in advance – which makes it hugely much worse. Imagine that level of hatred – it's terrifying. And then to carry it out, and manage to hide it afterwards. Acting all innocent and grief-stricken.'

Higgins was watching her intently, nodding his encouragement. 'Have you anybody specific in mind?' he asked.

She paused, and frowned. 'Not Jake. Not Imogen. Penny and Kirsty and Victor all seem perfectly ordinary and genuine. Umberto wasn't here and I haven't met Theresa.' She rattled off the names effortlessly, the family tree deeply imprinted on her mind. 'Which only leaves the mysterious Christian and Stefan. If it was family at all, then I think it's got to have been one of them. Or *both* of them together.' She sat up straight. 'What if it was a whole *team* of them? That would make the business with the vehicle much easier.'

Higgins kept on nodding. 'We thought of that,' he said, witheringly. 'And it actually doesn't make it that much easier. The damned thing still has to be *somewhere*. And if you've got more than one killer involved, the chances become very great that one of them will spill the beans. They're hostages to each other for the rest of their lives.'

'I suppose so. But they might not have understood that at the time. Only when it's too late.'

'And you left out the person who's practically at the top of the list.'

'You mean Ramon.' She realised that the boyfriend had been given the all-clear purely because Stephanie knew and liked him. 'He sounds too nice,' she said pathetically.

Higgins snorted, and asked, 'So who *isn't* nice?'

'Nobody, really. I wasn't too keen on Penny Rider. She's very bossy and big-sisterish. Oh – and I've left another person out. That man, Clifford Savage. He actually is a bit suspicious, at least in theory. The way he just turned up yesterday morning and showed off his knowledge of the family. It was a bit peculiar, I suppose, thinking about it. Although it does happen quite often – people showing up to talk to me, I mean. I thought he was just being nosy, or wanted to boast about how well he knows the Kinglys. But he could have been checking to see who was under suspicion, maybe.'

'What did you tell him?'

'I can't remember. It was yesterday. I still wasn't thinking straight. It was quite early in the morning.'

'I assume you reported all this to somebody?'

'I did,' she said firmly. 'I told Barkley the whole thing. She interviewed him when they did the house to house. She knows his sister, as it happens.'

Higgins closed his eyes and let his heavy head droop. 'I have a nasty sensation of going round and round the same circle and not getting anywhere.'

'Well, don't rely on me to set you going in the right direction,' she said tartly. 'It looks as if your only hope is the ferries and whatnot. And even that feels a bit silly. Why would they risk taking the vehicle abroad with broken headlights, when they could simply hide it somewhere and then get it scrapped?'

'There are things you don't know,' he said, to her surprise. 'You must understand we can't tell you every detail of the investigation.'

She digested this with some bitterness. 'So – if it was a member of the family who did it, all you have to do is find out which of them has gone missing while they take the car out of the country.'

He grimaced. 'If only it was that simple.'

'You mean they could have got someone else to take it.'

It was approaching three o'clock and Thea found herself counting the hours until Umberto came back and she could leave the dreary Oddingtons and go home to her family. Admittedly, Broad Campden had its dreary side as well, but at least there were two or three reliable neighbours who would bump into her outside the church and chat for a bit. There was something depressingly lifeless about Lower Oddington, and the atmosphere was only marginally better in its Upper sister. The abandoned church had perhaps cast a pall over the entire settlement, wreaking revenge for the way it had been treated.

Higgins was still watching her, probably wondering at her sudden silence. 'Sorry,' she said. 'I was getting fanciful for a minute. All I want really is to go home.'

'Which is when?'

'I told you – tomorrow. Umberto's due back around five. He's coming on the Shuttle with his van.'

Higgins grimaced again. 'If only we could pin it on him, all our worries would be over. Are you absolutely sure it wasn't his van you saw?'

She didn't dignify this with a reply. It was unworthy of him and he knew it. He sighed. 'Sorry. I think it's all getting to me – the Super's the same. We're all running around like decapitated hens, as Barkley would say.'

Thea laughed and showed him out.

'Only another twenty-four hours,' she muttered to her dog following faithfully at her heels.

She sat with a large mug of tea and reviewed the day, ignoring the pangs of conscience that told her she should be playing with the salukis. Their lack of motivation to exercise themselves was starting to annoy her. If she was Umberto, she'd be tempted to add a small flock of sheep or goats to the field and let the dogs enjoy chasing them around. Although that would probably count as gross cruelty to the ovines. Three dogs in a pack might well opt for actual slaughter.

The conversation with Imogen Peake was fading from her memory, overlaid by the meeting with Jake and the debriefing with Higgins. The whole day felt desperately short of actual facts, and too much loaded with speculation and guesses. Clever police work was doubtless going on, with hints as to some progress concerning movements in and out of the country. But there was a palpable absence of evidence, and with every passing hour the killer was going to cover his tracks more and more successfully. The headlight would be fixed, perhaps by some small Belgian outfit that kept little or no paperwork. If the plan had been to catch a ferry or train out of England on Monday evening, or early Tuesday, they could be in Greece or Poland or somewhere equally remote by now. It was, she suspected, almost entirely hopeless.

She went over what she had learnt about Gabriella, as reported by her brother. A bit of a prig, seemed to sum it up. Had she, then, wounded the sensibilities of her boyfriend? Had he fallen short of her standards and been castigated beyond endurance as a result? Was there some lurking scandal at school that had gone over Stephanie's head? The man sounded dangerously charismatic, with hormonal schoolgirls yearning for him. Had he succumbed to the charms of a nubile sixth-former and brought Gabriella's wrath down on his head as a result? It was a viable theory, without a single shred of supporting evidence. Never having met the man it was futile to speculate further.

Her thoughts went back to the Riders and their

comprehensive family knowledge. Did they have their own suspicions, which they knew better than to voice? Were they even perhaps sure in their own minds who had done the deed but were determined not to betray the person, for reasons of family loyalty? Had they even just possibly had reason to abhor their niece, and devised a watertight plan by which they could dispose of her? Penny Rider struck Thea as a person who might summon the necessary ruthlessness to commit murder by vehicle and then drive off to finish the job by evading detection. Even perhaps doing it all on her own, without her husband knowing a thing about it. His blundering ignorance would create a perfect smokescreen.

Her phone signalled an incoming text from Stephanie, which provided a welcome distraction. 'Mr Rodriguez would like to meet you. I said I'd introduce you. Can we come today? Same time as yesterday?'

Many thoughts ran through Thea's mind in the two seconds after reading this. Had Ramon gone back to work, then? Was there something slightly disconcerting about the 'we'? Who was going to drive? Did Drew know about it? And crowning it all was a sense of excitement and the possibility of real progress towards understanding Gabriella's death better.

She did not reply by text, but made a proper phone call, hoping that Stephanie would be walking home from school and free to talk.

'What's all this then?' she began, when the girl answered.

222

'What do you mean?'

'You and Mr Rodriguez. A lot seems to have happened since yesterday. Was he in school today? Does your father know what you're planning to do?'

Stephanie's sigh was almost palpable down the phone. 'Actually, he went to see Dad and talked to him about you and what happened in Oddington. Then he came to school in the lunch break and found me and told me. He's terribly upset. I said I'd ask you. Satisfied?'

It was a much sharper tone than Thea was used to in her stepdaughter. Somebody had annoyed or unsettled her, and it wasn't clear who. 'Okay. And why didn't Dad call me about it, instead of leaving it up to you?'

'He says it's nothing to do with him. He wasn't very happy about Mr Rodriguez turning up like that.'

'Ah – now I see.' Which she did, very clearly. It was far from the first time that Drew had objected to the amateur detecting that his daughter had suddenly got herself involved in. Since the end of the previous year, Stephanie had intruded into matters that her father believed to be very much too adult for her. In vain, she and Thea had reminded him that he himself had encouraged his daughter to face the realities of death and funerals. It seemed to them a small step from there to addressing the facts around crime, punishment and murder.

'He said all the usual things,' Stephanie went on. 'It's not a game. It could be dangerous. It'll give me all the wrong ideas about human nature. You know how he is.'

Thea was torn. 'Well, he's right, though. You are

awfully young. But I'm more concerned with what your teacher thinks he's doing, dragging you into it.'

'That's not what he did. Somebody else must have told him that you were there at the house, and he just connected the name to me and Dad. It wasn't difficult, was it? He already knew my father was an undertaker, and everybody knows you, and of course he's desperate to find who killed Miss Milner.' She gave an unhappy little laugh. 'I think he might want to kill them, if he can find them. I've never seen him like he is today.'

'Oh dear,' said Thea. 'I hope he didn't tell your father that.'

'No.' The voice brightened. 'But guess what? He says he wants us to do her funeral!! How about that?'

'Gosh,' said Thea faintly. 'That should make Drew happy.'

'It might, but not yet.'

'So, who's bringing you here this afternoon? That's if your father agrees that you can come. It might turn out to be much too grown up for you.'

'Dad won't stop me, but he isn't going to drive us. If you think it's all right, Mr Rodriguez will drive. I'm nearly home now, and if you say it's okay, he can collect me about quarter past four and we can come.'

'Surely your father won't let you do that?'

'He will, though. He says if anything happens to me it'll all be your fault. I think he must have been joking, but he is quite cross.'

'Nothing's going to happen to you,' said Thea heartily.

'But just to be sure, I'm going to call Caz and see if she can bring you both. I know this is the twenty-first century and people don't have chaperones any more, but . . .'

'That's a very good idea,' said Stephanie, with a startling level of relief. 'Let me know what she says.'

'Right. Oh, and give me Ramon's phone number, will you? I think I ought to have it.'

'I'll text it to you,' said the girl patiently. 'Thanks.'

Thea was very impressed with her own quick thinking, when she finished the call. There were incipient transgressions threatening to take place, with a very young girl at the centre of them. There was a real possibility that Ramon Rodriguez was a murderer, who wanted to gain some sort of hold over Thea via her stepdaughter.

Even so, it would not hurt at all to have the steady influence of Caz Barkley as backup.

Chapter Fifteen

Caz was not altogether co-operative when Thea tried to explain the situation. 'I can't just drop everything to act as nursemaid to your girl,' she protested. 'It's hectic here.'

'Think about it,' Thea ordered her. 'This could be the breakthrough. It'll take about an hour and a half, max, for you to do the whole thing. You're safeguarding a potential witness, overseeing a delicate development in the investigation. If you won't do it, I'll ask Gladwin. Or Higgins.'

'Honestly – you act as if the entire police force is at your beck and call. There are protocols, you know. Everything has to be logged, reported, shared with the team. I'll have to keep a record of everywhere I go and who I see and what they say. Nothing's simple.'

'Your phone can do all that for you. I'm assuming Ramon can be in Broad Campden in the next few minutes, so you can pick them up together, bring them here, listen to what he says, and take them back again.'

'It's compromising. I can't have them both in my car. Not with things at the stage they are now. But I can see it

226

might be useful as well. Why don't you tell Mr R. to make his own way to Oddington, and I'll go for Stephanie? That could work. It might even be quicker.' There was a pause. 'Actually – do we really need Stephanie to be there? Isn't she a bit young for all this sort of thing?'

'It was her idea. She really wants to come. I can't be so mean as to stop her now.'

'Well, all right then. From what I know of her, she'll have no great trouble coping with it.'

'Thanks.' Thea's excitement ratcheted up another level. 'You never know – this might resolve the whole case.'

'It won't,' said Barkley flatly. 'I'll see you around five, or a bit before.'

Thea called Ramon, who answered instantly, and agreed to the plan with no discernible hesitation. 'I'm really very grateful,' he said. His Spanish accent made him sound very masculine and not at all like Jake Milner. Thea realised that she had carelessly bracketed the two men together – brother and boyfriend of the deceased, both stricken by grief and perhaps slightly limp as a result. Ramon Rodriguez did not sound the least bit limp.

There was little to do while waiting for the visitors. The salukis had been short-changed all day, but the return of their beloved master was so imminent that it no longer seemed to matter very much. At least, she assumed he was beloved. As a breed these dogs did not appear to be especially demonstrative. If pressed, Thea would

227

put them on the snooty end of the spectrum, a long way from the undignified squirming displays of affection that a spaniel went in for. Their supper would either have to be very early or a bit late, given the timing of Stephanie's invasion – but that too would be readily tolerated. She threw them each a small biscuit to be going on with. And then she stood watching them for a few minutes, noting with mild dismay that Rocket was scratching her neck rather viciously and Dolly was chewing her own tail. 'I'll comb you all later on,' she promised.

Ramon was the first to arrive, walking confidently up to the gate. He had clearly been to the house before, probably several times. He and Gabriella must have been together for a while, then. Which meant that he very likely counted himself as part of the Kingly family. He was tall, with dark brown hair and broad shoulders. His eyes were deep-set and rather close together. Thea tried to grasp what it was about him that had won Stephanie's affection. If she remembered her own schooldays, the favourite teachers were the ones who gave you attention, praise and comprehensible information. Their appearance counted for very little. Perhaps none of that applied here. As far as Thea could recall, Stephanie had barely mentioned this particular teacher until now. There had been some stressing about a Spanish test a week or so ago, which had not felt very important. All this ran through her head as she opened the gate and let him in, having made a big play of gazing down the street in expectation of Barkley's car materialising.

'They'll be here in a minute,' she said. Something about this man made her earlier wariness seem entirely sensible. He did not smile, or even hold out a hand to shake. His eyes were unfocused and his nose looked pink. The air rippled with strong emotion as he headed for the front door, having said nothing at all. Hepzie stood out of his way, abandoning any expectation of being admired or even acknowledged.

The silence was contagious and Thea forbore from making small talk, other than offering a cup of tea. It was twenty to five – her assertion about the others soon arriving had been deliberately exaggerated. It struck her that in her efforts to protect Stephanie she had blundered into placing herself in a very awkward position. Without the girl, Thea and Ramon were in no kind of relationship. This again was entirely different from the way Jake Milner had behaved. There had been an easy assumption as to their reasons for getting together – admittedly facilitated by Barkley. Here on her own with the boyfriend, it was infinitely more difficult.

But Ramon was gathering himself together, with an effort. 'I like this house,' he said. 'Though it was nicer when Nonna was still here.'

For the first time, Thea made the connection between the Italian grandmother and the Spanish boyfriend. Had they shared nostalgic tales of Mediterranean experiences? Unlikely, she decided, when she remembered that Jocasta had lived the great bulk of her life in Gloucestershire.

Even so, there could well have been an affinity between them, surrounded as they were by cool British relatives and neighbours.

'When does Umberto get back?' The question was uttered carelessly, as if the answer mattered not at all.

'Tomorrow. About this time, or a bit later.'

'Right.' He looked at his watch.

'They'll be hitting the traffic,' said Thea, realising that Stephanie's idea of effecting an introduction had been spoilt by the change of plan regarding cars. 'They'll be coming through Stow, I suppose. It can be very slow.' *Slow through Stow*, she repeated stupidly to herself. There was a flickering threat of hysteria somewhere not too far below the surface. *What's the matter with me?* she wondered. Generally, this was what she did best – winning over potential suspects and extracting crucial information from them. This man came with too much emotion, too many possibilities of the wrong sort. He felt like an unexploded bomb sitting on Umberto's chair and staring at her.

'You're Stephanie's stepmother, is that right? What happened to her real mother?'

Thea frowned. Shouldn't he know that already? And why was he asking? What did it have to do with anything? Was he trying to undermine her in some subtle way?

'She died,' she said.

'Ah. Perhaps that explains it.'

'What?'

230

He leant forward and instantly seemed more human. 'Until a few weeks ago she was just another pupil. Nothing special. Average in her work. Quiet. Then she began to attract my attention. We were discussing Spanish culture and got onto the way we do funerals. She told me that her father is a funeral director. Undertaker. The class all knew it already, I think. But Stephanie gained size – I mean *stature*. A good word. Respect and attention. Because she had no anxiety about death as a thing to talk about. But she did not mention her mother.'

Thea listened in silence. What was there to say to this? Why was he telling her about it?

'You might know what they say about the Spanish and death? The bullfight, and fierce fighting. Hemingway. The Civil War.' He cocked his head at her. 'We are supposed to be unusually good at facing up to it. Did you know that?'

'Not really. I never thought about it.'

'Well, it's mostly just a myth, anyway. I don't think human beings face death very well, whoever they are. They just have different ways of deceiving themselves about it.'

Thea felt inadequate. Being married to an undertaker was no help at all at times like this. Ramon's eyes were glittering, the urgency and passion behind his words impossible to ignore. But she found herself no longer nervous of him. He wasn't going to hurt her, and his interest in Stephanie appeared to be reassuringly academic. 'My husband isn't very keen on Stephanie taking an interest in murder,' she said.

'So I understand. I went to see him today, you know.'

'And he wasn't very co-operative, according to Stephanie.'

Ramon shrugged. 'He loosened up after I said I'd like him to do Gabby's funeral.'

Thea felt embarrassed on her husband's behalf. 'I'm sorry about that,' she said. 'He probably didn't understand.' Then she wondered whether Ramon would have the right to decide on the funeral in any case. Perhaps Drew had realised that from the outset. 'You're not actually her next of kin, I assume?'

'That'll be her mother – or father. Both? I don't anticipate any difficulties, either way.'

Thea pulled herself up, and smiled. 'We should probably wait for the others before we say much more. Stephanie's going to be cross if we get everything settled without her.'

'Settled?' He glared at her. 'How do you think that's going to happen?'

'Sorry,' she said again. 'Let me go and make more tea.'

'That's them now,' said Ramon, apparently having detected a car engine from fifty yards away through closed windows. 'Look.'

'So it is,' said Thea, feeling less relief than she might have expected. She went to the gate and almost grabbed the young detective in one hand and Stephanie in the other. 'Was the traffic bad?' she asked.

232

'A bit. It's only just gone five,' said Barkley.

Stephanie went to find her teacher, the others following close behind. Thea watched as the girl went up to Ramon, stopping a foot away from his chair. 'Hello,' she said.

'Hi. We've been talking without you. Your mother thinks you might be angry about that.'

The girl laughed. 'Was it anything important?'

The man gave her a long look and did not answer. Thea interposed quickly. 'We were getting to know each other, that's all.'

Caz Barkley took a place on the sofa, and patted the cushion beside her, inviting Stephanie to take it. 'Settle down,' she said to the room in general. 'What's all this in aid of, anyway?'

'As Mrs Slocombe said – we're getting to know each other,' Ramon replied. 'I think we both felt we were missing something, not having met.'

Caz shook her head slightly. 'I'm not sure I did the right thing, bringing Stephanie here. I got the icy treatment from her father just now.'

'She's the one who links it all together,' said Ramon. 'She had to be here.'

'Actually, I would say it was Miss Milner who did that,' said Caz stoutly. 'Stephanie's just a coincidence.'

'Thanks very much!' said the girl indignantly. Thea understood how she felt – still under the control of adults, who could not always be trusted to do the right thing. The fact that she had been permitted to join this group of adults must seem like a remarkable triumph, that might yet be snatched away.

'What was she like?' Thea interposed again. 'Can you talk about her?'

It seemed to strike all four of them at once that the meeting was oddly artificial, achieved at the cost of Drew's temper and liable to do more harm than good. Even Stephanie faltered. 'I told you that,' she said in a low voice.

'Sweetheart – you only met her once.'

'She was the last person you could think of as a victim,' said Ramon. 'She was strong and certain, knowing her own mind.'

This chimed with what Jake Milner had said, Thea realised. 'Is that why someone killed her, then?' she asked, just as stoutly as Caz. 'She trampled on their feelings?'

'Hardly a motive for murder,' muttered the detective.

'You'd be surprised,' Thea told her, conscious that she had been involved in a lot more murders than the young police officer had. She addressed Ramon. 'Did you know about Christian and Stefan – Imogen's sons?'

'Know about them?' He snorted. 'I've met them. Gabby and I spent last Christmas with them in Innsbruck.'

It felt like a bombshell and the room went quiet. Stephanie wriggled impatiently, wanting an explanation. Barkley took out a notebook and flicked through the pages. Thea simply gazed at the man and tried to insert this revelation into the picture of the family she had constructed. A balance had been set askew somewhere. She was determined to learn more.

'Did the others know about that? Imogen? Umberto? Penny?'

He shook his head. 'Not even Gabriella's mother knew until we came back. But it was all down to her that it happened, really. She found the boys more or less by accident last year, and came home all excited about it. Gabby couldn't wait to tell everyone about it, but her mother swore her to secrecy. That didn't last long, though. Nonna soon got hold of the secret, and the shit hit the fan, as they say so rudely in this country.'

Stephanie giggled. Ramon went on, seeming keen to unburden himself now the dam had been breached. 'Gabby felt we owed her cousins some sort of explanation, I think. But it wasn't very successful. They were pretty frosty with us, to be honest.'

Thea was struggling to calculate the implications. Was it possible that Ramon was playing a complicated game of some kind? It did not feel like that. Rather, he was relieved that Thea had raised the subject of the absent cousins. Quite why she had done that remained obscure. It had suddenly felt as if the only way to cut through the inconsequential chat and make the whole encounter mean something was to address the most mysterious and perhaps even taboo element in the story. But there was ample scope for misunderstanding. Ramon might well have felt that she was trying to take control, manipulating him, or startling him into giving something away. In which case he had certainly called her bluff.

'Okay. What about since then? Christmas was ages ago.' She remembered that it could be helpful to ask *Why now?* in a murder investigation.

Caz Barkley was leaning forward, holding her notebook and opening her mouth as if to speak. But no words emerged. She shut it again. With a minimal gesture she indicated that Thea was welcome to continue the questioning, despite its obvious unorthodoxy.

'I don't know,' said Ramon, slumping back in his chair. 'I had a quarrel with Stefan on our last day and said I agreed with the family that it would have been better if we'd never found out they existed.'

'Who said that?' Somewhere Thea recalled having been told that the grandmother had deeply resented the way these boys had been hidden from her all their lives. 'I thought your Nonna was very upset at having missed seeing them grow up.'

'She was,' said Ramon, sounding more foreign than he had up to then. 'I'm talking more about Penny and Umberto, really. First Nonna was upset, and then when all the trouble began, she was angry. All on the same day – and then she had her stroke. Then another one, which killed her.'

'Trouble?' Caz had come to life at the word. 'When?'

'Well, I was not really involved. Nonna was like Gabriella – they both set high standards for behaviour. And Imogen had not been married to the father of her boys. She had raised them in secret, telling lies and never inviting her family to visit. There was a blazing row about it. Poor Imogen was ostracised. Nobody had any sympathy for her, except Kirsty, of course. Even though she became perfectly respectable after coming back to England and marrying Mr Peake. I never met him, actually.'

'Wait,' begged Thea. 'When did Imogen get married?'

'Oh – many years ago, twenty-five or so. Kirsty was born a few months later. It was a small affair, and the family were annoyed about that – when they realised it was because she was pregnant.' He laughed. 'I suppose that made her all the more determined not to admit to the existence of her sons.'

Caz groaned. Stephanie had given up and was ostentatiously fondling the spaniel which had found its way onto her lap. Thea was positively sparkling at all this new information. 'But it was Theresa who first discovered them?'

'So I understand. I think possibly Umberto knew more than he let on. When Gabriella got to know about it, she wanted to meet them right away. She was very shocked and angry with Imogen, but she was very glad to have more cousins. She told her grandmother about them, because they were always so close and it seemed such a big thing. That was last year. I was away visiting my family in Cadiz. Gabriella was unhappy when I got back, because Nonna did not thank her for what she did. It really stirred things up for everybody.' He spoke almost automatically, revealing facts with no emotion. Thea understood that none of it mattered any more, at least to him.

'Wait,' Thea said again. She looked at Caz. 'This must be it. The motive behind the murder. Something about Christian and Stefan being kept a secret.' She took a deep breath. 'But there are so many people involved, all of them close relatives. Is it possible that one of them could have so brutally slaughtered Gabriella?'

Stephanie looked up, startled by the harsh words. Thea threw her a reassuring smile.

Ramon's face drooped and darkened. 'That's the question that has kept me awake every night since Monday,' he said.

Chapter Sixteen

Barkley finally took charge and got to her feet. 'This has to be part of an official interview,' she asserted. 'Names, dates, *facts*. It all has to be recorded and processed. All we've got so far is a jumble of old history. Arguments happen in every family. It might not have any bearing on the case, once we give it a proper look.'

'What about that phone call?' Thea remembered. 'About who owns this house?'

Ramon frowned and Caz moaned. 'Enough!' said the detective. 'This is not the place for any further talk. It's all speculation and muddle as far as I can see. It needs to be set out logically.'

'It's not really a muddle, though,' said Stephanie softly. 'It's given you something to go on. I mean, you can start your police work on computers and stuff, now you've got all this. Can't you?'

'Out of the mouth of babes,' said Ramon, with a powerfully fond look at his pupil. 'That's my good girl.'

Stephanie blushed. Caz threw sharp looks around. Thea converted her sudden anxiety to more mundane matters. 'I've got to feed those dogs,' she said. 'It's an hour later than their usual time.'

'We'll go,' said Caz, with a face that said *If you think you're busy* . . .

'Thanks for bringing Stephanie. Tell Drew I'll phone him later on and try to mollify him. No harm done, eh Steph?'

The girl rolled her eyes. Thea hoped that did not mean she was being overoptimistic. Quite a lot of the conversation had been unsuitable listening for somebody so young, she supposed. The Spanish teacher hadn't helped, with his implication of a special bond between himself and his pupil. Such relationships were treated with extreme suspicion these days. Caz had been alerted, opening the possibility of further unpleasant scrutiny. The police position was probably that Ramon Rodriguez was still very much a person of interest, playing a clever game involving a profusion of smokescreens and red herrings. Stephanie was his unwitting foil and Thea herself a gullible interloper.

Ramon made for the front door without further ceremony. Thea suspected that he had embarrassed himself as well as Stephanie and was eager to get away. He pulled the door open and stepped out. Only then did he turn back. 'There's one more thing you should know about Gabriella,' he said. 'She was very religious.'

The surprise rendered Thea speechless for ten long seconds. 'So – why are you burying her in Drew's field?' she asked starkly. 'It's unconsecrated ground.'

Behind her, Thea heard Stephanie make a sound rather like *chssk*. She turned round and said 'What? What's wrong with that?'

'Because nothing else would fit,' said Ramon, before Stephanie could reply. 'Her religion was not like most people's. She could never give it a label. I called it Old Testament with overtones of Gaia Theory. She said that was simplistic.' He smiled thinly. 'But she never told me how she wanted her body to be disposed of. She was only twenty-five. A simple grave in a nice field is as good as we can get. Her mother thinks the same.'

'Oh,' said Thea helplessly. 'Okay.'

The dogs were reproachful on the topic of their delayed supper. They gathered around Thea's legs as she scooped food into their bowls. Then they ate voraciously as if the meal was two days late instead of under two hours. None of it made any impression on their temporary minder. Her head was whirling with the avalanche of impressions gained from all the different encounters there had been since breakfast. Names and theories, faces and facts thronged her mind and sparked an endless series of ideas and questions. And still there were gaping holes in the picture. Gabriella's parents for a start. And what would be the precise implications of the discovery of Christian and Stefan, first cousins lurking invisibly in Central Europe? From what she knew of the Kinglys, cousinhood was a big deal. Although . . . she revisited this notion while making herself a much-needed sandwich . . . did Kirsty, Jake and

Gabriella actually see very much of each other? The fact that there were so few of them suggested that they probably did behave more like three siblings, the Milners including Kirsty Peake in their lives. Especially as they all lived near each other. But Kirsty had not acquired new *cousins*, but two half-brothers. Had she always known about them, and been ordered by her mother to say nothing? Did people do that? Would it ever really work, if so?

And Gabriella herself, at last asserting herself as a real individual. Almost she had been characterised as 'difficult'. On reflection, the last-minute revelation of her religious beliefs fitted very well with her moral superiority and judgemental attitudes. Self-confident, sure of her own rightness, ideological, even perhaps insensitive. Not, then, a Quakerish sort of religion, such as still survived – just – in Broad Campden. The image Thea now entertained of Gabriella was more of a warrior queen, battling for her beliefs, lecturing others on the errors of their ways.

Such a person might well be so infuriating that somebody could be tempted to kill her.

Thea spent the next hour on the phone. First, she called Drew, thinking it might be best to speak to him before Stephanie got home. As it was, the girl arrived only five minutes into the conversation. Those minutes were mainly spent in carefully worded expressions of concern, in which both Drew and Thea strove to avoid accusations, whilst feeling hard done by. 'I really don't think you have any need to worry,' Thea repeated. 'Can you explain what it is that most bothers you?'

This was a line that Drew himself sometimes used, when trying to get to the heart of a problem. His response now was stiff and unsatisfactory. 'It's obviously not good for a child her age to be faced with something so unpleasant,' he said. 'That ought not to need saying.'

'I agree it's very unpleasant. But Stephanie got herself involved with no help from me. And once that had happened, I can't see what good it would have done to try and stop her from going further. Besides, Caz was with her.' Thea had been hoping for some acknowledgement that this had been an excellent idea.

'The saintly Caz,' said Drew with a very untypical scorn. 'A little clone of your beloved Gladwin, as far as I can see.'

'They're both very good at their job. They're both *good people*, Drew. You know they are.'

'And they're both stealing my wife and daughter from me,' he said in a low voice.

Her reaction was swift. 'They're not! That's ridiculous.' Then she hesitated. 'Is that how you see it? Really?'

'Can you blame me?'

'Gosh! We can't do this on the phone. I'm coming home tomorrow, don't forget. And I won't be going anywhere again for I don't know how long. There's nothing in the diary.' The empty diary suddenly acquired a bleak aspect. If she wasn't going anywhere, how was she going to spend her time? Being a good wife, as specified by some annoying code of conduct, was a very mixed prospect. Surely she could love Drew, admire him, support him, be a provider of emotional stability to his children and still have some freedom to do her own thing? Against growing evidence, she clung to a belief that there was a 'win-win' solution somewhere.

'My diary is pretty full,' he said, still cool and unyielding.

'And they want you to do the funeral for Gabriella Milner,' she remembered. 'Even though he's just told me she's religious. Ramon, I mean.'

'And you believe him? You really think they'll genuinely want one of my burials? Once they understand what the limitations are, I very much doubt if they'll go through with a funeral here. Besides, it'll be a media circus. There'll be film cameras and all that nonsense. Frankly, I'd rather duck out of that one.'

'Oh.'

'Stephanie's here now. She can tell me all about it – if I let her, that is. I might decide it's best to change the subject.'

'If you do that, you'll be deliberately excluding yourself from something important to her. You might want to think about that.'

'I might want to think about a lot of things,' he said, which coming from him felt like a very alarming threat.

'Talk to her, Drew. Let's make sure we all stay on the same side. You can be nasty to Caz if you want, but don't alienate Stephanie because you're angry with me. You know better than that.'

'I'll see you tomorrow,' he said, rendering Thea thankful that he had the sense not to say anything more. She already knew she herself had said too much.

'Yes. I love you, Drew,' she finished, choking on the words. They did not say them very often, but when they did it very much meant something.

'Hm,' came the grudging response. It was just about enough to give her hope that this latest glitch could be overcome.

The next phone conversation was with Caz Barkley. 'Where are you?' Thea asked.

'Parked in Broad Campden, a hundred yards from your house. What do we make of all that, then?'

'Ramon, you mean?'

'What else? Did you believe him? What was he leaving out? Is any of it getting us any closer to solving the case?'

'Not really for me to say,' Thea objected. 'You're the detective.'

'Don't be like that. You sound like your husband.'

'I've just been talking to him. He's in quite a strop. I think it's because we let Stephanie get involved.'

'Yeah. You can see his point.'

'I told him she'd be fine under your watchful eye.'

'Thanks.'

'Anyway – it never occurred to me not to believe Ramon. Which part do you mean exactly?'

'Most of it. It's more a matter of what he left out. It was a very threadbare story, when you think about it.'

'I haven't had much time to do that. It's been like that all day, one thing after another. I need some peace and quiet to do any proper thinking.'

'Well, I'll report in now, and then go home. We can have a look at those cousins in Austria or wherever it is. First, we need to know their surname . . . I'll get one of the plods to do that. I'm getting a few ideas, actually. Might move things along a bit at tomorrow's briefing. Bit of brainstorming . . .' She was thinking aloud, making no demands on Thea, who listened quietly.

'So – thanks for getting me to come along. You didn't have to do that. I thought it might have an inhibiting effect on the boyfriend, but he didn't seem to care, did he?'

'It was his idea to meet. I'm still not sure what it was he wanted. Oh – and Drew thinks the whole business of him doing Gabriella's funeral was just hot air. Something to get on the right side of him, because of Stephanie.'

'And if *that* was hot air, maybe the rest of it was as well. Maybe he was deliberately setting us chasing after a red herring, to divert attention from himself.'

'Stephanie's going to be terribly upset if it turns out to be him,' Thea worried.

'So is Drew,' said Caz with a little laugh.

Thea was slow to get the meaning of this. 'Why should Drew care?'

'Because he will have entrusted his precious child to

a murderer, however reluctantly. And he'll have to cope with the fallout if she's upset.'

'Except he *didn't* entrust her, did he? We got you to interpose yourself between them.'

'Oh well,' said Caz with an audible shrug. 'This won't get us anywhere. Let's leave it now until after tomorrow's meeting. I'll update you then. Or the uper will. She was saying earlier today that she hasn't seen you for at least a day. She'll be wanting to catch up.'

Thea entertained a vision of the whole police team constructing some sort of flowchart on the wall of their meeting room, full of arrows and question marks and an array of mugshots of the people involved. Was Umberto up there? she wondered. Or anyone she had not yet met or even heard of? Was the killer going to turn out to be a wholly unconnected stranger, after all? Or were they destined never to know – the case permanently unsolved?

It was half past seven, with a good two hours of daylight left. 'Walkies,' she announced to a rapturous Hepzibah. 'We both need to clear our heads. Let's go up to the old church again. We liked it there.'

She let the dog run ahead on the quiet little road that led to nowhere but the church. The sky had brightened gradually during the day, and was now a pearly layer of thin cloud, with a faint pinkness on the western horizon, patchily visible across the fields. The ground around Oddington undulated gently, with a scattering of trees here and there. Around the church the impression of a surviving ancient woodland was strong, but illusory. The big old beech trees were mere vestiges of the forest that must once have been there. Beyond the church, where Hepzie ran ahead and Thea contentedly followed, the band of trees widened slightly, and after a while relaxed its fierce insistence on privacy and actually admitted walkers through a small gate. On a whim, Thea went in and followed a path that looked as if it led somewhere.

There was nobody about and the light was dim under the canopy of spreading branches. The path was clear, and within a few minutes had taken them to the southern edge of the woodland. Stepping out, through another small gateway, the vista suddenly became almost ludicrously open. Great sweeping fields lay before Thea's gaze, with a new-looking roadway bordering them. Not far off was a busy highway, which she could not immediately identify. It seemed to be at the wrong angle to be the A436, but there was nothing else it could be. English roads did not run straight, after all, except where the Roman influence persisted. The sound of traffic came clear across the empty fields.

'This way,' she told the dog, turning to the right. That would take them back to the church along the smart new road that had perhaps until recently been a weed-strewn track inhospitable to ordinary cars. There were new houses, needing better access, and there was something hinting at industry or commerce further down to the left.

Another right turn at the corner of the woodland took them back the way they'd come, before diving into the woods. As they approached the church again, Thea glimpsed the top of a very distinctive head amongst the graves, and paused. There was an equally distinctive voice, and her natural curiosity was engaged. Who was he talking to?

'I can't do that!' The words came clear through the quiet evening. 'It would only lead to more trouble.'

Thea went closer. Cliff Savage was standing a few feet from the church door with his back to her, a phone held to his ear. The next words caught her attention more powerfully. 'You'll have to ask Imogen about that. She's your mother, not mine. Why would I know?'

Another pause while he listened to the person at the other end. 'Well, I can't see you need worry about that. It's been four days now . . . all right, three days . . . but you can tell they're not getting anywhere. But I'm telling you – stop trying to involve me more than I am already. It's never been my battle. I'm starting to think the price is far too high . . . Yes, I know. What's done is done, and it makes me sick . . . All right . . . I suppose so, but the way I feel now I could well be out of here next month and won't be coming back. It isn't worth it.'

Hepzie was still off the lead, and was all too likely to run and greet the man she might regard as a friend after a single encounter. This, Thea realised, would be a bad thing. There were some very alarming implications in what she had overheard and if he became aware that she was there things could get unpleasant. Better to dodge past unobserved, if that could be managed.

'This way,' she hissed at the dog, taking a few steps down the lane, hoping Savage would be too engrossed to notice. But was this the most sensible way to go? The ideal would be to hurry down to the village street and back to Positano, leaving the man in ignorance of her eavesdropping. But she was fatally reluctant to miss any further revelations in the phone conversation – which had not yet finished. Hepzie was looking puzzled, standing a little way further along the lane, close to the gate into the churchyard. Savage still had his back to them, making it reasonably safe to simply jog past and off before he saw them. But still she lingered. If she squatted down, she might safely wait another minute, in the hope of overhearing more incriminating words.

But then a squirrel jumped down from one of the big beech trees, flicked its tail flirtatiously at the spaniel and Hepzie gave loud and joyous chase. The man turned round, and instantly fixed his gaze on Thea, who could not conceal a guilty expression. Neither could Cliff Savage, who took his phone from his ear and looked at it as if trying to pretend he had not known it was in his hand. 'Oh!' he said. 'It's you.' Anger, anxiety, defiance all crossed his face.

'Can't stop,' breathed Thea, and made a show of running after the dog, which had vanished into the forbidden woods. 'Hepzie! Come here!' she called as she ran. If the man came after her, she would keep running and assume her faithful pet would follow. Or so she insisted to herself. But what if Hepzie didn't follow? And how would she get into Umberto's house, once Thea had closed the gate – which had no space through which anything larger than a mouse could pass? And Thea would have to close the gate because she was afraid the Savage man would chase her down and do whatever was necessary to stop her reporting what she had heard. All these worries were confirmed by a loud shout behind her. 'Hey! Come back!' It sounded horribly close.

Then things were further complicated by a sudden howl of pain that could only have come from the dog. Thea veered sharply to the right and was over the fence and into the shadowy wood before anything else entered her conscious mind. 'Where are you?' she shouted, before listening for a response. A whimper came from a point at the far edge of the small patch of trees. Hardly a forest, Thea reminded herself. The whole thing was probably less than fifty yards across. She found the dog thanks to the patch of white on her back. She was sitting on a slight mound, holding up one foot like a cartoon animal. *Trodden on a thorn* was the clear unspoken message. 'Come here,' ordered Thea. 'You idiot. We can't stop here.'

There was no sign or sound of the man. Was he simply waiting for her to go back the way she'd come? Or perhaps sneaking quietly after her, wary of alerting any listening residents – of which there were all too few. Or could it all be over already, with the man giving up and scurrying back to his rented house in the hope she had not heard enough to raise any suspicion? He would try to recall his exact words, and guess what she might make of them. He might consult the person at the other end and take advice. In any event, surely he was most unlikely to try and murder her, even if he was in close touch with Gabriella Milner's killer. That crime had been meticulously planned in advance and was increasingly unlikely to be solved. It would be a very unwise move to whack Umberto's house-sitter on the head without due preparation. Apart from anything else, what would he do with her dog? Nothing felt safe or sensible. There was little prospect of a helpful passer-by and no way of knowing what Savage intended.

Meanwhile, the animal was already having second thoughts about the extent of her injury. Thea fingered the dangling paw and found nothing wrong with it. This had happened before – Hepzie was a first-class wimp. 'Come on,' Thea whispered, and picked her up. 'We're going a different way.'

This felt like a clever strategy until she reached a much higher and stouter fence on the further edge of the wood, with a very well-kept garden on the other side. It was intended to keep deer, people and dogs out. There was barbed wire along the top. Thwarted, Thea followed it for a few yards, the dog under her arm, and came to a high wooden gate with a padlock keeping it closed. It had bars like a field gate. 'I'm climbing over,' she murmured. 'Brace yourself.'

It was awkward but not especially difficult to get halfway up, hoist the dog over the top bar and lower her

252

down the other side, before quickly following. The gate was barely three feet wide, and Thea's foot caught on the top, so she landed in an ungainly heap that caused some concern for her left wrist. 'At least it wasn't my ankle,' she breathed, and headed across the manicured lawn, letting the miraculously healed spaniel follow at her heels.

It was still light, but past most children's bedtime. She recognised the spectacular tree house that she had seen from the lane, but assumed there would be nobody in it. The chances were there was nobody in residence in the main house either. The more pressing issue was whether or not Cliff Savage had worked out where she was. He could very easily be lying in wait for her out in the road. But then she remembered that this property also had a gate, with a keypad and intercom. A smooth metal gate that would be tricky to climb. She was effectively locked in.

At that point a light went on in an upstairs room of the house and she took a deep breath and changed direction.

Chapter Seventeen

Before she could reach the front door of the house, across the enormous garden, her better sense caught up with her. What was she going to say to explain her presence? She was trespassing, with a dog running loose for added insult. Nobody had threatened her and she definitely did not want these unknown neighbours to call the police.

Not that they were even proper neighbours. It was nearly half a mile to Umberto's house from here. But she could *pretend* to be appealing to them, as a way of deterring Savage from doing anything incriminating. She could hide away for a while, until he gave up and left. Assuming, of course, that he had not already done so. He might well be almost home by now, with absolutely no intention of chasing or harming the house-sitter and her dog. There was no hard evidence as to his state of mind, after all.

It was still quite light, except for areas overshadowed by trees. Grabbing the spaniel, who was sulking at having been dropped over a high gate into a strange garden, Thea attached the lead again and crept around the edge of the property, hoping to remain invisible. The room with the light on had its curtains closed and there was no other sign of life. If there were people downstairs, they must be at the back. When she reached the furthest corner, in what she calculated must be the most easterly point, she began to breathe more comfortably. It was even rather good fun. Even better was the moment she came to a wooden fence with a door in it that turned out to be unlocked. Either this was an oversight or the people were on good terms with next door, because she stepped into a neighbouring garden, much smaller and less securely fortified than the first. In moments she had got past this second house, through a perfectly normal little gate and out into the lane that led down to the village street.

There was no sign of Clifford Savage. A car came towards her, slowing slightly, which she took to be a welcome sign. She even waved amicably at the driver, hoping he would remember her. At times like this, a witness could be invaluable. There was no answering wave, which Thea had found to be typical of the Cotswolds, but the purpose had probably been served just the same.

She got back to Positano completely unmolested, and admitted to herself that it had been rather a disappointing little adventure, with hindsight. Her phone was out of charge, so she had to stand by the plug in the kitchen while she called Gladwin. There were, she noted, no missed calls. There were people who would think her criminally negligent not to take the thing with her on a dangerous walk through the backwaters of Lower Oddington.

The danger might have been illusory, but the overheard phone call was not. *Imogen's your mother, not mine* repeated itself so insistently that much of the rest of Savage's words were lost. There had been an obvious reference to the police investigation and a strong implication that he knew the identity of the killer, and had very probably been speaking to him. Gladwin had to know – she should have known half an hour ago.

The detective answered her phone quickly. 'What now?' she snapped.

'Don't be like that. You're going to be extremely pleased with me when you hear what I've got to tell you.'

'Go on, then.'

Thea dispensed with preliminaries about woodlands and churchyards and went directly to the phone conversation. 'Clifford Savage knows who killed Gabriella. I've just heard him on the phone. It's one of Imogen Peake's sons.'

'Ri-i-i-ght,' said Gladwin slowly, but with definite energy. There was even something close to excitement. 'Does he know you heard him?'

It was not the question Thea had expected, but it made her feel nervous. 'Yes.'

'I'd better come, then. Give me twenty minutes. Don't go outside.'

* * *

She spent the next few minutes jotting down all she could remember of what Savage had said, before attending to the dogs and boiling the kettle. The salukis made it plain that this was different from their usual evening routine and were accordingly rather puzzled. Dolly took the role of spokesdog and approached Thea with slowly wagging tail. 'I know,' Thea said. 'It's all at sixes and sevens. But it's too late now for a proper run outside. Go and have a pee and then it'll be bedtime, okay? Daddy's home tomorrow, and everything'll be back to normal.' Or would it? She worried slightly about making false promises, even if it was to a pack of dogs with minimal understanding.

She was by the gate when Gladwin arrived, in contravention of the edict not to go outside. The risk of being shot by Savage felt small enough to manage. He would have to stand where she could see him, and it would be easy to duck behind the copper beech tree. And the chance of his being in possession of a gun felt small enough to ignore. Beyond that, she could not imagine any credible physical danger.

'We're almost there!' Gladwin declared girlishly, the moment they were in the kitchen, before Thea could make her report. 'Higgins thinks we've cracked it, but we're not quite at that stage yet.' She sighed happily. 'This is always the best part – watching the whole picture come together, and ferreting out the evidence.'

Thea felt mildly resentful that progress had been made without her. Looking back over the week, she had to acknowledge that her contribution had been minimal since Monday. All the same, she had been the one to set it all in motion. She also felt amused and affectionate towards a woman who could still relish her work and throw herself into it, after years of experience that must have shown her the very darkest aspects of humanity. 'You'll be the hero of the hour,' she said.

Gladwin grimaced. 'That's a part I really *don't* like. All the media attention. It's been crazy already, and if we charge somebody, it'll only get worse.'

'So you already suspected Stefan, did you?'

Gladwin blinked, and then stared. 'How did you know?'

'It's obvious when you think about it – except, you got there without me telling you about what happened this evening.' She frowned. 'Actually, it's not really at all obvious. But it does confirm what I brought you here to tell you.'

'Um . . . yes.' Gladwin looked very uncertain. 'You heard the man up the road talking on the phone to one of Imogen Peake's sons, implying that he knew the son, whichever one it was, had killed Gabriella and was keeping it a secret from the police.'

'More or less, yes.'

'Meanwhile we have good reason to think it was the woman's son, too. The one called Stefan.'

Thea stared down at the notes she had made. They suddenly seemed much less significant after Gladwin's words. 'Well, it all seems very neat. Did he bring the vehicle over here? Where is it now? What about his brother? And where does Clifford Savage come into it?'

'You're right that it isn't obvious at all. It's taken about a hundred hours on the computer to discover that a left-hand drive Land Rover Discovery came across on the Shuttle on Sunday and went back on Tuesday with a broken headlight and missing wing mirror. Its owner is a Mr Stefan Woltzer from Innsbruck. He is the cousin of the deceased and almost certain to be guilty of her murder.'

Thea felt a powerful sense of anticlimax. Could it possibly all be over and done with so easily? 'What was his motive?' she asked, in a muddled effort to undermine Gladwin's certainty.

'Unclear. Some family stuff, presumably.'

'Where is he now?'

'Back home. The Austrian police are questioning him. He says the car was "borrowed" while he was in England, and he has no idea who took it.'

'But they returned it, with the damage?'

'So he says. Not very credible, you'll agree.' She took a long swig of the coffee Thea had provided, and looked up. Thea was standing across the kitchen table from her, hands on the back of a chair. The detective met her gaze. 'So, tell me more about this phone call.'

'I can't remember many of the exact words. It wouldn't stand up in court. But I imagine you can check the records and find out who he was talking to. It must have been Stefan, surely?'

'Tell me all you can remember.'

'He said "You'll have to ask Imogen. She's your mother not mine". And "Well, it's done now and I feel sick about it". Then he said he was leaving here soon and never coming back. And something about the police investigation not getting anywhere. At least, that's what I took him to be talking about. I don't think he said anything quite as definite as that.'

'Right,' said Gladwin. 'Thanks.'

Thea tried to pin down the precise words she had heard, with little success. Gladwin's apparent unconcern made her feel perversely determined to get it right. 'He definitely said he felt sick.' A thought struck her. 'Oh – do you think he saw what happened on Monday as well – and lied about it? Because he knew the driver and wanted to protect him? It didn't really sound as if he'd helped to plan it or anything like that. But I was scared of him. I ran away.' Again, she felt the sinking awareness that nothing she could offer would look persuasive once dissected by a defence lawyer.

Gladwin nodded. 'That would certainly fit. Higgins is all for hunting down a male conspiracy against Gabriella. He's just been on some sort of awareness course about violence towards women, and now he sees sexism everywhere. Every man is a potential threat to every woman. He even wonders whether the boyfriend might be part of it. And the brother, Christian, I mean, not Jacob.' She shook her head. 'I thought we'd got past that sort of stuff years ago. But now it's back with a vengeance. And of course, much of the time, it's true. I just don't like wholesale generalising.'

'I hope Higgins doesn't suspect Jake Milner,' said Thea with a rush of sympathetic scepticism. 'He said his sister could be annoying.' She hesitated. 'Nearly everyone says that, one way or another.' A sudden flashback to events some years before in Lower Slaughter made her frown. 'You'd have to find an awful lot of evidence to prove it was Stefan in the car.'

Gladwin raised her eyebrows. 'It's his car. They'll be checking it for fingerprints and DNA and so forth as we speak, just to be sure.'

'No, Sonia. It won't do. It feels all wrong.' Thea spoke before she had fully considered her words. They emerged from somewhere too deep for easy access. Something in her gut that warned against easy assumptions.

'What do you mean? You've just provided a gold-plated piece of supporting evidence to what we had already more or less concluded. What's changed your mind?'

The answer came slowly, after a real effort to dredge up the source of her suspicions. 'I don't know exactly. Listen – will you let me go and see the Riders first thing tomorrow? Penny and Victor – remember? I think they were trying to tell me something on Wednesday, and I was too traumatised and dim to get it. That book – I should have let you have it, really. You might have found clues in it. But it's not at all obvious. Not the sort of thing the police could use.'

'You've lost me. You don't need my permission to go and see anybody. You've never bothered about that before.'

'No – but it would help if you could give me their address.' She smiled at her friend, who drained her coffee and got to her feet. 'And if I give you a call, make sure you answer right away.'

'Which takes us back to this Savage person. Higgins is there now, actually, trying to get the truth out of him. That's assuming he went home, of course. He might even have taken him in for formal questioning.'

'Just find out who he was talking to on the phone.'

Gladwin took a deep breath. 'We will, but there are procedures. Sometimes it takes days.'

'Make him hand over the phone, then. Won't it be right there on its screen? The damned things record every move you make, for heaven's sake.'

'True. But don't you think that in his position you might have hidden the damned thing in a tuft of long grass somewhere between here and wherever you heard him talking?'

'I suppose I might,' said Thea submissively.

Before she left, Gladwin had enquired about Drew and gleaned enough to rekindle a worry the detective had felt before. Thea's incorrigible proclivities towards amateur detecting had always sat awkwardly in the middle of her marriage. Drew had seldom welcomed Gladwin into the house, and yet it was a strong relationship, unusual for many reasons, and in need of consideration. 'Whatever happens tomorrow, you have to go home and mend some fences,' Gladwin instructed Thea. 'Anything else would be a betrayal of his patience.'

As always, there were numerous unanswered questions and neglected areas left behind when pressure of work demanded the detective hurry away. The revelation about the car belonging to Stefan Woltzer was huge and probably conclusive, despite Thea's reservations. But was she allowed to tell anybody about it? As she tried to rehearse what she would say to the Riders next day, it instantly became troublesome. As a general rule, what Thea Slocombe knew, everybody knew. Holding back created such complications that she could seldom sustain it for long. But Gladwin would have naturally assumed that the information was highly confidential. Even as a good friend as well as professional police officer, she ought not to have disclosed it. The fact that she had done so told Thea that, in Gladwin's mind, the case was already solved. All that was needed was enough supporting evidence to arrest, extradite and charge the man with murder. First-degree, premeditated and carefully planned murder, at that.

She wondered what had happened to Clifford Savage, purely as a result of the very unlucky – from his point of view – coincidence of Thea overhearing his phone call. She examined her conscience, as well as her memory, in an effort to justify what she had done. Could he possibly have *not* said 'Imogen' but some other name? Could he have been speaking to somebody wholly unconnected with the Kinglys? Perhaps he had been researching a grave, consulting somebody about ancient ancestry or local history. But no – she gave herself a free pass. Nothing he could find in a country churchyard could make him feel sick, or refer to something having occupied three days and got nowhere. Could it? The final reassuring detail concerned his phone. If he claimed to have lost it, or never to have had one, he would be incriminating himself. If he relinquished it calmly, and demonstrated that he had been speaking to a professor of genealogy in Carlisle, he would be in the clear. Simple.

But he had appeared so friendly and uncomplicated on Wednesday. Given what she had now witnessed, all that must have been an act, a deliberate pretence to win her confidence. The seemingly frank disclosures about Jocasta Kingly and her family had been harmless diversions away from the main issue. He had told her nothing she could not have found out for herself, from Rider's book or general chat with members of the family. It gave her a shaky sensation, as if nothing could be relied on. Anybody could tell outright lies, manipulate her and exploit her innate goodwill. It made her feel foolish and gullible.

And she still did not know what might have happened if he had caught her out there by the church, having realised what she had heard. He wasn't very big and showed little sign of physical strength. But Thea was smaller and made no claim at all to powerful muscle. She could run fairly fast, but had very little idea about self-defence. Somehow, it had never been required, regardless of all her encounters with violence. In films the woman poked the attacker's eye out, or kicked him hard in the testicles – or both. Thea could not imagine herself in such a state or terror or fury that she could do either of those things. She didn't even think she could scream very loudly. Her voice was quite deep for a small woman, and the high notes required for a scream eluded her.

Could she assume that he had told the truth about his work and other details when he called in on Wednesday? Did it matter? Was he now in danger of being charged with conspiracy to murder and thereby losing job, self-respect and social status? What had it been about Gabriella Milner that could make such a risk worth taking, if so?

Gladwin's apparent confidence that Savage could be made to talk was unsettling, too. If he was part of a careful plan to kill Gabriella, he would have a persuasive story oven-ready with alibis all in place. If he had driven Stefan Woltzer's murderous vehicle himself, then Thea would never trust another human being. Or so she believed. When she analysed this reaction, she found that it applied to almost everyone she had met in the past three days. Could Jake or Ramon or Victor Rider have done it, any more credibly than Cliff? Possibly Ramon, she conceded, in spite of Stephanie's affection for him. And if the plan had been exceptionally clever, then perhaps Umberto should be added to the list.

It was half past nine and she was still restlessly rerunning every conversation and every random idea that had come to her since Monday. The warbling of her phone took some seconds to penetrate her distracted attention.

'Just confirming timings for tomorrow,' came Umberto's voice, in a jarringly hearty tone. 'Seems I've been missing quite a lot. The story has even hit the headlines in Germany, would you believe?'

'It's been horrible,' she said repressively. 'I haven't seen any news all week. I don't think I could bear to hear what they're saying.'

'It's all been quite sensitively done, actually.' There was a hint of reproach in his voice. 'What *have* you been doing, then?'

'Looking after your dogs, of course,' she shot back. *What do you think?* was swallowed before she could say it. 'And dealing with quite a few visitors, including the police.'

'They haven't caught him, then?'

'Not as far as I know.' She felt no wish to pass on any more information than that. Umberto had removed himself and thereby very probably set the whole series of ghastly events in motion. That had been true of previous cases, at any rate. This time, when she stopped to think about it, might be different. Gabriella had presumably thought her uncle would be at home – or why else would she come calling at his house?

'Oh well. It'll all get sorted eventually,' he said

266

blandly. 'Meanwhile I'm in France tonight, about four hours from Calais. I'm aiming for the Shuttle that goes just after one tomorrow, but I might be a bit earlier or later. They never seem to mind if you use a different one. That should mean I get home something like four or five o'clock, all being well. Can you stay till then?'

'That was the arrangement. Thanks for confirming it all.'

'Listen – I really am sorry you've had such a bad time. You've done a great job, I'm sure. The dogs must be fine, or you'd have told me. I can't wait to see them again.'

'They've missed you. I don't meet all their expectations when it comes to the games. But they seem to be quite well. Eating everything I give them, anyway.'

'I've missed them. I guess I'm going to have to work something out if I intend to keep on doing these trips.'

'It went well, then?'

'It went brilliantly. Beyond my wildest dreams. There's a huge market over here – it'd be a waste not to exploit it. But that would involve a lot more travelling, in the UK as well as Germany.'

Thea was reminded of the fee he was paying her. If he were to sustain that level of outlay, his profits might look a lot less impressive. 'I expect you can work something out,' she said. *Get a wife* was one unspoken suggestion that she knew very well would be an outrageous idea to many people. Even so, she could see it working out pretty well, given the right woman.

'We'll see. I've got a lot to think about. It all got

sidelined last year with my mother and the dogs and everything, but now I have to get my act together, big time.'

Well bully for you, thought Thea as she ended the call. The air of complacency had irritated her. On Tuesday Umberto had expressed horror and grief at the death of his niece. Now it sounded as if he regarded it as little more than a temporary glitch in his life. He had seemed utterly unconcerned as to how the investigation was going, and whether someone he knew might be found guilty of a terrible crime. Finally, having mentally gone through the call again, Thea concluded that he was being deliberately evasive. Had someone from the family alerted him to be careful in what he said? Layer upon layer of loyalty, affection, shared history and secret resentments existed in most families, one way or another. In general, such realities went unmentioned, often forgotten as a result. But Thea had a sense that Jocasta Kingly, powerful matriarch, had exerted control over all her offspring. They had not wanted to let her down and had not dared to neglect her. There were hints that one specific incident had brought a lot of stuff to the surface, and been so shocking that Jocasta had died of it.

And that incident was, as far as Thea could work out, the discovery that her second daughter had given birth to two sons and never told her mother about them.

It was still a very skeletal outline to what must have been a dense and dramatic series of events, dating back forty years, reaching a crescendo last year, and now a stunning climax outside the family home. The inevitable complexities going back so far might never be understood by an outsider. If the police did gather enough evidence for a prosecution, little or none of it would emanate from Imogen's years in exile, which Thea had come to regard as probably the most fascinating chapter in the story.

It therefore made good sense to consult the eldest sister, and discover how much she knew and how much she was willing to divulge.

Chapter Eighteen

Friday started wet and windy. Rain lashed against the bedroom window, which Thea had left open the night before. It came in and made puddles on the sill. In the final moments of a dream, she believed herself to be on a boat of some kind. An open boat that refused to steer. When she opened her eyes it was broad daylight and her phone told her it was six twenty-five. 'Errggh,' she said and got up to close the window. The carpet was wet. 'What happened?' she asked the sky.

No doubt there had been some kind of warning on a forecast somewhere, but she had superstitiously shunned all news media since Tuesday. On that day there had been reporters at the end of the street outside, staring hungrily at the house, and all Thea could think to do was to pretend they weren't there. The police had kept them at a distance, and by the end of the day all but the one TV van had gone away.

The pounding rain felt quite alarming. Would there be floods? Where was the nearest river? Everyone in the area knew that Tewkesbury became an island in weather like this. Tewkesbury was twenty-five miles away, but there was something symbolic about it, with its abbey standing defiantly above the waters.

Closer to home, she would have to take the dogs outside, and then rub them dry when they came in again. If she could force them out at all. She had known dogs who loved getting wet, and others who found it horrifying. She had a suspicion that salukis were in the latter camp. One thing was sure – there would be no elaborate games this morning.

Hepzibah wasted no time in relieving herself on the closest patch of grass she could find and then scampering back indoors. Whatever had happened to the world, she did not like it. 'At least you'll be all right in the car, if I take you with me this morning,' Thea told her. Until that moment she had not given any thought as to what to do with the dog if the weather was uncooperative. The Riders might well not be willing to let her into their house. They had given the impression of not much approving of domestic pets.

There were other dilemmas looming. Should she contact the couple first and warn them of her visit? How could she be sure of finding them at home? Victor was retired, but Penny was very much employed, by her own account. The fact that she had shown up at Positano in the middle of a working Wednesday now struck Thea as incongruous. Gladwin had reluctantly supplied the address in Winchcombe and Thea had been diverted into a stream of fond memories for the unconventional little town with its mismatched buildings and eccentric museum and forgotten to ask for more information.

'Oh well,' she muttered. 'Nothing ventured, as they say.'

The salukis made their morning exercise into quite a drama. Gina stood shivering and wretched in the middle of the field, gazing at Thea in abject horror. Rocket slunk mutinously to the toilet corner, where she performed quickly, and then also stared accusingly at the woman who had permitted this dreadful soaking to take place. Dolly appeared to be on autopilot, her mind a blank. As a breed they obviously had coats designed for the steppes, where it was dry and flat and all you had to do all day was run. There was none of the dense water-resistant pelt found on a Labrador, or the quickly shaken-dry hair of a Jack Russell. These poor things got soaked to the skin, the coats flattened almost to invisibility. Tails and ears drooped pathetically.

There was a pile of dog towels in their room, which Thea used to get the worst of the wet off. The animals were evidently used to this, as they stood patiently, twisting and turning as required, like obedient customers at a poodle parlour. 'Good girls,' Thea murmured every few seconds. Dolly leant against her lovingly, when the drying was finished.

'I must admit I'll miss you,' Thea admitted. 'You haven't been any trouble at all, thank goodness.' There was even a chance that the rain might have washed away any remaining fleas. Wasn't there something about them not liking water?

* * *

She set out westwards for Winchcombe shortly before nine. At the last minute she decided to leave the spaniel behind. 'If you're in the car for ages, you'll steam it all up and make it smell of dog,' she explained.

There was no easy direct way to get there, despite the choice of two different routes. The A436 would be quicker, if only because it involved less hassle in Stow. The last few miles were along one of the more spectacular stretches of road in the region, through Brockhampton and past the sweetly named Humblebee Wood. Not that much of it would be visible through the relentless torrent of water falling from the sky.

She had not been to Winchcombe for quite some time. It was not on the way to anywhere, and there was no compelling attraction to take the children to. It was simply a unique piece of irrational architectural mish-mash, which made her happy just to contemplate. No two buildings were the same, even though they were all joined together in a fantasy terrace along the main street. The roofs were of different heights, the windows of different shapes and sizes. It was as if the only rule applied to the construction of them was that there must be no rule.

The Riders lived in one of these houses, Thea discovered with delight. There had to be something virtuous about people who would choose such a home. Something special and admirable, suggestive of a spirit of fun and adventure. None of which matched her initial impressions of them.

She was ahead of the usual rush of tourists, which meant there was still some parking space to be had. The house was twenty yards away and the rain was still just as heavy. She grabbed a big umbrella from the back seat and opened it. Even such a short distance would be enough to get unacceptably wet without it. Especially as she might have to stand on the doorstep for some time. With an unfamiliar flurry of nerves, she ran along the street, only now remembering why she was here. What was she going to say? The fact that she had done this many times before, labelling herself facetiously as 'She Who Knocks on Doors', there had usually been a somewhat better pretext than she had this time. Or perhaps that had only turned out to be the case with hindsight, because the people behind the doors had generally been remarkably amenable to her visitations.

Victor Rider turned out to be an exception. 'What do *you* want?' he asked starkly, holding the door half-open.

'Just to talk,' she said weakly. Then she squared her shoulders and brandished the dripping umbrella. 'I had a rather unpleasant phone call on Wednesday evening and wondered if I could tell you about it.' It was an unplanned piece of inspiration. Until that moment she had forgotten all about the call. 'It was anonymous,' she added, 'and had to do with the ownership of Umberto's house. The house he lives in,' she corrected herself.

'Sounds like nonsense,' he snapped. But he turned round and called 'Penny!' into the depths of the house. 'Can you come?'

'Just a minute!' came the reply.

Twenty seconds later, the woman appeared, peeling off thin white rubber gloves as she came down the passageway to the front door. There was something clinical about the action, as if she had just performed some sort of operation. 'Oh, it's you,' she said, more with resignation than annoyance. 'I was doing the compost.'

Quite what that entailed, given the weather, Thea was never to discover, but she smiled anyway. 'Sorry to interrupt. Your husband isn't very happy about it, I'm afraid. It's very *wet* out here.'

Victor blustered wordlessly, but Penny gave him a soothing pat. 'Don't you find that men always object to unannounced visitors, as a matter of principle?'

'I suppose they do,' said Thea, smiling even more broadly. The door had opened much wider now and she could see a piece of very old oak furniture halfway down the passage, which suggested both good taste and ample means. 'What a gorgeous chest!' she said, stepping in backwards, closing the brolly on the doorstep. 'Where can I put this?'

'There, look.' Penny indicated a ceramic stand with Chinese figures on it just inside the door. 'How did you find us?' the woman then asked, with a multilevel tone that warned Thea to be wary. She had not prepared for that question. She had not, she now realised, prepared very well at all. All she had intended was to somehow broach the topic of Penny's sister's mysterious sons and the strong possibility that one or both of them had murdered their cousin.

'Oh – Well . . . Um . . .' She found herself unable to admit that the Senior Investigating Officer into Gabriella's murder had given it to her. 'It was in an old phone book at Umberto's.' That was very stupid, she thought, the moment the words were out. There hadn't been proper phone books for years, and even if Umberto had one, the Riders were probably ex-directory.

'Fibber,' said Penny, carelessly. 'I suppose you got it from the police. There's no need to worry about what we might think, you know.'

She had led the way into the front room, which was of no great size, but was immaculately clean and tidy. The furniture was all beautiful, upholstered in Regency patterns and colours. A lot of stripes and fleurs-de-lis. The walls were papered, with clever lighting showing original paintings to best advantage. It all screamed *Money!* loud and clear. 'Was some of this your mother's?' she asked, waving a vague hand.

'What? The furniture and stuff? God, no. At least, not *my* mother's. Victor's family is out of a very different social drawer than mine. Most of this came to us from an aunt of his, if you must know.'

This gave rise to a host of further questions, which Thea firmly set aside. Victor Rider's forbears were not of immediate relevance, as far as she could tell. She focused the bulk of her attention onto Penny Rider's state of mind, which was at best complicated. Victor remained quietly hostile.

'Listen – I have to finish what I've started in the kitchen. It's a lot more important than it sounds. I signed up for some experimental work for the Ministry, which can be done from home. You really don't want to know the details. Give me ten minutes and I'm at your disposal. I can see you think you're owed a bit of consideration, given what you went through on Monday. I don't blame you for that. I also fully understand that you're working with the police and anything we might tell you will be reported within the hour. Which some people might think is an excellent reason for sending you away with nothing said. But, we do want to help get it all resolved if we can. Victor's got work to do upstairs, as well. So we're going to be very rude and leave you in here on your own. I'll bring you some coffee when I'm done.'

'That's all right,' said Thea. 'Serves me right for coming unannounced.'

'That's true,' said Penny and left the room, with her husband trailing after her.

There was no clock in the room, and nothing electronic. Even so, Thea was fairly sure the ten minutes turned out to be closer to twenty. She sat in a deep armchair that was much too comfortable to be genuine Regency. It had a cushion with a hand-embroidered

Jacobean design on it. The fireplace had a tile surround and a mantelpiece that could come from any point in the past two centuries. The tiles were probably genuine William De Morgan, she thought wryly. Two slender pewter candlesticks on the mantelpiece could easily be made by Charles Ashbee, local hero. A hand-knotted rug was spread before the hearth. Sitting quietly, letting her thoughts roam where they liked, she found herself in a timeless limbo where Charles Dickens might walk in, or Beatrice Webb or even John Ruskin. She forgot about murder and relevant questions and whether or not she ought to be taking notes.

When Penny came back, carrying two large mugs of coffee and a jug of milk on a shiny tray that could only be silver, Thea had difficulty in getting back to the present. 'There's something very soothing about this room,' she said.

'We like it.' The woman put her tray on a small mahogany table close to Thea's chair. 'We make a virtue of being as old-fashioned as possible.'

Thea laughed and poured milk into her coffee. It was obviously not the skimmed atrocity that almost everyone used. 'Creamy,' she said.

'We get it straight from the cows. There's a small dairy farm a mile or two away, and we go twice a week.'

'My first husband would approve.'

'But not the second?'

'He wouldn't mind. But it's not something he feels strongly about.'

Penny tossed her head as if to discard irrelevancies. 'You want to know whether I know who killed Gabriella, but you have no real expectation that I'll tell you. Because why would I tell *you* and not the police? All I have are vague and very troubling suspicions. I badly want it not to be somebody in the family, but have to accept the possibility. Do you understand?'

'Perfectly,' said Thea. She stared for a moment at the mug in her hand. It was plain brown earthenware, glazed inside but not out; taller and slimmer than most. A pattern had been worked on the lower half, simple grooves such as might have been used in the Stone Age.

'Local potter,' said Penny. 'So what do you want me to tell you?'

'Why Gabriella? Why now? What's this business of the house and who owns it? And what's Imogen's story?' It came out in a rush, almost without conscious thought, as if pent up to bursting point.

Penny settled herself on a big chaise longue that occupied much of the wall space under the window. Logically it ought to dominate the whole room, but somehow it did not. 'Let's start at the end, then. As you will have read in Victor's book, Imogen produced two sons when she was very young. They're both in their late thirties now. Stefan might even be forty. There's just over a year between them, and they have the same father. Imogen went to work in Austria as a secretary when she was seventeen. She spoke very good German and settled there instantly. Everything about it seemed to suit her, and we hardly saw her for some years. Umberto went to visit, and there were weekly letters between her and our mother. But there was never any mention of the children. Not so much as a hint.'

'Did Umberto know about them?'

'He swears not. He's so unobservant, it's easy to believe him. Even if they were in the house, they could be explained away somehow.'

'What about their father?'

Penny smiled. 'Funnily enough, people seldom ask about him. His name was Philippe, and he was no older than Imogen. They simply set up home together like any normal couple, without bothering to get married. The boys had his surname. He worked as an electrician and everything was peaceful and happy, as far as anyone can tell. It went on like that for years.'

'But Imogen came back here and had Kirsty. The boys must only have been young then.'

'Kirsty never knew she had brothers, until she was in her twenties. Philippe died and his mother grabbed the boys. Imogen didn't have any means of resisting. She was foreign, living with a huge secret, unmarried. And very little money. It was a foregone conclusion that their grandma would take them. Besides, the boys loved her and were glad to go and live with her. She had a big house in Innsbruck at the time. They both became expert skiers, and did well at school. She's dead now, of course.'

'So when Imogen came back, she was – what? – thirty or so? And she met a Mr Peake, right?'

'Martin Peake, yes. He was a fruit farmer near Worcester. She married him and Kirsty was born. Only just in that order, which didn't endear her to our mother, I can tell you.'

'Where is he now?'

'Gone. All part of the collateral damage from last year.'

Thea's head went up. 'Oh?'

'You'll have gathered much of it already, I'm sure. Our mother finally got to hear about Christian and Stefan, was massively hurt and angry, refused to have Imogen anywhere near her, and died very soon afterwards – everybody assumes because of the shock. It's difficult to convey to anybody outside the family how huge a thing it was. She had always been the unquestioned matriarch, involved in every detail of everyone's life. She micro-managed all our lives, ordering the girls about and casting judgement on everything they did. Gabriella never seemed to mind, but Kirsty didn't like it so much. But we never really questioned it. That's what she was like. She lived for the family.'

'It must have shaken you all up horribly when she died, then.'

'Indeed. We all took it for granted she'd live to be a hundred. We put ourselves out for her, with very little complaint. She wasn't a tyrant, you see – not at all. Everything was meant lovingly, even if it was oppressive. We never minded going to stay with her. Has anybody told you about that – the way we went in rotation?'

Thea nodded. 'And it was Umberto's turn when she died, so he just stayed on in the house.'

'Something like that. It was a bit more complicated than that, actually. It's not completely resolved even now.'

'Poor Imogen,' Thea commented, going back to what she suspected was the key subject. 'She must have felt awful.'

'Well, she had Kirsty, of course. They're very bonded. But she lost Martin. He never knew about Philippe and the boys, you see. He felt deeply, incurably betrayed. He walked out one day and never came back.'

'Do they keep in touch now? Christian and Stefan, I mean?'

'Barely. It all feels too late, I think. We get cards at Christmas, and there's some Facebook contact – that sort of thing.'

'So – Kirsty knew about them first. Before your mother or Martin Peake?'

'Apparently. Not before Gabriella, though. It emerged that she'd known for longer than anybody. She must have told Kirsty, and they agreed to keep it a secret from Nonna. They kept it from us all for a while. Even Kirsty's father. That was all part of his hurt feelings.'

'Would Imogen have inherited the house, do you think?'

'What? Oh – probably. Her need was greatest at the time. But of course, the whole family blamed her for my mother's sudden death, and would never have agreed to it.'

Thea closed her eyes, letting the information form pictures and implications, as well as throwing up an endless list of questions. 'So how did your mother find out?' she asked.

'Ah – there you have it. The very nub of the matter. We always assumed it was Theresa, because she'd been on holiday in Austria shortly before and might have somehow worked it out. But she flatly denied it, and we had to believe her in the end.'

'How could she have worked it out? They've got a surname she wouldn't have recognised. Unless one of them's the spitting image of his mother, I suppose.'

'It doesn't really matter,' said Penny tiredly. 'All that fades away in the face of this new horror. It's the final nail in the family coffin. We're destroyed by it, individually and collectively. I wake up in the night and can't begin to get my mind to accept the enormity of it.' She looked into Thea's eyes. 'And you know what? I don't even think it matters very much who did it. If anything, that's going to just make it all worse. It'll raise everybody's worst sides – revenge, mainly, I suppose. An endless feeling of rage and victimhood and helplessness. And Gabriella will still be dead in spite of it all.'

Thea had heard similar sentiments expressed before. 'I think the uncertainty would be harder and harder to bear, as time went on,' she offered. 'Like when a person goes missing and you never see them again and never have any idea what happened to them.'

Penny shook her head. 'It's not at all like that. We know exactly what happened.' She looked as if she might say more, but clamped her mouth shut instead.

'How did *you* feel when you heard about your unknown nephews?' This, Thea felt sure, remained a crucial element in the picture. 'Were you angry with Imogen?'

'Of course I was. It was unforgivable to deprive Nonna of two grandchildren. Boys, at that. She was forever bemoaning the fact that we'd been such poor breeders, annoyed with me and Victor for being childless.'

Thea smiled. 'I stopped at one. But my sisters had eight between them.'

'Good God.'

'Imogen?' Thea prompted. 'From what I can understand, she was in a pretty impossible situation. Your mother would have deplored the fact that she wasn't married to the boys' father, wouldn't she? She might well have cut them off, even if she'd known about them.'

'That's what Imogen tried to tell her. It just made the whole thing worse. My mother was not a very rational person, I have to admit. She was very good at rewriting history, and very bad at understanding herself. Victor always said she had power without responsibility. We all turned ourselves inside out trying to please her, never knowing for sure how she would take anything. She was impossibly inconsistent about most subjects. But I think she's right about those boys. I think she would have accepted them as lovingly as she did the others. They were the first grandchildren. Her husband had died. She could have gone out there to live near them. Everything would probably have been completely different.' She gazed at the tiled fireplace, following her train of thought. 'And Imogen might well have got the house.'

It was a leap that caught Thea unawares. 'Oh! I haven't told you about the phone message I got on Wednesday. Imogen thought at first it must have come from Stefan.' She went on to explain what had happened. 'But how could he have got my number?'

'And why should he?' Penny seemed confused. 'You've seen Imogen?'

'Yes. Twice. And Kirsty. I've seen the whole family except for Theresa.'

'How is she?'

'You mean Imogen? I would say she's struggling. Haven't you seen her yourself?'

Penny's face went hard. 'I have not seen her since last summer – at our mother's funeral. And then I refused to speak to her. I thought you would have understood by now – this whole ghastly mess is completely Imogen's fault. She is the bad apple in our generation. And it seems obvious that somebody thought Gabriella was the equivalent in hers.'

Thea realised that she was outstaying the grudging welcome, and got up to go. She was pleased with herself for withholding any privileged information concerning the police investigation. There was no danger of the Riders learning from her that Stefan was currently the prime suspect.

Chapter Nineteen

It was a quarter to eleven when Thea started the drive back to Lower Oddington, which felt impossibly early, given how much she had done already that day. The rain was easing off as she drove, with patches of blue visible in the western sky. She decided to vary the route by going back via the B4077, which was a road she knew quite well. It passed through areas where she had done a lot of house-sitting before she met Drew. The Cotswolds were gradually dividing into smaller regions, representing many different experiences and periods of her life. Over less than five years she had progressed from tormented recent widow, via girlfriend of a senior police officer, to wife of an undertaker. Throughout it all she had been accompanied by the spaniel and dogged by sudden violent deaths. She had become friendly with Gladwin, Barkley and Higgins, and had evolved an increasingly critical opinion of the whole area. Its beauty was obvious, but beneath it lay something much darker, based mainly on material wealth. And yet it took no more than a cursory glance at history to see that this had been true for centuries – and that the beauty relied quite heavily on the affluence.

Drew's ideological business of offering 'authentic' funerals that did no harm to the environment was a precious antidote to much that was wrong. The theory behind it all was beyond reproach and Thea embraced it without a single reservation. Only when it came to the actual in-your-face detail did she wince at times. She had intended to work at his side, arranging the burials and dealing with the bereaved families – only to discover that she was not very good at it. After one agonising incident, where the business was taken elsewhere, thanks to Thea's clumsy handling, she had lost her nerve completely and refused to try again. Despite Drew's insistence that such things happened even to him, and it was no reason to give up, she kept herself as clear of the undertaking as she could.

Now Stephanie was growing up so rapidly, it was becoming increasingly credible that she would take on much of the role that Thea had rejected. Already she was allowed to take the initial call from the family, in busy times. She had spent much of her preschool years in Drew's office, listening to the stories about death and loss and grief as she played quietly in a corner. She had seen her own mother die, and mused unflinchingly on the immense implications of death in all its forms.

Which left Timmy, Drew's younger child, bewildered and unsatisfied. For him death had been a perpetual disaster, a mystery and a frustration. Thea was nice to him, encouraging his interests, listening to his lesser worries, but she could do nothing to assuage his monumental loss. Timmy would never become an undertaker – more likely, said Drew, he would be an actor or an aeroplane pilot. Something that took you away from yourself. Thea had to agree.

She passed the turning to Temple Guiting, and carried on towards the Swells, which were close to Lower Slaughter. She had walked from one to the other, a time or two. She knew how the footpaths worked, linking the ancient settlements together in ways that were not always obvious from the map.

It was odd being alone in the car. Hepzibah was almost always on the passenger seat, patiently curled up, showing no curiosity about where they were going. It made her feel guilty at abandoning her pet, but also free to go into places where dogs were not allowed. And it reminded her that in a few more hours she would be driving them both back to Broad Campden, where normal life would be resumed and murder might be pushed to one side.

Which, she admitted to herself, as she came closer to Upper Swell and its twisty little bridge, was what she was doing already. She was resisting the nagging knowledge that Penny Rider had been trying to tell her something without putting it into incriminating words. The family was full of rage, hurt feelings, resentments and perhaps jealousies. That a young member of it had been viciously killed had somehow arisen from all these horrible emotions. It *could* have been Stefan, just as it could have been Ramon or even Jake, but none of them carried any real conviction in Thea's mind. Why would any of them do it?

There was a dawning answer to that question, which Penny had almost supplied. In fact, Thea had seen it sitting at the back of her eyes, too awful to be spoken. Nothing more than an idea, born of illogical leaps with no evidence whatever behind them. Nothing had been said to give the idea substance. Any hints were too remote and misty to grasp.

Imogen was accused of being a 'bad apple', which felt deeply unfair. The woman had struggled all her life, with much of it going wrong, repeatedly. Thea felt more and more sorry for her as she reran the story.

Upper Swell was right on the road, causing traffic to slow down for the much-photographed old bridge. Thea had a feeling that nobody objected to this impediment, since it gave drivers and passengers a chance to admire the glory of their surroundings. Gorgeous Cotswold stone houses, a well-behaved river, trees – all perfectly arranged to please the human eye. But as Thea slowed down behind a big blue van, she observed a tableau half-hidden by the large tree growing on the right-hand side of the road, adjacent to the bridge.

A woman was sitting on the ground, with another woman leaning over her apparently shouting. There was no overt sign of serious distress; no necessity for anybody to stop and offer help, apart from the odd place they had chosen to occupy in very damp conditions, and yet Thea could see there was trouble of some kind. Her special insight was due to the fact that she knew both the people.

She had to drive another hundred yards or more before she could get the car off the road. Then she walked back to where Imogen and Kirsty Peake had not changed position. Walking along the road was hazardous, and Thea was glad the bridge and the subsequent bends forced everything to slow down. She trotted the final yards and jumped onto the slight bank under the tree. 'Hello,' she said. 'What's the matter?'

Kirsty gave her a look that plainly said *Mind your own business*. She looked down at her mother with exasperation. 'For God's sake get up, will you? This is ridiculous.'

'Not until you stop shouting at me,' said Imogen. 'I can't take any more of it.'

'But it's all for your own good, you fool. Don't go dotty on me now. Just come back to the house before more people start interfering.'

'Is she ill?' asked Thea.

'You may well ask. She's not eating or sleeping. Won't talk to anybody. It's driving me mad.'

The tone was impatient, but worried. There was no anger directed towards Imogen that Thea could detect. The consistent impression she had formed of these two was of a genuinely devoted daughter, wanting whatever was best for her parent. 'Where's the house?' she asked.

'Over there.' Kirsty waved vaguely to the west, on the further side of the bridge. 'I don't know where she thought she was going. She's soaking wet, look.'

At some point, Thea had been grudgingly accepted, despite the rude remark about interference. 'I can't leave my car where it is for long,' she said. 'It's in somebody's gateway.'

'Who's asking you to?'

'I don't think you can get her back on your own, if she doesn't want to go. How about getting her into the car? It's only just down there, look.'

'How? We'll have to stop the traffic.'

'So what? Listen – I'll turn round and bring it up here, and we can bundle her in and drive you home. It'll only take a minute.'

'Bundle?' said Imogen. 'Now I'm a bundle, am I?' She laughed. 'Might as well be that as anything else, I suppose.'

'Will you do it, Ma? Get out of the wet and talk everything through. I still don't know where you thought you were going.'

'I was looking for a place to drown myself,' said Imogen flatly.

Thea's plan worked reasonably well. Imogen seemed to be close to hysteria, finding everything impossibly funny, whilst at the same time insisting she'd be better off dead. Traffic waited with a fair degree of patience as the three of them scrambled into Thea's car. 'Where now?' she asked.

'Next left. Then about a quarter of a mile,' Kirsty instructed.

There were puddles along the small road they drove down, but the sky had become much lighter in the past half-hour. 'Didn't it rain!' said Thea. 'Look at how wet everything is.'

'Including me,' said Imogen. She and her daughter were both in the back. 'That's what gave me the idea, you see. I thought the river would be nice and deep.'

'Stupid,' muttered Kirsty. 'First thing I do when I've got you dry is to book us a holiday. You'll go completely round the bend if you stay here any longer. Somewhere hot like Turkey.'

'Pish!' said Imogen. 'We can't go anywhere, can we? We'll miss Gabriella's funeral if we do. And we haven't got any money, remember.'

'Here. It's here,' said Kirsty, to Thea. She leant over the seat and pointed to a small track on the right. 'Go in there. We're on the left.'

The property she was pointing to was a low single-storey building that made Thea think of little houses on American prairies. It was only one or two steps up from a wartime prefab, as far as she could see. 'An ill-favoured thing, but our own,' said Imogen with a snort of laughter. 'It was all I could afford when Peake Esquire walked off with all the cash.'

'It's only temporary,' said Kirsty quickly. 'I'm going to get a mortgage on a proper house, when I've finished my course.'

'Tell that to the marines,' scoffed Imogen, causing Thea to seriously wonder about her mental state. Hysteria seemed too mild a word for it. She wondered whether she ought to offer to call somebody, although she had no idea who. The only person she wanted to talk to was Gladwin.

'Course?' she echoed.

'Operating drones,' came the terse reply. 'It's going to be very lucrative.'

293

'I'm sure,' said Thea faintly.

They were all out of the car and walking up a weedy path to the house. 'There's two acres of land with it, you know,' Imogen informed Thea. 'All that scrubby stuff over there is ours.'

The land in question had two vehicles sitting on it. One was a sturdy Volvo of considerable age, and the other was a medium-sized red saloon, with a registration plate clearly reading CV55 GNU.

'Whose car is that?' Thea asked.

'Which one?'

'The red one. I've seen it before.' She frowned in puzzlement. It could not have been Kirsty driving it at the garden centre when it almost hit Thea, because she had already arrived, and was in her mother's office. So how had she got there if not in the car? Or . . . her thought processes moved slowly . . . perhaps there had been a second person with her, who for some odd reason was driving the car around the lanes and car park. That was possible, if bizarre.

'Mine of course,' said Kirsty with an exaggerated sigh. 'And before you ask, yes the police have checked it out, the same as Ma's Volvo and every vehicle belonging to every member of the family.'

'Right,' said Thea, bracing herself. 'The thing is – I saw it yesterday at the garden centre. It nearly crashed into me. But you were in the office, so it can't have been you driving it.'

'That'd be Cliff,' said Kirsty with a glance at her mother. 'It's all perfectly simple. I don't know why you think it matters. Everyone's so *suspicious* these days. Eh, Ma?'

Imogen met her daughter's eyes. 'With good reason, if you ask me.'

Kirsty flushed and opened the front door. It had not been locked. Thea lingered on the threshold. 'You don't need me any more,' she said.

'We're in no fit state for company,' Imogen agreed. 'It looks as if I'm to be stripped naked and plunged into a hot bath.'

'That's right,' said Kirsty. 'But just for the record – when I went to the garden centre yesterday, it was because one of the staff had phoned me and said they thought my mother ought to be taken home. That meant there would be two cars, and I thought she would probably need me to drive her. She's fairly erratic at the best of times when it comes to driving. So I asked Cliff to come with me, and drive one of the cars back here. My guess is that he forgot something, which is when you saw him. Does all that make sense to you?' Her expression was of challenge and annoyance.

'Of course,' said Thea, thinking it very strange – and probably significant – that she had failed to notice Cliff Savage's orange hair as he drove towards her.

'So – thanks for the lift. We'll be fine now,' said Kirsty.

Thea looked at Imogen who was leaning against the wall inside the front door. From what she could see of the interior, it was drab, dark and dingy. About as far from stereotypical Cotswolds as it was possible to be. Also, a very long way from the affluent comfort of the Riders, or the cheerful carelessness of Umberto. 'She does look ill,' she said. 'Perhaps you should call a doctor.'

'She *is* ill. She's got leukaemia, if you must know,' said Kirsty. 'Which some of us think was made a lot worse by what happened last year.' And she took hold of her mother's arm and started propelling her further into the house. Thea departed with a very great deal to think about.

Gladwin answered only slightly less promptly than Thea would have wished. 'We're gearing up to arrest Stefan Woltzer and get him extradited,' was the opening remark. 'Unless you can provide cast-iron reasons why we shouldn't.'

'Yet again you're putting too much onto me,' Thea objected. 'But I have learnt a lot this morning. It just needs to be laid out logically—'

'There's no time for that,' Gladwin interrupted. 'This is just about the most high-profile murder I've had to deal with, and everything's got to be done yesterday. If we get it wrong we're in trouble, but at least it'd show we'd been making an effort. We can't go dithering about with vague stories about the grandmother's inheritance, or whatever it is.'

'I think it is that, actually. In some sort of a way. But I can't work out why it was Gabriella who was killed. Which I can see is fairly basic to the whole business.'

'Did you ask them about Stefan?'

'He was barely even mentioned, except for the stuff we already know. Listen, Sonya. I think it might well have been Stefan, but there are some things that don't fit. Kirsty's mother has got leukaemia. Kirsty's very pally with Cliff Savage. He drives her car. Or he did yesterday. That phone call I heard. And the message left on my mobile about the house. Penny Rider told me a whole lot about the history – which all came to a head last year. It's all in a horrible jumble in my head, but I think everything's there if I can just sort it out. And I also think that Penny Rider knows who did it and why. She was trying to tell me without involving herself too deeply. Everything was in code and I haven't deciphered it yet.'

'Okay, but as I said . . .' Gladwin tailed off as another voice came down the phone, distracting her. 'Right. Yes . . . All *right*,' she said to the other person. To Thea she said, 'You heard that? I've got to go. Sorry. We're fighting a losing battle with the bureaucracy here. Why don't you sit down with some paper and pencil and figure out the logic? But don't forget I need hard evidence. We're past the point of examining theories and speculating about motives. We've got the car, remember. And the car is ninety-nine per cent of the whole case.'

'I know,' said Thea.

'So, short of a very persuasive confession from someone else, I'm sticking with Stefan Woltzer. Damaged car the size and colour you witnessed, in the country on the day in question, its owner closely linked to the deceased – that's more than enough in itself. You can go home in the knowledge that your work is done. Have a think about motive, if you like, but the rest is pretty much sorted.'

'I know,' said Thea again. 'But it's wrong.'

Chapter Twenty

It was approaching midday and the dogs needed and deserved a last prolonged session in the garden. The grass was still wet, but the air was fresh and sweet-smelling and reasonably mild. The world looked very green and young. 'Come on, you lot. Time for some games,' Thea ordered. Everyone trooped outside and spent a whole forty minutes in an exhausting succession of games. Hepzie joined in once or twice, but mostly employed the time with sniffing idly around the bottom of the fence at the end of the field.

There was little opportunity for logical thinking, but nothing would prevent connections and images and forgotten details from swirling around in her head. Gabriella Milner's face came back to her. A pleasant collection of features: large eyes, small nose, broad cheeks along the same sort of lines as those of her uncle Umberto. Short, thick hair, nicely cut. And a mouth that Thea could almost swear was just beginning to smile in that last tiny second. The car had been left-hand drive – did that make any meaningful difference? The driver would be closer, easier to see as the vehicle rushed towards Gabriella and her Skoda. Would Gabriella smile at a scarcely known cousin? One whose existence had caused the death of her grandmother? Had it not been a smile after all, then?

People drove other people's vehicles. Clifford Savage, for one. The man who knew the family very well. He had revealed as much to Thea on Wednesday, and again on Thursday in his overheard phone call. He might well have been aiding and abetting the killing, despite finding it 'sickening'. He had kept silent about it – although Thea had not been told any outcome from his more rigorous police interview the evening before. Perhaps he could provide useful evidence again Stefan— 'Rocket! Come back here!' she called, as the dog suddenly hurtled down the field towards the spaniel. 'You're meant to be racing against Gina.'

But the saluki ignored the call and charged straight into the unsuspecting Hepzibah. Both animals ended up rolling in a tangled heap, uttering alarming snarls and squeals. Thea ran down to separate them, but not before the larger dog had torn a flap from the smaller one's ear. 'What did you do that for?' Thea demanded in total outrage. Answer came there none. Hepzie whimpered and blood dripped onto the ground. A spaniel's ear was a famously vulnerable thing. In America, they cut them short. In Hepzie's case, this was not the first time something like this had happened. 'It's okay,' Thea crooned. 'You won't die.' In fact, she could already see that it was probably going to be possible to get the damage reversed, with the right equipment. She carried her pet back to the house, leaving the salukis to their own devices. 'What did you *say* to her?' Thea wondered. She had not noticed any remotely provoking behaviour that had caused Rocket to act as she did. 'She must be psychotic,' she concluded.

There was a first-aid box in the dogs' quarters, which Thea made good use of. She washed and disinfected the wound, and then tried in vain to get sticking plaster to hold the bitten flap in place. 'All the hair needs to be shaved off,' she realised. The bleeding had stopped but the torn edges were swelling up, making the task even harder. 'I've a feeling you'll be disfigured for life,' she told the dog. 'Things being as they are, you're going to have to go without professional attention.' Her natural inclination, in any case, was to avoid going to a vet. Her father had made something close to a religion out of self-reliance, and the habit went deep. The whole family nursed a conviction that if more people sorted out their own problems, the world would be a better place. Instead, it was patently going in quite the opposite direction.

'You can stay in the kitchen with me,' she told Hepzie. 'After I've got the others in. They should be all right now until their master comes home.' Thankfulness at her imminent release flooded through her. What more could possibly go wrong between now and then?

Tempting fate, many people would say. Once more, Thea felt glad of the locked gate onto the street and the high fences at the back. The lurking presence of Clifford Savage, who might well have good reason to feel angry with her, prevented her from relaxing and simply counting the hours until Umberto came home. Despite regular assurances to herself to the effect that whatever harm she might have done it was too late to remedy it by slaughtering her, she was nervous. Nobody except Umberto had been particularly friendly towards her. If she had to rank them in order, it would probably go – Jake, Ramon, Kirsty, Penny, Imogen, Victor and Cliff. Then she shuffled them, and tried to create patterns in which they either protected or betrayed each other. The glaring omission was Theresa, mother of the victim, whose image had been entirely created by her son Jake.

With her spaniel cuddled beside her, at half past one Thea was on the sofa with a pad of paper she had taken from Umberto's unlocked desk. The diagrams she drew were varied and unhelpful. She did one with Jocasta Kingly at the centre, her four offspring radiating out. Then she tried another with Gabriella the pivotal point, which quickly became a hopeless mess. She added Stefan (with Christian in brackets) and the husbands and partners she knew about. She put Stephanie beside Ramon, which was a big mistake, because it made the child appear unnervingly close to the terrible violence that had set the whole thing going. She tried connecting Cliff Savage to Jocasta, Umberto, Stefan and Kirsty. No meaningful theory leapt out at her. She ended up much more confused than she had been at the start.

Having used three pages of the pad she tore them out and went to put the depleted thing back in the desk where she found it. It was an old-fashioned bureau with a flap that opened downwards. The flap had been down all week, the pad sitting on it along with a jam jar of pens and pencils, a scattering of letters and envelopes. It seemed obvious that it had belonged to Jocasta. With a careless curiosity, Thea fingered the contents of the cubbyholes. There surely wouldn't be any revealing secrets or unnoticed clues. It was more that this was an object from a past era. It reminded her of her own grandmother, who had just such a bureau, complete with a secret drawer. The Kingly specimen was a little piece of nostalgia. The cubbyholes were sparsely filled. Very old chequebook stubs; some postage stamps torn from their envelopes and kept for a non-existent family collector; two old keys that might come from wind-up clocks; a Post Office savings book. It was almost with relief that Thea found nothing to incriminate anybody. She had for a moment feared she might discover Umberto's current passport, proving he had never left the country. Or a letter from Imogen or Penny expressing murderous rage against Gabriella.

Even then it would not be actual evidence. If Gladwin could not extract a confession from Stefan or place his car within a whisker of Upper Oddington on the relevant date, then he might not be successfully charged with murder. Nobody would. It would remain forever unsolved. And there was still the baffling question of motive to consider. Revenge for getting Imogen into trouble with her mother was all anyone could think of, and that felt worryingly flimsy.

In the event, it all fell apart at two o'clock when the detective phoned Thea to report that the Austrian cousin had hard and incontrovertible proof that he was in Cheltenham amongst a group of eight or ten other men from midday to midnight on that fatal Monday. He had insisted as much from the first moment the police approached him and now the alibi was confirmed by at least four of the men in question. His car, however, was still not cleared of guilt. His brother had been in Germany throughout.

'You might remember he told us that somebody took the car and then returned it with the damage,' said Gladwin.

'And nobody believed him.'

'Right. So now we sort of *do*. There's supporting evidence in the shape of a traffic warden, who had to listen to the man's rantings when he saw the state of his car.'

'What was he doing for twelve hours in a big group of men?' Thea's imagination was running wild, as it so often did.

'As far as I can understand it, they were planning a sort of historical re-enactment thing in Northumberland in September. They were writing scenarios, designing costumes – all very harmless. There's an American, a Pole and an Icelander amongst them. Admirably cosmopolitan. I'm very unsure of the details, but it involves Vikings and Norse legends.'

'Sounds a bit childish.'

'Probably less so than what the Freemasons get up to. Or trainspotters. Men being men, in fact.'

Thea laughed and then quickly turned serious. 'So we're saying it couldn't have been Stefan after all, are we? Did somebody know he'd be safely out of the way, had access to his car key, drove it all the way over here, timing it exactly to the moment, did the deed and put it back where he found it? Is that even remotely credible?'

'It is, I suppose, admittedly remotely.'

'Which has to mean it's one of the family,' said Thea with deep regret. 'Who else would know how to get hold of the key?'

'He might have friends.'

'But they wouldn't want to kill Gabriella. Where exactly were they in Cheltenham?'

'They hired a meeting room at the George Hotel. It's right in the centre. There's a little road and a public car park at the back. No CCTV, amazingly. The car was returned to almost the same space it was in originally. Or so he says. He didn't keep the ticket, but vows he paid for a whole day.'

'A hit man!' said Thea. 'Got to be. Stefan paid somebody to do it with his car. Gave him the key, and told him where to find Gabriella … well, I can see a few snags in that theory,' she tailed off.

'Like where to find the victim. Again, it is remotely possible, given a very high degree of advance planning. She'd have to be persuaded to go to Oddington at a particular time. And even then, the chances of actually being able to mow her down with the car have got to be slim. So there would have to be alternative methods available. A weapon of some sort.'

'Hopeless,' said Thea. 'I haven't been of the slightest help to you, have I? All I've done is get to meet a lot of relatives, and realise what a very mixed bunch they are, considering they're supposed to be such a close-knit family. I get the impression they really don't like each other very much. And there's a massive imbalance in their incomes. I suppose you've heard how Imogen and Kirsty live? It's a hovel. And the Riders have a fabulous place in Winchcombe. I don't know about Theresa.'

'I'm disappointed in you. There's a gap in your report, Mrs Slocombe.' Gladwin chuckled. 'But I can tell you you haven't missed much. Mrs Milner is not very bright, not very rich and not very sensible. She lied to the officer who went to interview her, for absolutely no reason.'

'Jake said she was dim,' Thea remembered. 'And prone to lying her way out of trouble.'

'Except she wasn't *in* any trouble. We already knew she'd been at work all day Monday – in Witney. And she doesn't drive. Never has.'

'So what lie did she tell?'

'She said she hadn't seen Gabriella for a fortnight. But we knew the girl was there last Sunday because it was Jake's birthday and they had a little party for him. The cousin came as well.'

'Kirsty? Did she?' Something about that felt odd to Thea. 'I thought the Peakes had been ostracised.'

'What?'

'Because of Christian and Stefan,' said Thea patiently. 'Imogen was in disgrace for concealing them for all those years, due to the very upsetting fact that the shock of finding out about them killed the old mother – or so

305

they believed. Why hasn't anybody mentioned the party on Sunday? Who else was there? Was *Stefan* there? I'm assuming that Imogen wasn't.' Pieces of jigsaw were tumbling into place as she spoke.

'I don't know,' said Gladwin meekly. 'I'm not sure that we're as much in the picture as you obviously are when it comes to all these family dynamics. People don't like talking to the police about that sort of thing. And we don't know what questions to ask,' she almost wailed.

'They talked to me about it,' said Thea smugly. 'Every one of them splurged it all out, with hardly any encouragement. Gabriella was religious, for example. I bet you didn't know that.'

'I did not. Which is why you're so valuable to us.' The tone was mildly ironic.

'So who else was at the party?' Thea asked again. 'What about Clifford Savage? I wonder if he's friendly with Jake?' She could feel the excitement bubbling up. 'Isn't it obvious that whatever conspiracy there was must have been hatched then?'

'If you put it like that . . .' said Gladwin. 'I think we'd have to go back to Mrs Milner and ask.'

'No. Ask Jake,' said Thea firmly. An idea struck her. 'Or we could wait until Umberto gets back and I can ask him. He was probably there as well.'

'What time are you expecting him?'

'Somewhere about five, I think. He was rather vague about it. He seemed to think he could get any Shuttle train he fancied, regardless of what his ticket says.'

'That's right, actually. They don't make you stick to a time.'

'Well, I hope he's not late. I want to get home.'

'Meanwhile we've got cases stacking up here and I'm going to have to take people off this one, now we've done every interview we can think of. I might send Barkley over to speak to your Umberto as soon as he gets back. Let me know when he does, okay?'

'Wilco,' said Thea with a laugh. Then she had a little panic. 'But wait – what happened with the Savage man? Where is he now?'

Gladwin made a tutting sound. 'He's at home, I suppose. Or at work. He wasn't at all helpful, you know. Said his phone call was to a friend in North Wales and had nothing to do with anything. I really don't think you need worry about him.'

'But he's *lying*. Barefaced lies. Did you mention me to him? Have you checked his phone to see who he was talking to?'

'Of course not, Thea. Have some sense. We can't just do that without proper cause. Besides, an overheard phone conversation is not admissible as evidence and he obviously knows it. He was polite and pained and acted puzzled. He didn't mention you, either – although I suppose he must have known it was you who reported him. He won't send you a Christmas card, but I'm pretty sure he isn't going to kill you over it.'

'But I'm sure he knows who killed Gabriella. He might even have been actively involved.' Thea's heart was thumping. A belated idea jumped up and bit her.

'We're looking into it,' said Gladwin patiently. 'Meanwhile, just sit tight for a bit.'

'It could have been Christian that Cliff Savage was speaking to,' Thea realised. 'Nobody's said much about him.'

'Stop it, will you? If and when we charge somebody, then we'll get back to Savage and see if he'll change his story then. We'll be in a better position to put the screws on him, if he was an accomplice.'

'He'll still know there's no proper evidence against him, won't he, even if he was the hit man.' Thea remembered only too vividly how she had run away from the man, across a garden in real terror. 'And he *chased* me,' she added.

'Did he, though? Are you sure?'

The images in Thea's memory began to reform. 'Well, I'm sure he *would* have done, if he'd known where I'd gone. He probably knew there were people in the house, who would hear if I screamed. There was a light on.'

'We checked that – didn't anyone tell you? There aren't any people – it's one of those systems that puts lights on at random to fool the burglar.'

'Oh! How sneaky.'

'And how very Cotswolds.' Gladwin snorted, with her undiluted Northern scorn for the soft affluence of the region. 'Look – I absolutely must go now.'

'Yes. Sorry.'

'I'll speak to you later. Keep your phone handy – okay?'

'Yes, ma'am,' said Thea.

Hepzie was still playing the part of an invalid, nose on paws, large eyes shiny with self-pity. The skin around the wound had turned purple, but the swelling had gone down somewhat. The bitten flap was unlikely to reattach itself, Thea assumed. It was already looking slightly shrivelled, as if it would never fit back properly. 'It's only small,' Thea told the dog. 'You'll just have a funny ear, that's all. I don't suppose it even hurts any more, does it?'

The dog made no reply, and Thea spent a few moments convincing herself that she was doing the kindest thing by avoiding professional assistance. Stitches, antibiotics, bewilderment – and a hefty bill. It could all be dodged quite easily, whatever cultural expectations might decree. You ran to your GP if you had a pimple and you rushed your dog to the vet if it shed a drop of blood. She heard again her father's voice, insisting that good sense ought to prevail and the medical services be reserved for genuinely serious matters.

'It'll be fine,' she assured the spaniel. 'All forgotten by bedtime.'

But bedtime still felt a long way off. The news about Stefan and his alibi had been of such great significance that at first she had not fully taken it in. The party on the previous Sunday had been pushed aside by worries over Savage. There was just too much to compute, added as it was to everything else she had gleaned that day. The solution was in there somewhere. She could almost grasp it, almost hear a voice telling her what it was.

The diagram she had drawn was still relevant, even

if some of the balances had been altered as a result of Gladwin's latest information. The Sunday party had to be crucial – giving a perfect opportunity for conspiracy and misdirection. If, for example, Stefan Woltzer had taken Jake Milner to one side and exploited any resentments or jealousies he might have towards his sister. They might have only joked about it – how it would only be natural justice if she was mown down by a lorry, given how annoying she was.

But *was* Gabriella annoying? Self-righteous, judgemental, sanctimonious – words of that sort had been attached to her, in the past few days. Only Umberto had sincerely expressed liking for her. The others were shocked, appalled, incredulous, even wounded, by the news of her death. But hardly anybody had said they had actually loved her. Imogen seemed the most distraught, on the face of it. Ramon and Jake were obviously bemused; Kirsty and Penny were both hard to read emotionally. Gabriella had not been immediately important to either of them, as far as Thea could tell, once the two girl cousins had drifted apart. That was how it went with cousins – you were thrown together as small children and then forgot about each other.

The really big question was: what had Gabriella done that had been so bad that someone wanted to kill her for it? Assembling all the small items of information gleaned over the past four days the only possible answer that emerged was that she had told her grandmother about the existence of Imogen's two secret sons, thereby betraying her aunt and causing Jocasta such a surge of fury that she died of it. This scenario had solidified little by little until it felt highly persuasive. It also meant the motive was strongest in Imogen. And that could perhaps fit with the use of Stefan's vehicle for the deed – his mother would know how to sneak away with it while he was otherwise engaged. But Imogen had been fond of Gabriella all the girl's life. Was such an act of violence within her capability – even if he could prove that he had not been driving it? Had she deputised someone else to do it with Stefan's collusion? Someone like Clifford Savage? And if so, would the others – Jake, Kirsty, Ramon, Penny – all make accurate guesses as to who did what and why? And what about Umberto?

She thought some more about Imogen. She was ill and almost penniless. Her life story was one of mistakes and isolation. Even when she came back from Austria, the family might not have embraced her with total enthusiasm. She married a Mr Peake and produced a daughter with objectionable timing. Then – many years later – the man had pocketed all her money and disappeared. Did he fit anywhere in the picture? It was hard to see how. And then there was the most mysterious character of all – Theresa, mother of the deceased.

It bothered Thea to have one of the set missing. Nobody in the family other than Jake had said anything meaningful about Theresa – the youngest sister, who did not get along too well with Gabriella and was in want of a husband. Gladwin had dismissed her as dim and dishonest, but not guilty of murder.

It was probably too late now, Thea supposed, to try

and see the woman for herself. She could examine her in the wall of photos, and that was all.

Her main informant had been Jake, closely followed by Penny Rider and Ramon Rodriguez. Jake especially had been free with his disclosures, showing no anxiety as to what she might make of them. Jake's own life appeared to have a similar absence of passion and engagement to that of his uncle Umberto. Neither had a partner, or conspicuous money, or even much of a social group. They didn't mention friends or commitments. Not like Penny Rider with her mysteriously important work, or Imogen with her struggling garden centre. Umberto bought and sold old cameras and had ambitions for his dogs. It felt as if he had rather little to show for a man in his late fifties.

And so it went round and round in Thea's head. The matriarch hovered over it all, her standards and expectations, her possessions and the power they wielded – everything combined to make her the central figure in the picture. It all radiated out from her. And here was her only son, living in her house by himself, with a dubious legal right to do so. The anonymous phone call suggested that not everyone was content with that state of affairs.

It was half past two. The dogs had been left free to be inside or out, as they liked. Rocket's attack on Hepzie's ear had repelled Thea more than she first realised. She had no wish to go near the animals again. She wasn't going to give them any supper, in the expectation that their master would do it on his return. Whatever Rocket's motive had been, the effect was severe. Thea would probably be within her rights to sue Umberto, or at least demand some compensation. She wouldn't do that, but she was going to warn him that the dog was unreliable. Even if it was due to female hormones, or a sudden brainstorm, it could not be allowed to pass unmentioned. It might even be a symptom of some incipient disease that Umberto ought to know about.

However much she tried to push it away, there remained a strong sense of obligation to find a way to help the police bring Gabriella's killer to justice. Just sitting in a shadowy room on a June day was bad enough, but when there was still a murder to solve and only two or three hours left in which to do it, it felt almost criminal.

And yet – what could she do? How would it help to try to accost Cliff Savage, for example? He would probably be at work, anyway. Likewise, almost everybody else in the story. Ramon was probably still on compassionate leave, but she could think of nothing useful she could ask him or say to him. There had to be *somebody*. But contemporary English villages no longer had an all-seeing postmistress, or a local tramp who spent his days sitting on roadside verges observing every movement. Even the houses that appeared to be occupied were not. They had clever robotic lights that made it look as if people were there. How terribly sad that seemed. What an indictment of modern living!

And then – just as she was thinking she might try phoning her husband as a last resort – she heard an engine right outside the gate. When she went to look, she saw the gate was opening. Umberto Kingly had come home.

Chapter Twenty-One

The man paying her to watch over his dogs came into the house with a weary step. 'Got an earlier Shuttle,' he said, without preamble. 'Back on British soil by one. But it's a bloody long drive from Folkestone and that M20's a swine on a Friday.'

'You've made quite good time, even so,' said Thea.

'What happened to your dog's ear? Don't tell me Rocket did it.'

'Actually. . .'

'I thought she'd stopped that game. She does go a bit bonkers when it rains – I noticed that. And there's something about ears. Must be a saluki thing. Is it bad?' His lack of genuine concern was annoying. Had he felt no obligation to give Thea a warning before letting her innocent spaniel near the volatile Rocket?

She gave a tight reply. 'It won't kill her, but it's going to leave a hole. I should probably have rushed her off to be stitched up, but I didn't. It won't show too badly when the hair grows back, I suppose. It didn't occur to me that your dog could be so treacherous.'

Umberto nodded vaguely, and said, 'Otherwise . . .?'

They were still standing in the hall, the weight of

the week's events pressing down on them until they could hardly speak. There was a sense that they each wanted to talk about entirely different things. Umberto had his adventures in Germany to relate and Thea was inwardly reciting the many questions she had for him. Or perhaps he was the one with the questions. If so, she would quite like to dodge any more conversation. All she wanted was to go home and forget all about the Kingly family. But she had told Gladwin she would ask about Sunday's party and who was there and what horrible conspiracy they could have devised between them. For the moment, however, they remained with the safer subject of dogs.

'Otherwise they've been fine. Plenty of exercise, good appetites, no problems.'

'I blame myself. I should have warned you it was risky to bring your own dog. But she seemed such a placid little thing. I thought it would be all right.'

'Well . . .' said Thea. In the overall scale of things, she had to admit that a torn ear carried little importance. 'These things happen.'

'That's very sporting of you. Give me five minutes with them and then we might sit down? I got up at five this morning, and I can hardly keep my eyes open.'

The dogs had already detected his presence and were whining and scratching at the door of their room. Umberto headed for it, as Thea spoke to his back. 'I'll make some tea. Then I should go. I can get back in time to have supper with my husband and the kids, at this rate.'

He made no reply, but disappeared into the back room. Thea left him to it and put the kettle on. It was not much more than five minutes before they were sitting together in the front room with mugs of tea and a plate of biscuits.

Umberto leant back against the cushions, looking plump and relaxed. 'Am I to expect a visitation from the CID, do you think? I had a call from my sister that implied that was on the cards.'

'Which sister?'

'Oh – Penny, of course. Imogen wouldn't phone me. Nor Theresa. Especially not Theresa.'

Thea tried not to read anything into this remark. Umberto's lack of curiosity as to how she had spent her week was beginning to rankle. Where was his concern for her welfare? And he had yet to pay her fee for the house-sitting.

He was on the sofa, with the wall of family portraits behind him. As Thea gave them a glance, she found herself foolishly hoping that one of them would somehow shimmer or twitch with guilt. One of them was very probably a killer – ought not Gabriella Milner's ghost arrange for a sign of some kind? One of them could crash inexplicably to the floor perhaps, or the glass suddenly crack. Instead, they all seemed to fade into smudgy marks on paper with very little meaning.

'So what do you think?' said Umberto. 'About the cops?'

'I really don't know. The investigation has made a lot

of progress. I think they've got to grips with most of the background, and there's quite a bit of evidence about the vehicle.' She was being as careful as she knew how, wary of conveying anything that he couldn't learn anywhere else. Already she might have said too much.

'Penny said they've got nowhere. Just going round in circles.'

'Did she?' Thea clamped her lips together, resisting the urge to say more.

'You're the one who knows most, aren't you?' He narrowed his eyes at her. 'You've got detectives on your list of friends, and a long history of helping them out at times like this. So who do *you* think killed my poor little niece?'

Thea had always been slow to admit to herself that there might be actual danger close by. She habitually rationalised herself into believing that everything was all right. Granted there had been a few exceptions, not least only a day or two ago finding herself in a quiet evening lane with a man who had just made self-incriminating statements in a phone call – and who knew she had heard him. And yet, that might well not have been genuinely dangerous, either. She had run away unscathed and afterwards assured herself he was never intending to hurt her. The fact was that not once in her life had she been physically hurt by anybody, man or woman. No one had ever laid a violent hand on her. And when it came to it – unlike most of the population – Thea Slocombe put experience before theory.

But verbal attack was different. She had been criticised, accused, blamed, a great many times. She had been told about her failings and defects in ringing tones. It was always unpleasant, making her go cold and wobbly inside.

'I saw it happen,' she said in a low voice. 'I was *involved*.'

'All right,' he said, looking even more tired and really not at all threatening. 'It's a complete mess – I can see that. You know – I was going to let Gabriella and Ramon have this house. It's what my mother would have wanted. I don't have any proper right to it. But I needed to get some money together first and work out what I should do with myself. As Penny would tell you, my career so far has been sadly inglorious.' He smiled weakly, and Thea could see that he was genuinely exhausted.

'Oh?' she said, feeling rather weary herself. Here was a new fact that might well impinge on the murder. It might comprise the whole motive, in fact. 'But what about Christian and Stefan? I know about them.' She frowned, wondering what had prompted her to say that. 'I mean – it looks as if everything centres on them. Do you think?'

Umberto shrugged. 'Everybody knows about them now. Imogen's dark secret exploded in all our faces nearly a year ago. But that dust has settled. In fact, I saw Christian on Wednesday. He came over to Munich to meet me. He's a very decent chap. Actually offered to start another little branch of the business in Vienna. There could be a good market there for the cameras, if we do a bit of research.'

'Did you sell the ones you took?'

'Nearly all of them, at very good prices. It's going to work out very nicely, with just a few bits of luck and ironing out the glitches.' He looked at her speculatively. 'For a start, I can't afford to have you here every time I go over. It's taking nearly half my profit.' He laughed bitterly. 'And see what happens when I go away.'

It felt to Thea as if the conversation was dense with implications and important clues. The house, the dogs, the cameras, the relatives – everything jumbled up together and all of it carrying strong feelings and old animosities, to use Victor Rider's word. In there somewhere was a towering passion that had led to murder. She reviewed the faces of each member of the family in turn, searching for a sign. Like testing an egg for fertility, its weight suggesting a growing chick inside it. Somebody she had met in the past three days could well be a killer, carrying a burden of guilt – surely there had to be *something* about that person that would give him – or her – away?

Clifford Savage would be her favourite candidate, despite his apparent denial in the phone conversation she had heard. Ramon was probably volatile and deeply involved emotionally— she stopped herself. Hadn't she gone through all this already? Weren't they past that point – with Umberto here in front of her, full of relevant knowledge, if only she knew how to extract it.

'What are they like? Christian and Stefan. What do they think about you and the rest of the family?' The mysterious nephews had been gaining in stature in her mind ever since she first heard about them. 'It must have been a huge surprise when you discovered they existed.'

'Not as huge as hearing that Gabriella had been murdered,' he said with a reproachful look. Evidently, she was not supposed to be so excited about last year's drama. 'I can't understand why you're talking about them. They've been accepted as part of the family, but we've missed too much of their lives for it ever to feel they really belong. They both look like their father, and they don't speak very good English.'

Thea felt she was being dishonest, keeping too much from him. But she had assumed from Gladwin that none of the Kinglys knew that the police had proof of the identity of the vehicle that had killed their girl. It was definitely not her place to wreck everything by splurging to Umberto. And yet treachery was lurking on all sides and she did not want to be part of it. 'I saw Imogen and Kirsty today,' she said, aware of a wish to startle him, or at least impress him with her knowledge of his family. 'And before that I went to see the Riders.'

'Why?' Again his eyes were narrow. 'What have you been playing at?'

This time she felt no trepidation. Umberto was not going to hurt her, or even say anything very wounding. He was half-asleep, and despite his claims to have financial worries and a potential loss of the house, he appeared to be perfectly calm. Like an otter with its impervious pelt, everything she told him simply slid off, leaving him unaffected.

'I was involved,' she said again, without emphasis. 'And I had time on my hands.'

'It sounds to me as if you're convinced that somebody in my family murdered my niece. That's not very nice of you, is it? Who says it wasn't some total stranger? A maniac with a big car, driving too fast down the village street. She must have stepped out in front of him.'

'She didn't,' said Thea clearly. 'I saw what happened.'

'I know you did – but it can't have been a very good view. Which room were you in?'

'Upstairs. It didn't happen by accident.'

He patted his thighs in a gesture that implied he had finished with the subject. 'I'll phone Theresa later on,' he said. 'There might be a plan for the funeral by now.'

But Thea was not done yet. 'There was a party on Sunday at her house, wasn't there? Did you go? Who else was there? How about Stefan?'

'Oh, stop it, you silly woman. Just take your money and your dog and go home. Your work here is finished. You've done your best to get under the skin of my family, but it's an impossible task. Ask Victor Rider. He's spent twenty years or more at it, and still barely scratched the surface.'

'He's not the only one.'

The voice came from the hallway. With a huge thump,

Thea's heart registered genuine fear. On her lap, the spaniel jerked and yapped like an echo of her mistress's reaction. A small agitated red-headed man appeared in the doorway, confirming Thea's instant identification from his voice. 'How did you get in?' she asked, speaking for Umberto, who seemed to be paralysed not so much from fear as total surprise.

'Across a field, over the fence and through an open door,' said Clifford Savage. 'I didn't think you would let me in through the front.'

'Cliff,' said Umberto. 'What's going on, mate?'

'More than I can explain in the time available. I've come for the deeds of the house, old *mate*.' The word was an attempt at a sneer, but he was too tense for it to work properly. Thea had an impression of a man playing a part that really didn't suit him. He came over like a panicky understudy suddenly thrust onto the stage with no choice but to see it through. 'I'm not letting it go, just because someone's slaughtered one of your nieces. That's just a distraction. Kirsty and I are the rightful heirs to this house and have been from the start. Just go and get the papers, and we'll say no more.' A flicker of something like pleading crossed his face.

Thea was thinking back to Wednesday. 'You told me a whole lot of absolute barefaced lies,' she accused the intruder. 'Coming over here pretending to be worried about me. Not a word of truth in anything you said.' She stared at him, remembering how frightened she had been for a few moments out by the church. 'And what about last night, scaring me like that?'

'I didn't do anything to scare you,' he said. 'You ran off before I could say a word. And on Wednesday, all I did was let you think I was a lot less well acquainted with the family than I really am.'

'And what about your sister being at school with Caz?'

'That's true. Those girls bullied me mercilessly.'

Umberto interrupted. 'I'm not giving you the deeds and that's final,' he said, as if he'd just arrived at a firm decision. 'The idea is preposterous. Pure fantasy.'

'You'll have to in the end. You've got no claim on the house and you know it. I just want to get things moving more quickly.'

It was barely two years since Thea had sold a house. She knew something of the procedure. 'The papers don't mean anything these days,' she said in a voice that was as wobbly and uncontrolled as Savage's. Only Umberto seemed calm. 'Everything's online now at the Land Registry. You can't just grab a house simply because you've got the deeds.'

'Well, that's where you're wrong,' said Savage with more confidence. 'This house has been in the same hands for fifty-five years. It doesn't concern the Land Registry. I checked, if you must know. With Jocasta dead, it's been in limbo for a year already. She left no will, but the family in their wisdom chose the sainted Gabriella to have it, once she married her Spaniard. Now she's been conveniently removed, it can only be

Kirsty in line for it. God knows she's earned it.'

'And Kirsty's mother? Is she going to live here as well?'

He shrugged. 'If she lasts that long.'

Thea frowned at him, waiting for her pulse to stabilise. Had her wits deserted her or was this very close indeed to a confession to murder? Before she could speak, Umberto said it for her. 'Are we right in thinking that you and Kirsty murdered poor little Gabby, then?' His calm was unnerving. Thea and Savage both manifested far more agitation.

Savage choked out a furious response. 'Are you mad? Gabriella died under the wheels of some hit-and-run drug-addicted lunatic. Granted the family's bizarre and complicated, but nobody in it would commit *murder*.'

'Except they did,' shouted Thea in a sudden fury. 'And you know it. It's long past the point where anyone could believe otherwise. And it's all about Imogen and her sons. Isn't it?' she demanded. Then she looked at Umberto. 'Except it can't possibly have been Kirsty...'

Umberto held her gaze, with slightly raised eyebrows. *Can't it?* he was silently asking.

Savage said nothing. He looked from Thea to Umberto and back, as if waiting for one of them to say something he could relate to. Finally, he exhaled, a long-held breath released, and said, 'Well I didn't kill her either. The whole thing was sickening.'

Thea's memory flashed. 'That's what you said on the phone. You were talking to the person who killed

Gabriella, and you said Imogen was their mother. That narrows it down to three people, and Kirsty—' Again she stopped. What had she been going to say? The logic was so stark and incontrovertible that it stood like a brick wall in front of her. There was no getting around it.

'Leave it out,' said Savage flatly. 'Just admit that we've got a good claim to this house. That's all I came for. Fetch the deeds and I'll leave you in peace.'

Thea was floundering, clutching her spaniel to her in near-panic. This was the moment of truth and she was tempted to turn away and leave it out, as Savage instructed. Her brain had gone numb. There had been a horrible murder and it was incumbent on them all to see justice done. It was outrageous that both these men seemed content to let it slide, as if other matters outweighed it in importance.

'I'm not leaving it out,' she said. 'No way. I want to know the whole thing. Were you at the famous party as well? Did you hear Stefan and the others planning it all?'

Savage flapped an impatient hand at the question. It dawned on Thea to be thankful that the hand did not hold a gun. The man had come unarmed, both materially and emotionally. His eyes were glistening with adrenaline, his words jerky and largely rehearsed. 'Get the deeds,' he repeated.

'Or what?' said Umberto.

'Or I'll make so much trouble for you and your family, you'll curse yourself for refusing me.'

Umberto's bravado subsided a notch or two. Thea was in no doubt that the threat carried considerable heft. The sense that she had barely scratched the surface of the Kingly secrets, with the whole edifice already cracking, gave credence to Savage's words. 'But why is it so important to you?' she asked. 'You told me you were only here for a few more weeks. You told the person on the phone you were leaving even sooner than that. What is it that you *want*?'

'I want Kirsty,' came the simple answer. 'Whatever I have to do to get her.'

'Oh Lord!' groaned Umberto. 'You poor fool. She sent you to collect the house deeds, I suppose. What else has she made you do?'

Thea forced herself to review everything she had seen and learnt of Kirsty Peake, and then reran the overheard phone call the previous evening. She knew already what the conclusion would be. 'You were speaking to *Kirsty* last night, weren't you?' She looked at Umberto. 'I was right just now, and you know it as well, don't you?' She turned to Savage. 'You more or less admitted it yourself. Never mind some crazy convenient hit-and-run driver. You two killed Gabriella. It's been plain for days, if I had but faced up to it. Everything's been pointing that way.' She paused, still doubting. 'Except . . .' She remembered Kirsty's concern for her mother, and obvious lack of organisation. The unconvincing assertions that things would come right, and the troubles were only temporary. She had glimpsed

326

someone struggling desperately to stay afloat in a treacherous world. *Poor Kirsty*, she found herself thinking, before sternly correcting herself.

'We did not,' said the man loudly. 'There is no way they could find any evidence pointing to her – or me. I was at work, with a hundred people to say so. And Kirsty's always been fond of Gabriella. They were like sisters. And there's obviously not a scrap of evidence,' he repeated.

Thea was briefly tempted to accept his denials and let the whole thing go. It was nearly four o'clock and she badly wanted to go home. Unless Kirsty actually confessed, with a full explanation of how and why she had done the deed, it was probably right that there would never be enough evidence to charge her. But then there was the matter of the house. What would happen to Umberto? And was it remotely acceptable that a killer should not only get away with her crime, but also actually *benefit* from it? And, weirdly, she felt a sudden urge to protect little Cliff Savage from a woman who was probably both predatory and ruthless. 'Wouldn't you be scared to live with her, knowing what she'd done?' she asked, really wanting to know.

He stared her down, with his shining eyes. 'I'd be in heaven,' he said.

'She's bewitched you, mate,' said Umberto with a small cynical laugh. 'As only a woman can.' He looked at Thea. 'This is another one. They don't even know they're doing it half the time. You just can't trust them, you know.'

She remembered the way he had eyed her at the beginning of the week. Appreciation, knowledge, but no real engagement. Had a woman broken him in his early years, immunising him against feminine charms for the rest of his life? It would explain a lot, if so. She could find nothing to say to him, sensing yet more betrayal in his past, its damage never-ending.

'I can trust Kirsty. She's the only one in this damned family that *is* trustworthy.'

'If you believe that, there's no hope for you,' said Umberto.

'It's true. Compared to bloody Gabriella, Kirsty's a rock.'

'And you're going to break your stupid head on her before you know what's happened,' predicted the older man.

'Shut up!'

Thea was doing her best to assess the degree of responsibility she held, now that there was so little doubt as to who killed Gabriella. The picture was still very out of focus, with the morality even more obscure. If Kirsty was sent to prison, what would happen to Imogen? And how closely involved had Stefan been? The loose ends were still there, albeit slightly fewer and of lesser importance than before.

'You said on the phone you were leaving and never coming back. What changed?'

'None of your business.' Which Thea had to accept was true. Up to a point.

The sheer lack of drama was making everything more difficult. If Savage had burst in waving a gun, that would have felt more fitted to the situation. If Umberto had suddenly hurled himself out of his comfortable spot on the sofa and called the police while sitting on Clifford's back, it would have made a good finale. As it was, there were scattered pieces of the story lying all around the room, amounting to a solid solution to the crime, and yet nothing had been proved or admitted.

Then Thea's mobile jingled, breaking the tension at the same time as being an irritating cliché. She assumed it would be Gladwin, and was already worrying about what she ought to say, when she looked at the screen. 'Stephanie' it said.

'Hey – are you all right?' she responded.

'No, I'm not. It's Mr Rodriguez. It's on Facebook. It says he killed himself today, in his car.'

Chapter Twenty-Two

Ramon the boyfriend, the handsome Spanish teacher beloved of her stepdaughter, was dead. He had driven down a small track into a clump of trees and filled his car with lethal carbon monoxide. He was found just too late by a woman and her dog at ten o'clock that morning. Somehow the news was out by midday and anyone who knew the man was bleating about it online.

Stephanie was inconsolable. 'They all say it means that he killed Miss Milner,' she wailed.

Thea understood that the police would be very tempted to adopt this line and declare the investigation closed. She also knew that no such thing could be allowed to happen. Ramon had no access to Stefan Woltzer's car, surely? And did he not have a bulletproof alibi? For the moment, Thea could not remember where he said he had been on Monday, or why she had so readily dismissed him from her list of suspects. Then it came back to her that he had in fact been unable to demonstrate precisely where he had been. He could all too easily have left school as usual, somehow got hold of the car in Cheltenham, used it and returned it, and nobody the wiser. If he hid his own vehicle somewhere out of sight, he might have done it and got away with it. Although there had to be cameras galore all along his route from Chipping Campden to Cheltenham that would have recorded his progress. And flakes of his skin or loose hairs from his head would have been left behind in Stefan's car. And Thea now knew with utter certainty that the man was innocent. He was collateral damage, broken by the horror of his loss and all its implications.

'It's absolutely terrible,' she told the girl on the phone. 'The poor man.'

'When are you coming home?'

'Soon. Is Dad there?'

'In the office. With a woman.'

'For a funeral?'

'I s'pose so.'

'Well, try not to get too upset about Ramon. He must have been very unhappy. We might try and get Caz to come over tomorrow and talk to us about it.' Stephanie had formed a devoted bond with the young detective, which Thea hoped was beneficial to them both.

'But what if he *did* kill Miss Milner?'

'He didn't, Steph. I know he didn't. Do you believe me?'

'I don't know.'

'Listen, I'm going now. There are only one or two more things to do here and then I'll be home. What's for supper?'

'Fish and chips,' said Stephanie. 'It's meant to be

a surprise. Dad said if you're not back by the time he fetches it, we'll eat your share. I don't think I'll be able to eat anything, though. I feel all full – sort of choked.'

'Oh, Steph. You poor thing. I'm coming as soon as I can, I promise.'

'All right.'

She ended the call and faced the two men, who had been shamelessly listening. 'The boyfriend died,' said Umberto flatly. 'Presumably by his own hand.'

'The guilt too much for him,' said Savage with an intolerable smugness.

Thea suddenly got up. 'Come on, Heps,' she said. 'We're going now.' She looked at Umberto. 'My bag's all packed. If you'll just give me my money, I'll get out of your way. I'm needed at home.'

'Let me have your bank details and I'll do a transfer.'

'No – we agreed you'd pay me in cash. That was part of the deal.' The matter was not important, and yet she seized it as if it was crucial. It felt like a deliberate slight, on top of everything else she'd been forced to endure.

'Was it?'

'What sort of idiot uses cash these days?' said Savage wonderingly.

'Idiots like me. Oddly enough, I find it easier, quicker and more secure.' It was true – only a few months previously she had had her own little epiphany, standing in a lengthening queue behind someone whose debit card wasn't working. With an exasperated sigh, the person on the counter had said, 'Is anybody paying in cash?' And the

332

fortunate few had shifted to a different till and escaped in moments.

Since then, the advantages had burgeoned. It was a revelation. She was almost at the point of boycotting any establishment that refused cash. She had written angrily to Timmy's school, which had announced itself as cashless. 'I'm going to get a T-shirt printed with CASH IS KING on it,' she proclaimed. So far that had not happened.

'Well, I haven't got any on me,' said Umberto, with implacable finality.

Thea became aware of a volcanic fury building inside her. Everyone she had met over the past week had been annoying, in retrospect. Even Gabriella Milner, being careless enough to get herself killed right under Thea's nose. Her brother Jake was limp and pathetic. Penny Rider was bossy and cold-hearted. Clifford Savage was devious and sinister. But Umberto took the prize. Everything was very much his fault. She glared at him. 'Don't you ever keep your promises?' she demanded.

He shrank away. 'I'll get some tomorrow, if it's that important to you. You can come over and collect it.'

This did nothing to assuage her rage. 'And find you're out, or have forgotten all about it. No,' she snarled, 'do the bank thing. I don't ever want to come here again.' She fished in her bag for her wallet and provided the necessary numbers.

Then she and her dog marched to the front door, where she had left her bag. Making a suitable exit seemed to be important. The fact that she was unsure of the whereabouts of her car keys, and an uncertainty as to whether the outrageous gate would open at her command both slowed her progress slightly. As she rummaged again in her bag for the keys, and paused inside the gate, the legion of loose ends and unanswered questions caught up with her. Could she really just drive away from it all?

She could, she decided. There was a loving family waiting for her. The dog was gazing at her, wondering why the gate didn't open. Gladwin would be sifting every detail and creating a case that would stand every kind of scrutiny.

But a case against who? Or should that be *whom*? Even though the identity of the killer had become crystal clear to Thea over the past hour, through the layers of treachery that comprised the Kingly family, she knew the police would have great difficulty in proving it. And she knew she had no choice but to ensure that Gladwin got it right.

The gate opened obediently and woman and dog passed through into the village street. At the same moment a car pulled to a halt right beside her, giving a toot on the horn as it did so. 'Caught you!' said Gladwin, jumping out of the driving seat. Given her line of work, this struck Thea as a trifle ill-chosen as a greeting.

'Why? What have I done?' she asked.

'Nothing criminal, as far as I know. I've got someone here who wants to talk to Umberto – and you.'

The passenger eased herself out of the car much more slowly than Gladwin had done. 'Imogen!' said Thea, marvelling that she could still be surprised.

'I've come to apologise,' said the woman. Her face was even more haggard than it had been earlier in the day, her voice breathy. 'I killed Gabriella. Stefan let me have his car, without knowing why I wanted it. I made sure there was no evidence against him – or me, if possible. We cooked up the whole thing between us.'

Thea kept her eyes on the woman's face. 'You didn't, though, did you? You're covering for Kirsty, now you've worked it all out, the same as I have. And it wasn't you who cooked the whole thing up – you're just saying that to try to convince the police. You think you've got nothing to lose.'

'That's rubbish,' Imogen insisted. 'I wanted to tell you I was sorry you had to witness it. That's been nagging at me all along. You're a nice person. You shouldn't have seen such an awful thing.'

'No, I shouldn't.' They were standing outside the gate, which had clanged shut behind Thea. She looked longingly at her own little car, parked barely thirty yards away. 'But it wasn't you. Nobody will ever believe it was.'

Imogen ignored her words. 'I hated her, you see. She betrayed me to my mother, lost me this house, made sure the whole family ostracised me, and did her best to alienate me from my sons. She never showed a morsel of remorse about it, either. She deserved what she got.'

Thea turned to Gladwin. 'Have you told her about Ramon?'

Gladwin gave her a bitter look and shook her head. 'You never will mind your tongue, will you?' she accused.

Imogen coughed painfully. 'What about him? He's better off without her – he'll soon realise. He was far too good for her and never got any credit for anything.'

'He killed himself today,' said Thea flatly, without looking at Gladwin. 'It's difficult to see why, unless he wanted everyone to think he killed Gabriella. Which seems to be working, according to my stepdaughter.'

'Oh!' Imogen moaned and sank to the ground. 'Not Ramon!'

'Another victim of the killer,' said Thea relentlessly. 'My guess is that he just couldn't face life without Gabriella. He seemed to have a fair idea of what she was like, and loved her anyway. He put everything into the relationship.'

Imogen shook her head weakly, while Gladwin hovered anxiously. 'We should get her inside,' said the detective. 'She's really not at all well.'

Imogen pushed away her hand, refusing to be helped. 'No, you've got that wrong. Ramon was planning to leave Gabriella for Kirsty. They'd got together only a few weeks ago, and he was going to tell her on Sunday. She only confessed that to me today. She's feeling very bad about it.'

Thea almost laughed. 'That can't possibly be true. Cliff Savage has just told me that *he* and Kirsty have every intention of living together here in this house. Your daughter is playing games with you – can't you see?'

'She's had a very hard time, this past year,' whispered the woman, before closing her eyes. 'I can't betray her after everything she's done for me. She did it all for me, you see.'

Thea left Gladwin to deal with everything, once Umberto had come out to help manhandle Imogen into the house. 'It was Kirsty Peake who killed her cousin,' she said loudly, before turning away.

'Yes, I know,' said the detective superintendent.

She wanted desperately to get home, to the fish and chips and Friday evening lethargy. And yet she knew quite well that that was not how it would be. Stephanie was distraught. Drew would be disapproving and perhaps accusing. In her current frame of mind, Thea feared she would only make everything worse. She was sick, sad, sorry and very much on the brink of tears. Everybody she had met through the week had been knocked sideways, betrayed and battered by events. The details niggled at her, and there was still no cessation of the annoying questions. What had Stefan's part been? What did the Riders make of it all? And Jake? Theresa? Gabriella was well out of it, viewed from one perspective. It had all been her own fault, some might say. Thea had a feeling Umberto might take such a view. The death of Jocasta had been Gabriella's

337

doing, and that in itself warranted some kind of justice.

But murder could never be excused.

She had to find a way to debrief herself before she could inflict her miserable presence on the family. On the outskirts of Stow-on-the-Wold she pulled off the road and parked beside a little row of shops. It was twenty to five. She could afford half an hour before showing up for the fish and chips. Time enough, perhaps, to pull herself together. Especially if she could recruit someone to help her.

Miraculously, Caz Barkley answered her phone quickly. 'They've gone to arrest Kirsty Peake,' she said. 'I expect you know as much as I do about how that came about.'

'It was horrible. Her mother—'

'Yes, so I gather. Gladwin phoned it through ten minutes ago. It's all moving really fast now. Those of us still here have been trying to piece it all together.'

'Those poor people,' Thea tried again. 'I feel sorry for them all.'

'Treacherous lot, from what I can work out.'

'Not really. I'm still struggling with the motive. Kirsty and Gabriella were like sisters when they were small. How could one murder the other like that?'

'Sisters can hate each other, you know.'

Thea gave that some thought. She loved her sister Jocelyn unreservedly and always had. But Emily – well, she was harder to love, or to understand. 'I'll have to take your word for that,' she told Barkley. 'It's beyond my imagination.'

'Why did you phone me? Is there something we've missed?'

'I'm past trying to help your investigation. It's down to you to make the case. It probably isn't going to be easy, but my part in it is finished. I'm just left carrying a whole bucketful of crap. All the dark feelings and misery. It doesn't really feel fair.'

'Since when was anything ever fair?' snapped Barkley. 'Haven't we agreed on that ages ago?'

'Stephanie's been caught up in it, as well. Her beloved Mr Rodriguez is dead, don't forget. What's that going to do to her?'

'She'll dump it on her father, I expect. Isn't that what he's best at?'

'She'll want to understand everything about the murder. Who and why and how. It might come best from you. Will you have a moment to come over, tomorrow or Sunday?'

'No, Thea,' said Caz with unusual firmness. 'It wouldn't be my place to do that, on a number of levels. You and your family have to deal with it in your own way. No good could come of police involvement at this stage.'

'Oh,' said Thea. 'I might have to think about that.'

'I'm not saying you can't ask questions. All the loose ends and so forth need looking at. But you can probably figure most of it out at least as well as we can here. Email me with anything factual you want to know. Otherwise, trust me when I say you'll manage fine on your own.'

Most of the drive home was done on autopilot, but when she took the final turn into Broad Campden Thea could no longer avoid the fact that Drew had been very angry with her when they last spoke. She was going to have to abase herself and do everything possible to propitiate him. She would be expected to spend all weekend putting him first and staying off the subject of murder or house-sitting. It was basically a rather depressing rerun of earlier occasions where he had been frosty about her activities.

All the doors and windows were open when she reached the house. The day had slowly got drier after the morning downpour, but it was still far from summery. Drew, however, believed in the value of fresh air and rural sounds and smells and welcomed them into his house. After the repressive levels of security in Oddington, it was a blessed relief. It was, however, unusual for the front door to be standing quite so widely open. Hepzie ran ahead to announce their return and all became clear.

An unknown female voice chirped, 'Oh! And who might this be?'

'Thea?' came Drew's familiar tones.

Two people came forward and stood together in the doorway. One was Thea's husband and the other was a smiling woman in her early thirties, with dimples and curly hair. She was the same height as Drew. Standing side by side, they looked horribly like a couple.

Thea was six years older than him and had never once considered that to be a relevant factor in their marriage.

She was pretty, small, intelligent and headstrong. And a lot more. Here was a tall, young, lovely woman who he obviously liked. Even Thea, confident and blithe as she might be, experienced a violent shock of fear and jealousy. Surely he wouldn't? Surely of all the men in the world, she could at least trust Drew Slocombe? Or had she finally pushed him too far and here was his revenge? Could he possibly betray her in such a clichéd way?

'This is Vicky,' he said with a smile. 'We've been arranging her grandmother's funeral.'

Oh yes – it looks like it, Thea wanted to snarl. Anyone less grief-stricken or funereal would be hard to imagine. 'Hello,' she managed.

'I've been here practically the whole afternoon,' trilled Vicky. 'I don't know where the time went.'

'Stephanie phoned me about her teacher,' said Thea, holding nothing back. 'He killed himself, and she's very upset. I assume you haven't been available for her to talk to?'

'Good Lord!' said Drew. 'I had no idea.'

'She's been trained not to interrupt you when you've got a customer.' She gave Vicky a look that she hoped made the word sound suitably scathing. Drew tried to avoid using either 'customer' or 'client' about the people who came to arrange a funeral. Mostly he called them 'families' or 'relatives'.

'Yes,' he said.

'That's my cue to get a move on,' said the woman with outrageous aplomb. 'Thank you, Drew, for everything you're doing. It's been a revelation, you know. An absolute revelation. What you're doing is quite remarkable. Everything I heard is true, but only a tiny fraction of the whole business. And thanks for the way you introduced me.' She laughed.

'Till next week, then,' he said, and watched her departure with an infuriating glow.

'Bloody hell, Drew,' said Thea when they'd gone back indoors. 'What's come over you?'

'You've no idea who that was, have you?'

'A person called Vicky with a dead grandmother. What else is there to know?'

'She's the Honourable Victoria Troutbeck, daughter of one of the oldest and richest families in the land. Her grandmother was from an even older and richer line. They want her to be buried in *my* field. Have you any idea what that's going to do for the business? She thinks they'll get masses of media coverage. It all went to my head a bit. I started burbling about black horses. She spent most of the time talking me down.' He stopped and looked at her. 'Why? What's the matter?' He had forgotten his bad temper, forgotten what his wife had been doing or why it bothered him.

She couldn't tell him. At least, not in any direct way. 'She's so young and beautiful,' she mumbled. 'And she seemed so smitten with you.'

He put his hands on her shoulders and gave her a little shake. 'And I freely admit that if I was ever tempted to run off with another woman, she would be my ideal.

All that lovely money! Big cars, fancy holidays. Sailing. Skiing. And silly old me – it never even crossed my mind.'

'Ignore me,' she said humbly. 'I've had a week listening to one horrible betrayal after another, and it's shaken my faith.'

'Well, you needn't lose your faith in me. I'm very happy indeed to have you home again. I believe I was rather cross with you, but that's all flown away now. So, explain what's the trouble with poor old Stephanie?'

'I told you – her Mr Rodriguez died. But I should never have dumped it on you in front of Lady Whatnot. That can wait until later. A little mouse told me there was fish and chips on the menu this evening. Are you fetching it or am I?'

'Neither. Fiona's getting it. She'll be here in about an hour.'

'Oh. They're eating with us, are they?' The prospect of the Emersons' company on her first evening home was not especially appealing.

'Of course not. They've got more sense than to intrude on one of your homecomings. Fiona's just being a delivery person. She seems to think it's part of her job. Like taking Stephanie to school when it's raining.'

Chapter Twenty-Three

Stephanie was valiantly striving to get recent events into perspective. She ate a few chips, and waved away Drew's efforts to show sympathy. 'It probably wasn't just about Miss Milner,' she said. 'His mother died at Easter, as well. He told me about it, and said it made him think there couldn't be a God after all. She was only fifty-five.'

Thea stared at her. 'Blimey, Steph! When was this?' The mention of God was no surprise. Stephanie had given a lot of thought to religion in the past six months or so.

'Oh – just before half-term. I asked him if he was going home to Spain and he said there was no point, and then we just got on to it and he told me the whole story. He knows about Dad and the funerals. People often talk to me about death,' she finished with a little sigh.

'So Gabriella was the final straw for him,' said Thea, a trifle briskly. 'Do you think?'

'I think he had quite a lot of worries, that's all,' said the girl. 'One of the boys at school said something this morning – before we knew what had happened.'

'What sort of something?' asked Drew.

'It was about Mr Rodriguez and me. Teacher's little pet, and some people thinking it might be a little bit more than that. It was the look on his face as he said it – I could tell people had been talking about us.'

'Oh Steph,' moaned Thea. 'Aren't people awful!'

'You saw how it was, yesterday. He was only being friendly. But he might have heard what they were saying and got upset about it.'

Drew caught Thea's eye, and grimaced as if to say *Now what do we do?*

'Poor man,' said Thea weakly. 'Everything just got too much for him.'

'Maybe he and Gabriella will be together in heaven,' said Timmy with a grin.

'Yes, they will,' Stephanie told him sternly. She gave her father a hopeful look. 'Do you think they might be buried together in our field?'

Again Drew seemed to be out of his depth. 'We'll have to see,' he mumbled. 'But I dare say there's a chance it could happen.'

Epilogue

Some satisfaction of Thea's need for a final update came from a surprising quarter. On Saturday afternoon she had a call from Umberto Kingly. 'Just checking you're all right,' he said. 'You left with things in rather a muddle here.'

'That's very nice of you. We're doing our best to settle back into normal family life, but I must admit I still get a few flashbacks.' She refrained from telling him about the dream that woke her in a cold sweat at three that morning.

'The police phoned me at lunchtime. Just a courtesy call, they said, but they were surprisingly forthcoming. And I've got Penny here beside me, crossing all the t's, as they say. And Imogen's upstairs, feeling very poorly, poor old girl.'

Thea had no wish to talk to Penny Rider. Even Umberto was something of a strain. 'Oh,' she said.

'I found a flea on Gina,' he went on, as if this was at least as momentous as the murder of his niece. 'Do I have your spaniel to thank for that?'

'I hope not,' said Thea, feeling hot with shame.

'Oh well, it's easily fixed. After what my awful family put you through, I can hardly make a fuss, can I? We must seem quite bizarre to you.'

'Well . . .'

'It's partly being such strong Catholics, I suppose. Well, my mother and Theresa, anyway. A lot of faith in power beyond the grave and sticking to solemn promises. It rubbed off on the girls, of course, and got somewhat distorted in the process.'

'We're very upset about Ramon. Does Kirsty realise she's responsible for his death as well?'

'Possibly she does. I'm really not party to her thought processes. Imogen keeps insisting Kirsty was just taking revenge for what Gabby did to her and our mother.'

Thea could think of nothing to say to that. Kirsty Peake had to be severely disturbed to do what she did. She changed the subject. 'Are you staying in that house?'

'I hope so. But Immy's going to share it with me. That's what ought to have happened from the start, I see now. I'll have to acquire some nursing skills. She's really quite ill, you know.'

'Just one last question,' said Thea, assembling her thoughts with an effort. 'What about Stefan? Did he know Kirsty had taken his car?'

Umberto grunted. 'Nobody seems too sure about that. He had every reason to be critical of Gabby – but he's a perfectly sensible chap, and Penny insists he was just a useful element in Kirsty's plan. They were both at that party on Sunday – Theresa insisted on inviting Stefan, knowing he was in the country, and thinking it was at least something she could do for Imogen. Being nice to her son was as close as she could get to mending the breach with her sister. Gabriella didn't like it at all, of course. Kirsty made a big thing of showing him off, and making them all talk to him. I guess he must have said enough about his plans for her to decide she could take his car – which would be ideal for the purpose. She actually went back to Cheltenham with him that evening and stayed the night in his hotel room. Then she pretended to go home on a bus, but in reality she hung about until she was sure she could borrow the car without him noticing.'

'How do you know all that?'

'Imogen worked it out. She was suspicious right from the start, but kept pushing it away, until that didn't work any more.'

'But how did Kirsty know where Gabriella would be at the exact right time?' asked Thea.

'Oh – that's where you come in. And me, indirectly. Apparently, I said rather a lot about having to pay a house-sitter a steep sum to be sure everything would be okay with the dogs. Jake said something about you being famous for things going wrong, and wasn't I worried. Gabriella said she'd come round here after work and check up on you. All Kirsty had to do was hang about somewhere in Upper Oddington until she saw Gabriella drive past. It was probably all too horribly easy.' He gave a little cough. 'Is that everything now?'

'Just one more thing. Clifford Savage. Did he help Kirsty?'

'Well, there your guess is as good as mine. For what it's worth, I think she was using him almost more than anybody else. She wanted this house and thought he might come in handy, being on the spot. Something like that. Then he could have worked out the truth after the event, the same as Immy did.'

'Right,' said Thea with a sigh.

'Oh – Penny wants a word before you go,' he said suddenly. There was a moment's silence while the phone was transferred.

'Hello?' said the big sister. 'I won't keep you. I just wanted to add that Kirsty made a full confession to the police last night. I'm not sure you realise that. There won't be any need for you to appear in court as a witness or anything.'

'Thanks for that,' said Thea, with mixed feelings. It might have been oddly cathartic to include in her testimony that Gabriella Milner had been just about to smile when her cousin killed her with a large car.